ZEN LEE

HEROES OF SHOALIN
Through the Wooden Men Lane

Other   tual,

                                                                                        ly coincidental.

ISBN 978-1906221-546

Cover Design by Kieran Robert Leighton

FSC   **Mixed Sources**
Product group from well-managed
forests and other controlled sources
www.fsc.org Cert no. TT-COC-2082
© 1996 Forest Stewardship Council

Typeset in 12pt Bembo by Troubador Publishing Ltd, Leicester, UK
Printed in the UK by The Cromwell Press Ltd, Trowbridge, Wilts, UK

Matador is an imprint of Troubador Publishing Ltd

HEROES OF SHOALIN
Through the Wooden Men Lane

Map of China in Early Qing Dyn

Ru

Wuliyasutai

Xinjiang

Afghanistan

Gansu

I

Qinghai

Tibet

Si

Eme

Nepal

India

Erhai Lake
Dali

Yunnan

Burma

Thailand

ty

Long white mountain

Heilongjiang

Jilin

Mongolia)

Liaodong

Zhili

°Shenyang

Jinzhou

Ningyuan

Shanhaiguan

Beijing O

Tianjin

Korea

Japan

ngolia

Wutaishan

Shanxi

Shandong

Yellow   River

Kaifeng

Zhengzhou

Shaolin Monastery

Jiangsu

Xian°

Henan

Nanjing

haanxi

Anhui

Shanghai

Wudangshan

Hangzhou

ang River

Hubei

Zhejiang

Hunan

Jiangxi

zhou

Fujian

Taiwan

Guangxi

Guangdong

Guangzhou°

Hong Kong

Macao

Hainan

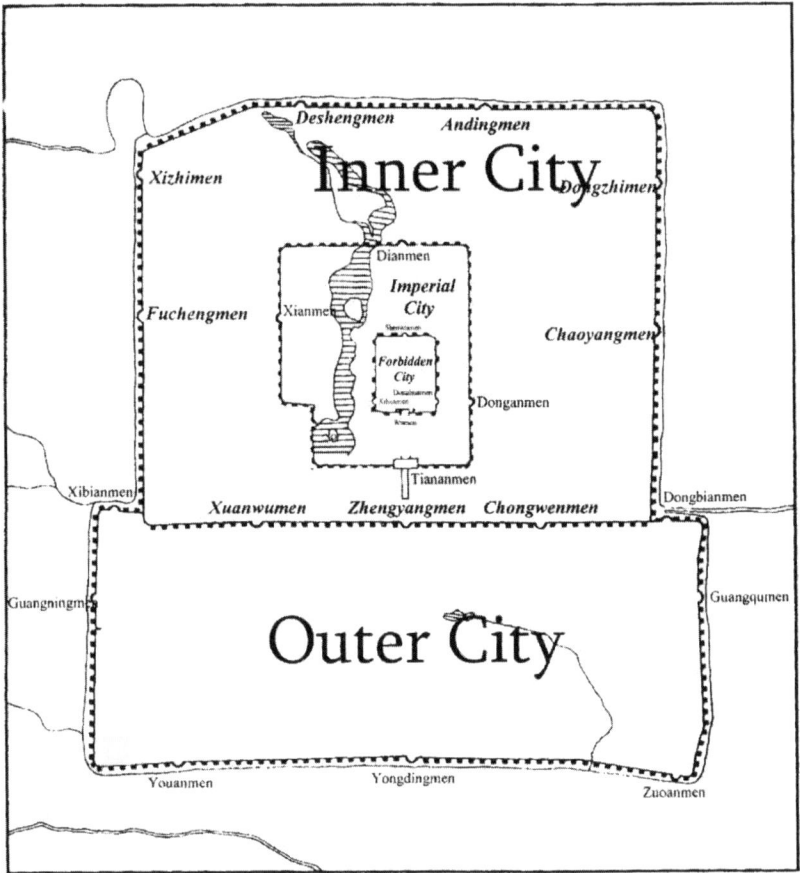

Gates of Beijing in Early Qing Dynasty

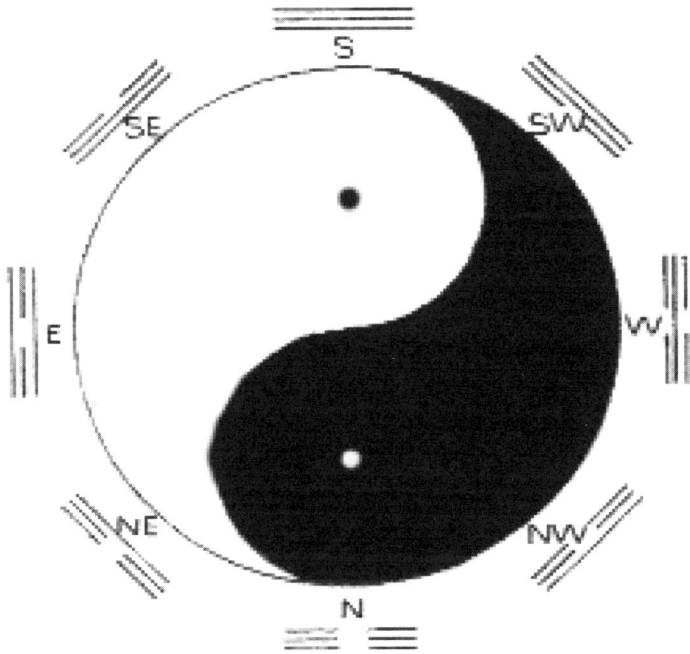

Yin-yang and 8-Trigrams (Bagua) diagram

GLOSSARY OF TERMS

Dark Way – A section of the Brotherhood of River and Lake whose members were mostly hardened criminals and convicts. They included bandits, robbers, thieves, pirates, smugglers, drug dealers, arsonists, assassins and gangsters.

Haohan – The literal meaning is 'good fellas'. These men were respected by the Brotherhood of 'River and Lake' for their bravery, honour and loyalty.

Kung Fu Terms –

(1) External Kung Fu trains a person in the skills and techniques of a kung fu style. The training develops the muscles, tendons, bones and physical fitness.

(2) Internal Kung Fu develops and treats the *Qi* (Internal Energy) in the body.

(3) Qingong means 'the art of lightness'. The body is trained to be 'light as feather' so that a person can run at great speed, leap high and drop down softly on the tip of the toe.

(4) Closing or Opening Energy Points is a specialized skill in martial arts. When pressure is applied to a person's energy point, he can be immobilised or even die. Similarly, the 'closed' energy point can be 'opened' or re-activated so that the person can move again.

(5) Energy Points These are acupuncture points located on the external pathway of the *Qi* channels.

(6) Fighting Pose Each kung fu style has a practice routine

which is made up of a series of fighting poses. There is no minimum or maximum number of fighting poses. Fighting poses can be joined together in sequences and the sequences can be varied. Each pose is given a descriptive phrase, for example 'Black Tiger Steals Heart', a straight punch at the chest from Shaolin kung fu.

Martial Arts Fellowship − Include all practitioners of martial arts.

Martial Arts Levels −
> *Level 1*, *Jing* (Essence) − to train the muscles, tendons and bones. This leads to the development of External Kung Fu (*Wai-Gong*).
> *Level 2*, *Qi* (Internal Energy) − to develop, treat and refine the internal energy. This leads to the development of Internal Kung Fu (*Nei-Gong*).
> *Level 3*, *Shen* (Mind and Spirit) − to attain spiritual fulfilment. In Buddhism, one is said to have reached 'enlightenment', and in Daoism, one is in union with the *Dao* or Way.

River and Lake (Jianghu) −
'River and Lake' is the literary translation of the Chinese term '*Jianghu*'. It was an alternative world which existed in parallel to the Confucian establishment of the day. In a narrow sense, it was an underground world of outlaws and vagabonds. But in the wider sense, it embraced people from all segments of society who were bonded by the same code of conduct. In this alternative world, relationships of honour, loyalty, love, hatred and revenge were resolved in accordance with the ways of the 'River and Lake', outside the legal framework or norms of a Confucian society.

River and Lake, Brotherhood of − People in the world of 'River and Lake' were regarded as brothers and sisters, sharing the same understanding and observing the same code of conduct.

PROLOGUE

On 6th June, 1644, Manchu troops entered Beijing and put their own six year old Emperor on the throne in the Forbidden City under the reign title 'Shun Zhi'. The name of the Dynasty was changed by the conquerors from 'Ming' to 'Qing'. Hence began the history of the Manchu rule in China which lasted for 267 years, ending in 1911.

Anti-Manchu feeling remained strong among the Han Chinese. The resistance movement continued with vigour, igniting in the hearts of millions of Chinese people the hope of 'Overthrowing the Qing and Restoring the Ming'.

The story begins in the eighth year of the reign of Kang Xi[1]. Kang Xi succeeded Shun Zhi who was the first Qing emperor to rule in China. It is 25 years since the Manchu Conquest of China. The literary inquisition is still in progress. Many well-known and respected Chinese scholars have been arrested, some are still imprisoned, and others have been executed, their properties confiscated and their family members beheaded, enslaved or exiled.

---

[1] 1669A.D.

I

THE BROTHERHOOD

It was drizzling in the city of Kaifeng. Summer rain had started early. Broad brimmed bamboo hats and straw rain capes filled the already congested streets. Kaifeng was an ancient city, the capital of seven dynasties in the early history of China. Although it had lost its capital status to Beijing, it was still bustling. Shops lined the streets. Hawk and falcon traders, horse traders, pearl and silk traders, salt merchants and peddlers flocked here for business. The city retained its importance as a trading centre because it was at the hub of the busy waterways, situated only a few miles south of the Yellow River.

Not far from the waterfront stood a two-storied tavern, a handsome structure with eaves, carved beams and decorative vermillion pillars. A pair of blue banners hung from a tall pole advertising 'Riverside Inn' and 'Top Quality Wine'. The inn was popular and every table was occupied with people eating and drinking. The shouts and laughter and the flurry of activity were such that no one paid attention when a Daoist priest and his acolyte walked in.

The Daoist was in his late thirties, tall and powerfully built, with a large mouth and bulbous nose. His eyebrows were bushy and his face half covered with wild, tangled beard. A black bandanna bound his head, and he wore a short black robe. From a silk sash around his waist hung two pouches. His feet were clad in hemp sandals with many eyelets, and a pair of old bronze swords swung from his back. Following behind was his acolyte, a young lad of around 15 years. The boy carried over his shoulder a cloth sack made from a large square scarf, the four corners tied in a knot in the centre. Anywhere else, the Daoist would have attracted the attention of the crowd. But this inn was used to accommodating strangers. From the four corners of the land traders gathered in Kaifeng, and there was no better place than the *Riverside Inn* to meet, talk business and take a bowl of wine. The hoteliers were accustomed to turning a blind eye.

The Daoist and his acolyte could not find a seat, so they climbed the stairs to the first floor and found a table by the window facing the waterfront. Food and wine arrived, steamed buns, noodles, braised beef, five-spice bean–curd slices, vegetables, and large bowls filled to the brim with wine. The Daoist was hungry and ate voraciously, gulping down bowl after bowl of wine. His young acolyte was gentle and well mannered. He picked delicately at the vegetables with his chopsticks, and slowly sipped his tea.

At the next table, five men were deep in conversation. A tall, fair-faced man wearing the dress of a scholar said, 'There have been sightings of the Third Prince. Someone saw him in Guangzhou, some have seen him in Hangzhou. Only two months ago, someone saw him in Fujian.' The scholar was nicknamed 'The Iron-Fan Scholar', because he used an iron fan as his weapon. Deadly darts were hidden in the ribs of the fan. With a flick of the hand, darts fired in all directions to hit their targets. The fan had razor sharp edges and could cut, strike or slide. It could be also used to strike vital energy points, paralysing opponents. The scholar was an ambitious young man, but he had been born at the wrong time and in the wrong place. His grandfather and father had served in the Ming courts. His father had told him that a man could not serve two masters, and so, being a filial son and a Ming Loyalist, the scholar could not serve the Manchus.

'Are you saying that Prince Zhu San, the third son of Emperor Chong Zhen, is alive?' the man next to him demanded. He was tall with a horse-like face, and wore a leather band round his head. On this early summer day, he was still wearing his leather boots. He was a horse trader from Shanxi and had earned his nickname 'The Phantom Rider', because of his superior riding skills and his ability to tame any horse. His weapon was a soft whip made from cow tendons which he disguised as a girdle round his waist.

The scholar nodded. 'Rumour has it that when the city of Beijing fell to the rebels, Emperor Chong Zhen's pregnant concubine of the Western Palace fled to Yunnan. There she gave birth to the Third Prince. Nobody had heard of him, but now suddenly he has appeared and is claiming to be the rightful heir to the Throne.' He took a swig of wine. 'When Li ZiCheng and his rebel army captured Beijing, Emperor Chong Zhen hanged himself on Coal Hill. That was the end of the Ming Dynasty. Li had the throne within his grasp. Who would have thought at the time that in less than two months, he would have lost his throne to the Manchus. And all because of the woman Chen Yuan Yuan.'

Another man at the table spat on the floor. 'That filthy traitor Wu SanGui's favourite concubine. When Li saw her in Beijing, he was struck by her beauty, and decided to keep her for himself. Wu went mad. Instead of fighting it out with Li, Wu went to the Tartar barbarians for help. He led the barbarians to Beijing. He betrayed his country for a whore!' The speaker was a short man with a swarthy complexion and high cheek bones. He wore a tattered bandanna and an old tunic which opened in front to reveal a well toned body and skin that gleamed like dark oil. He was a fisherman from Fujian, nicknamed 'The Flying Fish'. His fighting skills were deadlier under water than on land.

'Slut! Son of turtle egg!' A booming voice caught the attention of other diners in the room. It was a butcher from Guangdong, a short bulky man nicknamed 'The Hurricane'. His weapon was a nine-ring sabre which rattled loudly in action. The fisherman motioned to him to keep his voice down.

The five companions continued to eat and drink in silence. After a while, the fifth diner at the table grumbled, 'I would like to chop him into a mince ball and feed him to the dogs!' This was a hunter from Liaodong, a descendant of a Ming Commander stationed there before the Manchu occupation. His chest was tattooed with a two-headed green snake, and he gained his nickname 'The Magical Archer', because he was able to fire two arrows in quick succession so that they hissed like a two-headed snake in the air. 'Was Wu daft, handing our country on a plate to the Tartar barbarians? What did he think he was doing?'

The scholar smiled, 'Dear brother, Wu was not stupid. He was only a Ming General then. He got rid of the rebel leader Li, and is now the Prince of the Western Region, answerable to only one man, the Emperor himself. He is many times wealthier and more powerful than before. If he had tried to challenge Li, who knows who would have come out victor? 'A hill does not have room for two tigers'. It was a safe bet for Wu to get help from the Manchus to make sure Li was eliminated. Did Wu betray his country for a woman? Probably! Don't forget that Chen YuanYuan is the most beautiful woman on earth. Since the beginning of time, heroes and beauties have always gone together. If a man's ego is big, a hero's ego is even bigger. Can you imagine him suffering the humiliation of losing his woman to another man?'

The fisherman said sourly, 'The four Ming Generals have all done well for themselves. Since surrendering to the Tartar barbarians, they have all been made Princes of the Manchu Empire.'

'There are only three left now,' the scholar reminded him. 'Both Kong YouDe and Geng ZhongMing died long ago. Kong left behind only a daughter. Geng ZhongMing is succeeded by his son, Geng JiMao.'

'Yeah, I know,' replied the fisherman. 'On top of mountains of privileges, the three of them, Geng, Shang and Wu have been granted huge territories. Sometimes I wonder whether the Tartar barbarians can sleep at night after giving so much power and wealth to these three.'

The scholar laughed. 'Mark my words, they will not last long. The Manchus need time to recover from their long years of war. For the moment they have neither the resources nor the energies to fight. It is convenient to let the three Chinese generals govern the south and keep in check the Han Chinese. But everyone hates these traitors. The Manchus do not see them as a threat to their rule yet.'

'Why did we lose, brother Li? We are a hundred times the number of Tartar barbarians. We have generals, scholars, ministers, yet we lost to the Tartars. Why?' the fisherman grumbled.

'The Ming Emperors did not trust their honest and capable

ministers,' the scholar explained bitterly. 'They let those half-wit, half-man eunuchs run the country's affairs. The result is pretty obvious. The country began to rot like an apple from the core. The population was hungry and oppressed. The rebel chief, Li ZiCheng, became the people's hope. People were excited at first and called him 'The Daring King'. But once in the Capital, Li let his soldiers kill, rape and pillage. He got caught up in the corrupt lifestyle of the court. People's lives became as miserable as before. Li let the people down, and that's why the Manchus were able to get rid of him. Even without Wu's concubine, the country would have imploded.'

The fisherman lowered his voice. It happened that the Daoist priest sitting at the next table was adept in both External and Internal Kung Fu. He concentrated his mind and summoned his internal force so that he could hear every word.

'Listen,' said the fisherman. 'The Tartar barbarians have started witch-hunting the scholars again. Two days ago, they captured our famous scholar Gu YanWu, in a village near Kaifeng. At this very moment Scholar Gu is being escorted by military guards to Beijing where he will be tried by the Board of Punishment. That's only a rubber stamp and he's certain to be found guilty. The man who ordered his arrest was none other than Regent Oboi. Who'd dare go against his orders? Oboi is the most powerful man in the country. Even the Emperor himself would not dare challenge his decision. The prisoner and his guards will soon be at the waterfront where their boats are waiting for them. They will use the river route taking them north through Shandong Province to Tianjin. From there, they will travel by land to Beijing. We have our hooked spears ready. We can use them to chop the legs of the guards' horses when they arrive, and rescue Scholar Gu. Are you with me?'

It was not long before a clattering of horses' hooves could be heard approaching the waterfront. The five men drew their weapons and rushed to the window. A detachment of 20 or 30 military guards, led by a smartly dressed captain, rode towards the inn. In their midst, a man in plain clothes sat awkwardly on a horse which was joined to two other horses, one on each side, with iron bars and chains. Scholar Gu was about 50 years of age.

His hair hung loosely on his shoulders, his beard grey and untidy. He was manacled, and he clung wearily to the reins of his horse as he was dragged along.

The hunter at the window of the inn drew his bow, and with a twang two arrows hit the guards either side of Scholar Gu. The five men pulled on broad brimmed bamboo hats and jumped from the window.

The horse-trader lashed out his whip to coil around the captain's neck, but the captain ducked and leapt from his horse so that instead the whip broke the horse's neck. The captain waved a halberd in his right hand, and on the shield in his left hand were nine inverted hooks. Again, the horse-trader whirled his whip round the captain. Faster and faster moved the whip, round and round the captain danced and parried with his shield. The horse trader took a step forward, and the tip of his whip caught on the hooks of the shield. The captain, seizing the opportunity, thrust his halberd. The halberd was within an inch of the horse-trader's throat when it was knocked aside by an object. It was a chopstick which flew like an arrow from a window of the tavern. The horse-trader pulled a dagger from the handle of his whip and stabbed the hand holding the shield. The captain let the shield fall.

The scholar tackled the two lieutenants. One lieutenant bore a trident with a three-pronged metal head, the prongs flat with sharp edges. The other carried a pair of 'Tiger Head Double Hooks' fitted with a crescent over the handle, designed to cut at very short range. The trident and hook together were effective for cutting, stabbing, hooking and blocking. The scholar himself held a spear with a steel tip shaped like a brush pen in his right hand and the iron fan in his left. He used his spear to block the trident and his fan to strike at the Tiger Head Hook.

The captain continued to attack the horse-trader with his halberd. The horse-trader ducked and darted to disentangle his whip which was still caught in the captain's shield. The captain moved quickly and again he aimed his halberd at the horse-trader, but the halberd dropped from his hand when he was struck a second time, by a dart from the scholar's fan. The scholar had seen the horse trader in trouble, and fired the dart to pierce the captain's shoulder and force him to drop the halberd. The scholar performed a feint, dodged the two lieutenants, and leapt to the rescue of the horse-trader. With his fan he struck the 'Spirit Tower' vital energy point on the captain's back. The captain went down, unable to move.

The lieutenants chased after the scholar. The horse-trader, his whip now retrieved, lashed out at them. He coiled his whip around one lieutenant's waist, hauled him into the air, and with his left hand, thrust his dagger into his chest, killing him instantly. He cracked his whip again and the other lieutenant turned and ran.

The butcher was responsible for rescuing Scholar Gu. Holding his nine-ring sabre, he jumped from the window of the tavern directly onto Scholar Gu's horse. The two dead guards, arrows in their backs, sat either side on their horses, feet still in stirrups and their bodies swaying. With two mighty blows, the butcher cracked the iron chains linking the horses and rode off with the scholar.

The fisherman and the hunter dealt with the remaining guards. They used their hooked spears to chop the horses' legs so that horses and guards fell like dominoes. The horse trader gave a whistle and five black stallions came galloping towards him. The remaining four men jumped on to the horses, one riderless horse following behind, and disappeared in a cloud of dust.

Back inside the tavern, the Daoist priest was doubled over with pain. It had taken all his internal force to fling the chopstick which saved the horse trader. The exertion had split open his wound and blood seeped from his chest. The young acolyte bent over him. 'Are you all right?'

'I'll be fine. The men are heading for the East Gate of the City. They should be safe there at the Jewish Settlement. I think the scholar with the iron fan is related to one of the Jewish clans.'

'Who were those men?'

'Experts from the Martial Arts Fellowship, *haohans* from the Brotherhood of 'River and Lake'.'

'Really? I have read in the 'The Water Margin' about the 108 outlaws of Mount Liang. *Haohans* are brave men who would go through fire and water for their honour and stand together to live and die with their friends. But that's all I know about them.'

'The Martial Arts Fellowship includes only those who practise kung fu. It is part of the Brotherhood of River and Lake.'

'I have heard that the 'River and Lake' is a shadowy world with an underground culture,' said the young acolyte disapprovingly.

'Yes, you could say that. The Brotherhood includes both knights-errant and hardened criminals. That's why the world of 'River and Lake' is fraught with danger because you never know whose path you may cross.'

The young acolyte thought for a moment. 'Even if the Brotherhood does include knights-errant, it is still an outlaw fraternity. A knight-errant may save a poor girl by killing the villain, but by taking matters into his own hands, he is an outlaw.'

'Yes, it is a world of vagabonds and outlaws. However, the Brotherhood bonds those who share the same understanding and who abide by the same code of ethics. They come from all segments of society. They can be storytellers, performing acrobats, medicine peddlers, bodyguards, captains, sergeants, monks, nuns, scholars, merchants, bandits…virtually any one.'

'If the Brotherhood can accommodate criminals, I am surprised that it has a 'code of ethics'.'

'We in the Brotherhood have our own rules of conduct: loyalty and honour are the two most important things. You do not betray your friends; you do not break your promises; you do not play dirty; you do not harm the old, the sick, young children and pregnant women. The outlaws of Mount Liang are regarded as *haohans* because they put their honour and loyalty before their own lives.'

'What happens if someone breaks the rules?'

'He would be despised as 'scum of River and Lake'. Every righteous man in the Brotherhood would then have a duty to get rid of him.'

'Who is the Brotherhood leader then?' the acolyte asked.

'There's no leader now. No one has the clout to rally all those in the Brotherhood to follow him. To be a leader you need to be champion in martial arts. You have to prove you're the best. Until there is a formal contest no one will emerge as champion. The Brotherhood is dominated by the Martial Arts Fellowship. The champion of the Fellowship is automatically leader of the Brotherhood.'

'Just because someone is a champion doesn't mean he is also a good leader. He could be a bad man.'

'If a leader cannot command respect, the *haohans* in the Brotherhood will not listen to him. He'll be like a king without subjects.' He sighed, 'If we had a leader, we would be a force unto ourselves. We could take on the Tartar barbarians and restore the Ming Dynasty.'

The acolyte looked up at the Daoist. 'So do you know those men who rescued the scholar?'

'They are probably followers of Koxinga, the leader of the anti-Manchu resistance.'

'You mean Zheng ChengGong.'

'His surname was Zheng, but he was granted the use of the Imperial Surname 'Zhu' by a Ming Prince in recognition of his loyalty to the Ming Empire. Out of respect, people called him 'Koxinga', meaning the 'Lord with the Imperial Surname'.'

The young acolyte was surprised by the way his teacher's face lit up at the mention of Koxinga. 'You admired that Zheng ChengGong, didn't you?'

'Yes, I did.' The Daoist exclaimed. 'Every Chinese admired Koxinga. He was our hero. He fought the Tartar barbarians and refused to surrender. He took his army to Taiwan, drove the red hairy devils from the island, and continued the resistance movement there. The Tartar barbarians were powerless against him.'

'Red hairy devils. You mean the Dutch?'

'Could be. They were from somewhere in the west.'

'But Zheng ChengGong died seven years ago,' the pupil pointed out.

'When he died, he was succeeded by his son…er..'

'Zheng Jing,' his pupil reminded him.

'Yes, Zheng Jing inherited the title 'Prince of Yanping' from his father. He has vowed to continue the resistance movement and lead the Chinese to overthrow the Qing and restore the Ming.'

It was the first time the acolyte had seen such animation in his teacher. 'Taiwan was part of China before the foreign occupations, right?'

'Right, but Taiwan has not submitted to the Tartar barbarians. Never! The Taiwanese people are Ming loyalists and support the resistance movement.'

'Aren't they afraid of the Qing army?' asked the acolyte.

The Daoist laughed. 'The Taiwan Strait separates the island from the mainland. Taiwan has battleships and men who'd hold off any attack from the sea. The Tartars can ride on horseback, but ask them to cross the Strait, they'll be dead fish. The Tartar barbarians can't swim!'

'It is only a matter of time before Taiwan is fully integrated with the mainland. Taiwan is and shall always be an inseparable and inalienable part of China,' said the young acolyte with a seriousness beyond his years.

The Daoist shrugged and called for the bill. Then he rose from his seat, covering his chest wound with the cloth sack, and together with his acolyte he left the tavern.

II

YIN AND YANG

It was Flint's fifteenth birthday. He had come to Shaolin Monastery at the age of six. As a small child he had lived in a mountain cave, a labyrinth of winding and twisting tunnels providing a natural refuge from strangers. Everything in the cave came from round about. Wooden tables and chairs were fashioned from oak trees. Bowls and dishes were seashells, and mirrors were polished stones. The cave had little natural light, but the ceilings were scattered with pearls which shone like evening stars. Coloured stones littered the cave floor: red, green, amber, blue and black. He was too young to recognise these precious gems which men would die to lay their hands on.

There were four of them living in the cave. There was the beautiful woman whom Flint called *Shifu*[2]; his *Shifu's Shifu,* Miao Shan *ShiTai*[3]; and there was his dear old nanny. Flint did not know his parents. He adored his *Shifu* and would like to think that she was his mother. Although she kept her distance, he felt close to her. Her eyes betrayed her emotion, tender and loving whenever she looked at him. They would not tell him about his parents, saying only that one day he would meet them.

For a time, he did not even have a name. He came to be called 'Flint' by Miao Shan *ShiTai* because he liked to collect flint stones, fascinated by their rainbow colours. He would line them up in his corner of the cave. Under the glow of the pearl light, the stones captured the colours of the sky.

The old nanny went away twice a year to replenish supplies. Whenever she came back she brought something for him. Sometimes it was a mountain hare, sometimes a toad and once, a sea-lion and a golden-haired monkey. He liked to ride a giant

2 *Shifu* -Teacher
3 *ShiTai* - Abbess

tortoise under the water and play ball with the sea lion. He played with his sparrowhawk which was trained to zoom in at his whistle. Other sparrowhawks were kept in the aviary behind the cave, but his was the brightest and swiftest of them all. The sparrowhawks were fitted with steel tips at their beaks and claws.

Flint grew up with his animal friends. Once he rose from his bed an hour before dawn, and imitated the morning crow of the cock. The birds in the garden responded and woke the others in the cave. His mischief brought him an extra hour of exercise. He overheard Miao Shan *ShiTai* say to his *Shifu*, 'The child is intelligent and creative. He has good bone structure. One day he will become a great martial artist.' By imitating the sounds of animals, Flint unwittingly built up the *Qi* in his body and he surprised his *Shifu* by his progress in kung fu exercises. The breathing, rhythm, pitch and volume enhanced his *Qi* development. The most powerful use of sound in martial arts is the 'Lion's Roar', which if exercised by someone with immense *Qi* can shatter eardrums.

Miao Shan *ShiTai* and Flint's *Shifu* were Daoist nuns. Most Daoists practise both External and Internal Alchemy. External Alchemy involves the use of furnaces and cauldrons in which minerals and herbs are compounded into pills or elixirs that are believed to bring immortality. Internal Alchemy proposes that all essential ingredients are to be found inside the human body, and can be refined to achieve longevity without the use of elixir. The Daoist Internal Alchemy is concerned with the cultivation of *Qi* and *Qi* flow based on the pattern of *Yin* and *Yang*. It gives rise to the development of the style of kung fu known as Internal Kung Fu. Daoists believe in total serenity and tranquillity of the mind bereft of emotion and passion, withdrawal from the affairs of the world and following the course of nature. Flint was too young to realise that being a Daoist nun, his *Shifu* could not allow human emotions to disturb her tranquillity of mind.

Flint was taught to use Abdominal Breathing from a very young age. Air was channelled into the abdominal area, so that the abdomen expanded during inhalation and contracted during exhalation. He learned Reverse Abdominal Breathing, where the abdomen contracted while inhaling and expanded during exhalation. The breathing exercises stimulated and guided the flow of *Qi* and were essential training in the development of *Qi* in the body. Almost as soon as he could walk, his play took the form of physical training. Games were devised to stress balance, agility and flexibility, and as he grew older, the games became more advanced. He would practise rolling, jumping, leaping and tumbling. He practised somersaults, front flips, back flips and body drops. He could drop from a 30 foot high tree and perform 10 somersaults before hitting the ground. He did not realise he was being trained in the fundamentals of kung fu. By the time of his sixth birthday, he was a strong and healthy boy.

He had also learned to hold his breath and summon his *Qi* as he began *Qingong*, 'the art of lightness', which trained the body to become light as feather. When an expert in *Qingong* runs, he is so fast and so light on his feet that it is like a passing breeze. *Qingong* enables one to leap high in the air and come down softly on the tip of the toe.

Flint was beginning the more complicated steps of the mystical *Qingong* style 'The 72 Cloud Steps' and progressing well in his exercises when he suffered an accident and became so ill that he had to stop all his exercises.

It was the morning after his sixth birthday. He was, as every day, swimming under water when he noticed a small crack in the rocks. He managed to squeeze his small body through the crack, crawling along a long narrow tunnel. When he reached the other side, he realized that the cave which he called his home was in fact at the bottom of a great waterfall. Despite the ferocity of the cascading water and the fast current, he managed to swim to the point where the waterfall flowed into the river. The river was squeezed between the steep flanks of a gigantic gorge.

He sat against a boulder on the river bank to rest. The grass was lush and green. The mountain slopes were scattered with richly coloured flowers. With the flowers came bees and butterflies and birds. Flint saw a black-headed greenfinch, a chestnut-tailed starling and a white-tailed robin. There were wild rabbits and foxes.

He lazed on the river bank enjoying the fresh air, the light breeze and the fragrant smell of flowers, and whistled for his sparrowhawk to join him. He wondered whether his nanny travelled down this river to the outside world. The river seemed long and endless.

Flint possessed a rare gift. He was born with a sense akin to an animal instinct. He could sense a change in surroundings before others became aware of it. As he stretched out on the grass, he felt an approaching danger. The world was still. The birds stopped singing and fluttered frantically away. Animals disappeared from sight.

He looked around to see ripples on the surface of the water. Something was swimming towards the river bank. The water churned, and from the water sprung a large head with glassy eyes. A snake-like creature crawled ashore, black in colour and very, very long. It had two fins in front and two fins at the back. Its head was like an eel's, but was bigger than Flint's thigh. It made a small cry, like a dolphin. Flint jumped up and ran behind a boulder hoping the creature would go away. But the creature followed him. He began to run. The creature caught up with him and coiled itself round his body. Its head was now poised directly above his face, and the glassy eyes glared at him coldly.

He could not move. The coil round his body grew tighter. The creature flicked out its tongue, its breath foul like rotten fish. A slimy tongue licked his face, and he saw sharp fangs. Then came the 'keck-keck-keck' calls of his sparrowhawk. The creature raised its head towards the sound and made a threatening cry. The sparrowhawk weaved around them, at times closing in with its steel tipped claws, at times disappearing out of sight, then reappearing to scratch and peck at the creature. The creature strained its head to follow the bird, lashing out its tongue. Suddenly, the sparrowhawk dipped down with closed wings and dug its claws into the neck of the creature, pecking at its throat, piercing it. Blood spouted and Flint put his mouth to the hole to suck the creature's blood. He thought that if he sucked out its blood, the creature would die. The coil around his body began to loosen. Flint lost consciousness.

When he came to, he was shivering with cold despite being covered with a large deer skin. His arms and legs were numb, and his hands and feet felt cold as ice. His breathing was slow and shallow, and his skin had turned purple.

There were tears in his *Shifu*'s eyes. She told him, 'You were attacked by a sea serpent.'

'A sea snake?'

'Not a snake exactly. Sea snakes don't have gills or fins, and their tails are larger than their heads. The sea monster had a tail like the tail of a tadpole. We had thought sea serpents were legendary until now. Don't be afraid. The monster is dead. You're safe now.'

When he woke again, he heard Miao Shan *ShiTai* talking with his *Shifu*. 'The blood of the sea monster is very poisonous. It contains tremendous *Yin* energy. By drinking the blood of the sea monster, the child has become overwhelmed with *Yin*. This has caused disharmony of the *Yin-Yang* in his body. As a result of this excess *Yin*, the child is suffering a 'cold illness'. He has more *Yin* energy than I could handle otherwise I could help him channel it to the right place. Our style of kung fu has already built up *Yin* energy in our bodies, and the transfer of our energies to the child would only aggravate his illness. I have fed him the Golden Pearl of Elixir. The Elixir pill has stopped the excess *Yin* energy from spreading to his heart and to his internal organs. But now his *Qi* flow is blocked.'

'I'm most grateful, *Shifu*. I know that it took you 20 years to collect the ingredients for the Elixir pills, and that in all that time you have only been able to make three pills.' She wept softly. 'What has the child done to deserve such kindness? I am forever indebted to you, *Shifu*.'

Flint had never seen the face of Miao Shan *ShiTai*. Her face was always covered by a black veil, and he had wondered what she looked like. She must be older than his *Shifu* because she was his *Shifu's Shifu*. He was rather afraid of her. She always spoke in a voice devoid of emotion. When she walked, she made no sound, as if she were floating on air.

Miao Shao *ShiTai* said, 'I've tried using acupuncture with needles in the boy's energy points, but it's of no effect'.

'*Shifu*, is there no hope at all?'

Miao Shan *Shi Tai* replied with her usual calm, 'We have tried bear's gall bladder, ginseng, and other precious herbs but they have not been effective. I have even given the child Five Poisons Wine containing poisons from five types of venomous creature, centipedes, scorpions, snakes, spiders and toads, to produce *Yang* energy. This provided only temporary relief and has not cured the root of his illness. I cannot go on giving him the Wine. Too much will kill him. The only way that his life may be saved is to find someone who has developed tremendous *Yang* energy, and to transfer that *Yang* energy to the child. At the same time we must get the child to practise the *Yang* style of kung fu to generate his own *Yang* energy to balance the excess *Yin*. I am thinking of sending the child to Shaolin Monastery. The Abbot there is an expert in the *Yang* style kung fu'

'My elder adoptive brother is a disciple of the Abbot. I shall write to him at once.'

'Even before this incident, I had thought of sending the child to Shaolin. He needs to be with children of his own age. Our religious order is meant for women. He cannot stay with us indefinitely.'

Flint began his journey to Shaolin Monastery accompanied by his old nanny. He could not understand why he was so ill. She told him about the *Yin* energy in his body. A girl was *Yin* and a boy was *Yang*. He was confused. If he was *Yang*, why did he have excess *Yin*?

'Everyone has both *Yin* and *Yang* in the body. The *Yin* and *Yang* must balance, as excess *Yin* will cause 'cold illness', and excess *Yang* will cause 'hot illness'. It is only when *Yin* and *Yang* are in harmony that you can enjoy good health and a long life,' his nanny explained.

When they arrived at Shaolin Monastery, Flint was in a semi-conscious state and was taken to see a monk whose religious name was Xuan Kui. The monk was the elder adoptive brother of Flint's *Shifu*. When he saw Flint's condition, the monk took him immediately to the Abbot's room. The Abbot read the letter from Miao Shan *Shi Tai*, holding the boy on his knees.

'He looks very ill indeed.'

He put his hand on Flint's back. Flint felt warmth flow from the Abbot's palm into his body. It was the first time after many days of suffering that he had felt comfortable. He no longer shivered. He felt as though he was sunbathing on a warm summer's day, and he drifted into sleep. When he woke again, he found himself lying on a bed. The monk Xuan Kui was talking to his nanny in the other corner of the room.

'How is my sister Miss Anya?'

'Miss Anya has joined our Daoist Order. Her religious name is 'Wu Si'. She is learning kung fu from Miao Shan *ShiTai*. I am maid to Miao Shan *ShiTai*.'

'I gather from Miao Shan *ShiTai*'s letter that she is successor to the Ice Maiden who founded the Daoist order, The Way of the Great Perfection, famous for the kung fu style known as the Black Ice Palm.'

'My mistress took refuge in a mountain cave to hide from an enemy. There she discovered the relic of the Ice Maiden and the secret manual of the Black Ice Palm. It was written in the Will of the Ice Maiden that whoever found her relic and practised her style of kung fu would become her successor. My mistress kowtowed before the relic, and from that day on, she was successor to the Ice Maiden and head of her Daoist order.'

Monk Xuan Kui read the letter sent by Flint's *Shifu*. He became lost in thought. The monk now understood what had happened to his sister during the years since she had left home. He looked at the boy before him. He was only six but it was clear that he had inherited his father's chiselled good looks and aquiline nose. The monk remembered the eyes of the boy's father; sharp and cold. But this boy had inherited his mother's eyes and mouth. His eyes were warm and intense. The corners of his mouth curved slightly upwards like his mother's. He took an instant liking to the boy. He agreed that it would be best not to disclose to the boy who his parents were until he grew older.

"Flint' is a perfect name for the boy,' said the monk. 'I hope when he grows up, he will be as tough as flint stone, and that he will ignite the fire that gives light and warmth to those around him. Please leave the boy with me and tell Nun Wu Si that I will take good care of him and that he will recover from his illness.' The monk hoped in his heart that the boy would grow up a stronger person than his mother and a warmer person than his father.

During Flint's first week in Shaolin, the Abbot and other senior monks took turns to place their hands on his back every other hour, transferring their *Yang* energies into his body to combat the excess *Yin*. By passing the *Qi* to him, the monks became weak themselves and needed time to regenerate the *Qi* in their own bodies. The *Qi* transfer exercises were gradually reduced and after four weeks, twice daily was enough, once by the Abbot and once by the monk Xuan Kui. After a further three months, this was reduced again to once a day. Flint was taught simple Shaolin *Qi* exercises such as 'Lifting the Sky' to enable the *Qi* to flow to his arms and hands; 'Carrying the Moon' to strengthen the spine; and meditation exercises to calm the mind. In time, Flint was able to practise on his own to gain limited flow of *Qi* in his body.

Flint learned more about his illness. His *Shifu* in Shaolin asked Flint to think of the shady side of the hill as *Yin*, with the sunny side as *Yang*. *Yin* and *Yang* are direct opposites. Whilst *Yang* stands for the positive side of things, *Yin* stands for the negative. It follows that *Yang* represents the sun, heaven, day, fire, heat, and anything relating to brightness and happiness. And *Yin* stands for the moon, earth, night, water, coldness, darkness and sadness. Flint came to understand that *Qi* was the vital and intrinsic energy in the body. Like blood which flows in blood vessels, *Qi* flows in *Qi* channels. There are twelve 'primary' *Qi* channels, eight 'extraordinary' *Qi* vessels and numerous smaller energy pathways branching from the energy channels.

All the energy points lie on the external pathway of the channels. Of the eight extraordinary vessels, only the Conception Vessel and Governing Vessel have energy points of their own. Knowledge of the location of energy points is essential for a martial artist. One way of defeating an adversary is to attack the adversary's energy points, to paralyse him.

Flint's illness had been difficult to cure because the excess *Yin* energy had spread to the 'extraordinary' vessels. It was due to the Elixir pill that the *Yin* energy had stopped spreading into the 'primary' channels. This, however, had the adverse effect of blocking the *Qi* flow, as the excess *Yin* energy became stuck in the 'extraordinary' vessels. Normally when the *Qi* flow was blocked, one would die within seven days. It was the miraculous power of the Elixir pill that had kept him hanging by a breath until he reached Shaolin Monastery. To cure his illness, he would need to concentrate on the *Qi* exercises to unblock his *Qi* flow. Almost all types of kung fu require fundamental training in *Qi* development. The deployment of *Qi* enables the exponent to move fast and forcefully without shortage of breath. The stronger the *Qi* in the body, the more powerful the kung fu skills. Training in the development of *Qi* is 'Internal' kung fu.

When Flint was thirteen years old, the old Abbot Tong Ti went into seclusion. He appointed the monk Xuan Kui, adoptive brother of Flint's *Shifu*, as the new Abbot of Shaolin.

Two more years passed, Flint was approaching fifteen. The new Abbot Xuan Kui was concerned to find a way to cure Flint's lingering illness. Flint had improved significantly during his time at Shaolin, and Xuan Kui thought he was ready for a 'small universe' breakthrough which might eradicate the root of his illness. The 'small universe' energy flow is the continuous flow of *Qi* around the Conception Vessel and the Governing Vessel. It is universally heralded by martial artists that if a person has attained the 'small universe' energy flow, he will 'eliminate a hundred illnesses'; if he has attained the 'big universe' energy flow, he will 'live a hundred years'.

Abbot Xuan Kui realised that he alone could not help Flint achieve a 'small universe' breakthrough. Flint had been taught breathing techniques by Miao Shan *ShiTai* since babyhood and the *Qi* flow in the *Yin* channels was very different from the Shaolin style of breathing. This explained why Flint's right hand was cold and his left hand was hot. His face was paler on the right side. In addition to building up *Yang* energy, Flint must also learn how to channel the *Yin* energy to the proper places. This meant that he would need to develop both a *Yang* style kung fu and a *Yin* style kung fu. The only person who could help Flint was Miao Shan *ShiTai*, who was the Abbot's equal in *Qi*. Together they could help Flint reach a 'small universe' energy flow. The series of exercises would take 49 days, and the best time to practise was midnight.

Miao Shan *ShiTai* came to Shaolin at the Abbot's invitation. Each night, at midnight, Flint climbed the hill behind the monastery to practise the 'small universe' exercises with the Abbot and Miao Shan *ShiTai*. The Abbot had warned him not to let the other boys know about their night-time exercises. Any disturbance during the *Qi* exercise could put all three of them at risk of their lives. Disturbance during the *Qi* meditation can result in the body back-firing, and the *Qi* running riot, disrupting the *Qi* flow. A person could end up paralysed and even die.

By day, Flint met secretly with Miao Shan *ShiTai* in the woods to learn the Black Ice Palm kung fu. This consisted of a series of 72 fighting poses with numerous variations. To be effective, the Black Ice Palm also required combination of the special *Qingong* steps created by the Ice Maiden. Flint had stopped learning the *Qingong* '72 Cloud Steps' after he was attacked by the sea serpent. Miao Shan *ShiTai* demonstrated the *Qingong* steps and the Black Ice Palm kung fu. She encouraged Flint to memorise everything so that he could practise on his own. She also taught him Tortoise and Foetal Breathing. Tortoise Breathing imitates a tortoise's way of breathing inside its shell where the breath is very faint. Foetal Breathing combines Tortoise Breathing and abdominal movement with inhalation and exhalation, imitating the way a foetus breathes inside the womb. The midnight exercises lasted for 49 days, and were to finish on Flint's fifteenth birthday.

Flint looked forward to his birthday for another reason. He had made many friends in his time at the monastery, but his closest friends were two young boys named Bussie and Tobie, and a man named Storm who tended a vegetable plot behind the monastery. Storm had been away travelling and he had promised Flint that he would be back for his birthday.

III

ALL ROADS LEAD TO SHAOLIN

The Daoist priest and his acolyte were weary, their eyes red from lack of sleep and their mouths parched. They had been riding for days, and had barely stopped even for food. Finally they arrived in Dengfeng County, Henan Province, and ahead of them rose Mount Song, one of the five holy mountains of martial arts on the northern China plains.

The Daoist had grown fond of his pupil. The lad had followed him patiently, never complaining. Tired and thirsty himself, the Daoist called, 'Look! We are nearly at the foot of Shaoshi Hill. The Shaolin Monastery faces ShaoShi Hill to the south and backs onto Five-Breast Peak to the north. We don't have long to go now.'

The countryside grew more lush as they trudged on, until they heard the trickle of a mountain stream. 'Water!' cried the Daoist priest, 'If we follow upstream, we'll soon reach Shaolin.' They pushed their horses to the stream and jumped down to drink. Together they sat on the bank, refreshed. It looked as though they had at last shaken off their pursuers.

'The water from this stream flows down from the mountain. I bet you've never tasted water so good', said the Daoist.

'The water is fine,' replied his acolyte.

The Daoist filled his gourd. 'The spring source is right in front of the monastery and it flows eastward from there. It provides the monastery with a constant supply of water. We use it for our tea. I tell you, once you've tried our tea, you won't want tea from anywhere else.'

The lad nodded, but did not seem particularly impressed. 'So we are heading for Shaolin Monastery?'

'That's where I'm going and you're coming with me. We'll

soon be able to get rid of these hideous Daoist habits. Look at me! Do I look like a Daoist priest? There's not 'a single Daoist bone or a puff of Daoist air of spiritualism' in me. With my looks and size, I'd be better off in a guard's uniform or even dressed as a highwayman,' the Daoist chuckled.

'Are you a Shaolin monk?'

'I almost became one. I was made to learn the Shaolin rules which include 10 prohibitions, 12 moral codes, 10 obligations, and hundreds of rules. But after a few drinks, all the rules flew out of my head and I ended up fighting with the monks. They said I was disrespectful to my seniors.'

'So why did you join the Monastery?'

'I came to Shaolin because I once killed a man while I was drunk, a local ruffian who used to ride roughshod in the villages. He bullied the villagers, beating them half to death and taking their property and their women. Everyone was scared of him because he was nephew to that turtle egg Wu SanGui. I had wanted to sort him out for a long time. One evening after drinking with my friends, I came across him trying to snatch a young girl from a poor old man, claiming that the old man owed him money. With just one blow, I knocked him dead.'

'You could have taken him to the magistrate's court.'

'You don't know what it is like out there. Everyone knows Wu SanGui is the most powerful man in the Western Region. The magistrates, the governors, the damned lot of them are all in Wu's pocket and take orders from him. There's a saying, 'The Mountain is high, and the Emperor is far away.' In the Western Region, Wu is King. I've killed a nephew of Wu. Even if you were Emperor, you could not save my life.'

The acolyte raised his eyebrows. 'So what happened then?'

'I became a fugitive. I left the Western Region and travelled east. On the way I met a friend who wrote a letter recommending me to the Abbot of Shaolin Monastery. That was how I came to Shaolin. There I was banned from drinking. Not only because Shaolin prohibits the consumption of wine and meat, it was also the Abbot's fear that I would lose control once I started drinking again.'

'Banned from drinking? That must have been tough!' teased the acolyte.

'OK. So I did have a drink now and then.'

'I suppose a little wine doesn't do any harm.' said the acolyte to save his teacher from embarrassment.

'Damn it, I did try at the beginning. All would have been fine had people not kept reporting me to the Abbot. Something happened on the night before I was due to take my vow. I don't remember much, but the monks told me later that I was caught drinking. I was completely befuddled and apparently I started hitting out wildly at the monks. I injured several people that night and caused so much mayhem that I was asked to leave next morning. The old Abbot was a kindly man, and he wanted to find some use for me. There was a vegetable plot some five miles from the Monastery. The farm was in a mess because none of the monks liked the job. He said I could live there. I was happy with the arrangement because there I could be left alone. Since then I have not been asked to take my vow.'

'Am I to stay at the monastery then?'

'I don't see why not. After all, you saved my life. If you don't like the monastery, you can always come and stay with me on my farm.'

They sat silent for a while, each thinking about their arrival at the monastery. Suddenly the Daoist cried, 'Bloody hell, you're a damn good rider. We gave those bastards a hell of a chase.'

'The ancestors of the Manchus were nomads.' the lad said proudly. 'They roamed the northern plains for centuries, hunting and shooting. Every Manchu learns how to ride almost as soon as he can walk.'

'Are you a Manchu then?'

'My father was a Manchu but my mother was Han Chinese.'

'So you are half Han. That makes things a bit easier. Are your parents still alive?'

'No.'

He was saved having to say more by the sound of a carriage coming at speed along the path following the bend of the stream. The carriage was exquisite, black lacquered with gold inlay.

Alongside rode men on fine steeds. The retinue nearly rode into the priest and his pupil. Angered, the Daoist picked up a pebble and aimed it at the leg of a horse. The horse shied and the rider nearly fell. Managing to rein the horse in, the rider shouted, 'Damn it! You stinking priest, what do you think you're doing?'

'You blind turtle. Can't you look where you're going?' retorted the Daoist.

The rider leapt from his horse, a burly man with a luxuriant growth of neatly trimmed beard. He wore a sky blue riding jacket with circular floral motif. He pulled off his jacket to reveal a hairy chest and muscular body. He was ready to fight.

The carriage drew up beside him, and from the window, a man leaned out, a young and handsome man in a light yellow taffeta robe and a matching silk jacket fastened in the centre with solid gold buttons. On his head sat a black silk hat, a piece of white jade in front and two round pearls on each side. This was the attire of a very wealthy man.

The man waved a hand from the window of the carriage. His fingers were long and slender and his nails were beautifully manicured. He wore a large jadeite ring. He looked with disdain at the priest and his acolyte, and with a flick of his wrist he signalled the burly rider to move on. The rider bowed, and without another word, donned his jacket and re-mounted his horse. Within a moment, they were gone.

Two riders at the back of the retinue caught the attention of the Daoist. One was a stout Tibetan lama with a ruddy complexion. Although of heavy build, he was so light on his horse that the horse appeared to float, its feet barely touching the ground. Only a man with immense internal force could control a horse like that. The Daoist had never known a Tibetan lama with such superior kung fu. The other rider the Daoist thought he recognised. He was short and dark, with small beady eyes. Despite his small physique, he had long arms, the muscles gnarled and knotted like an old oak tree. His hands were claws with bulging knuckles and long sharp nails. The Daoist had long heard of such a man and the force that could be unleashed by this pair of hands. This could be Wan YunLong, the second pupil of the legendary Wang Lang.

Wang Lang was a lay Shaolin disciple who created the Praying Mantis kung fu in the late Ming Dynasty. This style of kung fu became so powerful that it began to outshine many Shaolin traditional styles. On the advice of his Shaolin *Shifu*, Wang Lang had left the monastery and travelled the country to study other styles of kung fu to further improve his footwork and refine his Praying Mantis techniques. In the course of his travels, he had taken on three pupils. The brightest of them was Wan YunLong, his second disciple.

The young acolyte watched the carriage and riders disappear. 'Who was the man in the carriage?'

'Jade, godson of Prince Geng JiMao of the Southern Region. I met him and his steward in a brothel in Beijing when his steward had a fight with another guest over a sing-song girl that Jade fancied.'

The young lad was surprised. 'I was not aware that Geng JiMao had a godson. Do you think that Jade and his paladins are also heading for the Shaolin Monastery? It would be interesting to meet them.'

★★★

'Look, a stream. Let's stop here. I'm so tired. I simply can't walk any further'. A young girl dressed in red ran to the water. Her companion, dressed in green, followed behind. They too had been travelling all night. They splashed water on their faces, but drank only from the water sac they carried with them. The girl in red took off her riding shoes and sat dangling her feet in the stream. Her hair was arranged in two buns in the hairstyle of unmarried girls. She wore a light strawberry red silk jacket and skirt. On her neck was a pearl necklace, and from the girdle round her waist hung a beautifully embroidered silk purse. She was petite, nearly fifteen but looked younger than her age.

Her companion was plain by comparison, taller, and wearing a simple jacket and skirt. The quality of her clothing suggested a servant. She looked older and more mature but was in fact a little younger. She had run away from home a few months earlier and had been found wandering the streets, hungry and cold. She was taken in and from then on, had become maid and companion to the only daughter in one of the most prestigious households in the country. She was called 'Greenie' because of her unusual green eyes. Greenie told her new master that she had run away because she was ill treated by her stepmother. But there was an air of grace about her. She was soon treated by the family more as a friend than a maid.

'My papa doesn't love me any more,' the girl in red said tearfully.

'No, Miss Minnie, you are wrong, your Papa loves you very much.'

'He scolded me. He has never scolded me before. All I wanted was some steamed buns from the Riverside Inn in Kaifeng.'

'But that was miles away.'

'I was hungry. We had many fast horses. It would have taken only a couple of hours to get the buns. Papa said everyone was busy preparing for the road and I was being disruptive. He has never uttered a harsh word to me before. He always says he loves me and my mother the most in the world. He has never refused me anything before.' She kicked at the water with her dainty foot.

Her father had just collected her from the E-mei School of Martial Arts where she was learning kung fu, and she was on her way home for the holidays. As they would pass through Henan Province, she had suggested a visit to the Shaolin Monastery. Her father went along with the idea as he too was interested in visiting the monastery. It had been many years since he was last in Mount Song. It was while they were resting at an inn at the foot of Mount Song that her father had berated her over the small matter of the buns. Her feelings were injured, and she decided to run away with her companion in the night, but they became lost in the woods, So when the girls found a path winding up the mountain, they thought the best thing was to head to the monastery by themselves.

'Miss, please may I help you put on your shoes? I've a feeling we're being watched.'

'Oh, really?' Surprised, Minnie looked around coquettishly.

'You are teasing. I don't see anyone.' She stretched a leg above the water. 'Do you think my foot is beautiful?' She arched her foot to show its lovely curve. Her toes were small and neatly aligned like a string of small pearls on a piece of silk cloth. The foot was like carved marble, smooth and spotless, and with a lustre only possessed by young girls. She was pleased with what she saw and waited with child-like expectation for admiration.

'Oh, yes, Miss Minnie, your feet are beautiful. Ma'am says that with such lovely hands and feet, you are destined to be a future empress.'

Minnie had small feet but they were not bound. After the Manchu Conquest foot binding had been banned, although many Han Chinese families upheld the tradition. Minnie's father had refused to allow his daughter's feet to be bound. Minnie was his only child and he hoped that she would learn kung fu and be like a son to him. Most importantly, his family was close to the centre of Manchu power and he could not be seen as a reactionary. Minnie's mother was a strong headed woman, and it was surprising that on this issue she gave in to her husband.

Suddenly Greenie picked up a pebble and took aim at a bush. 'Ouch!' Three young boys emerged cautiously from the foliage. The oldest was nearly sixteen years old and he rubbed his forehead where Greenie's pebble had landed. He was not particularly tall, and not the most handsome of boys, but neither was he unpleasant. His nickname was Leo, because he fought like a leopard and was one of the most outstanding youngsters at Shaolin Monastery, a junior monk who had not yet taken his vow. There was rivalry between the junior monks and the lay pupils. They were boys all around the same age, with the usual rows, scuffles and peer rivalry, but Leo was popular with both camps. He switched sides frequently, like a leopard changing its spots.

The boy next to him was a year younger but already taller, a big, strong boy, dark as charcoal. He had a fiery temper. His actions worked faster than his brain. At the slightest provocation, his fists were out. When he fought, he was fearless, without regard

27

for human life, including his own. He was born with unusual strength. He could kill a tiger with one blow and could without effort lift an ox over his shoulder. This gift from Heaven was admired by the senior monks, and enabled him to stay on at the monastery, even though he had caused endless trouble and could now go out only with permission and under the supervision of a senior pupil. His frequent bust-ups and explosive temper had earned him the nickname 'Bussie'.

The third boy was the youngest, short and chubby with a face as round as a full moon and the tip of his nose at the centre of a perfect circle. When he smiled, his eyes narrowed and two dimples appeared in his cheeks. His nickname was Tobie. He was shy. When he saw Minnie and Greenie, he hid timidly behind his friends.

Minnie jumped up to look for her shoes, but they were not there. Greenie said crossly, 'Give us back our shoes!' Leo stood speechless.

Minnie looked exquisite in her beautiful red dress. She began to cry, but was soon distracted by the sound of a carriage. The carriage pulled to a stop when it reached them and Jade stepped out. Greenie explained what had happened. 'You rascals, give the young lady back her shoes,' he ordered.

Tobie stepped forward to hand Minnie her shoes, and Greenie helped her put them on. Jade watched, casting furtive glances at Minnie's pretty feet. Minnie watched this handsome young man before her, mature and sophisticated in his yellow robe and fine jewellery. When she looked up at him, she blushed.

Someone ran towards them from the path. '*Shimei*[4], thank heaven, I've found you.' Minnie went to him, '*San Shixiong.*[5]' The young man was the third pupil of Minnie's father, nicknamed Madaha because he was a scatterbrain. '*Shifu* is waiting for you at the inn. He has been really worried and he sent all of us out to look for you.' He saw that Minnie was upset. 'What happened? Have they hurt you?' Mahada clenched his fists ready to fight.

This was what Bussie had been waiting for. He had been

---

[4] younger kung fu sister
[5] third elder kung fu brother

annoyed by Jade, and wanted to lash out at him but had been restrained by Leo. Now he did not hesitate and out went his fist. To his surprise, he missed. A fat Tibetan lama pointed a finger at him and his arm drooped.

Jade went to Madaha, clasped his hands in salutation and introduced himself. Madaha returned the courtesy and introduced himself and his *Shimei*.

Minnie's father was the famous Ma QingLing, a contender for the championship of the Martial Arts Fellowship. He owned the largest armed escort delivery service in the country with branches in ten provinces, a business founded by Minnie's grandfather, who had ten disciples, each disciple in charge of one province. The grandfather had retired and was succeeded by his son. Minnie's father was an only child, so this made Minnie very precious indeed from the moment she was born. Minnie's father had hoped for a boy, but his wife had had a difficult pregnancy and could not give him another child. Minnie did not disappoint her parents and grandparents. She grew up beautiful and intelligent and was perfection in their eyes.

Jade was impressed. The girl before him was the daughter of one of the most powerful men in the country. He smiled, looking his most charming. He offered to take Minnie, her *Shixiong* Madaha, and Greenie with him in his carriage as he was also on his way to the inn at the foot of Mount Song. He needed to drop his calling card at the Shaolin Monastery, and after that, he would take them back to the inn.

Through all the commotion, there was another boy in the bush who had not shown himself. Flint had just finished his kung fu exercises with Miao Shan *ShiTai*, and was watching out for his friend Storm. He saw the carriage and the riders stop by Minnie and Greenie. He wanted to get back to the monastery in case Storm had arrived by a different route, so decided to hitch a ride. He slid under the carriage. To his surprise, someone was there already, holding on for dear life, a very young boy, scruffy and dirty. As the carriage moved, the boy tried to bump Flint off but Flint held fast. The carriage rocked from side to side. Suddenly Flint grabbed the boy's arm and pulled him from the carriage, so that they both rolled into the undergrowth. The lama had spotted them hiding underneath the carriage, and had aimed a blow at them. Flint and the boy jumped off just in time. As soon as they were on safe ground, the boy ran away like a whiff of wind.

Flint walked the rest of the way back. The carriage stood in front of the monastery. He heard Jade say to the lama, 'Don't worry about them. Probably some local urchins. Now we have someone important to meet. He is waiting for us at the entrance gate.' Flint looked to the mountain gate, where stood Master Zheng, the Senior Master in charge of Shaolin's disciplinary matters. Flint decided to return to his dormitory and wait there for his friends Bussie and Tobie.

IV

NUMBER ONE MONASTERY
UNDER HEAVEN

Shaolin Monastery was the foremost monastery in China and the cradle of Chinese martial arts. Shaolin had the usual eaves and roof lines of a Buddhist building, large but not grandiose. It was built in 496AD by Emperor Wen Di of the Northern Wei Dynasty. The site was chosen by an Indian Buddhist monk, Batuo, who had come to China to spread Theravada Buddhism. The land had the shape of a lotus in full bloom. It was surrounded by hills, woods, and streams, and the air was fresh and clear. The remote mountaintop was an ideal place to practise meditation, to free the mind from worldly desires.

In 527AD another Buddhist monk Bodhidharma arrived at Shaolin Monastery. Bodhidharma was born a prince, the third son of the Indian King Brahman. Bodhidharma left his comfortable life to become a Buddhist monk. He travelled from India to China through the Himalayas to spread Mahayana Buddhism.

Theravada or 'Small Vehicle' Buddhism is one of the early schools of Buddhism. It conveys the early teachings of Buddha and the attainment of Buddhahood by one's own efforts. A later movement led to a new school of Buddhism known as the Mahayana, or 'Great Vehicle' Buddhism, which emphasises compassion and an aspiration to full Buddhahood for the benefit of all sentient beings. In the course of time, Mahayana Buddhism produced many schools of its own, including Zen Buddhism.

Shaolin Monastery is a Zen monastery. To attain the goals of Mahayana Buddhism, the Buddhist monk Bodhidharma promoted deep meditation in a sitting posture for long periods of time. The sitting form of meditation in the lotus Buddha pose became a characteristic of Zen Buddhism. But this deep meditation was not good for the limbs of the monks. So Bodhidharma devised exercises to help the monks reactivate their limbs and grow stronger and healthier, exercises which were improved upon by monks over generations. But it is Bodhidharma who is accredited as the founder of Shaolin kung fu and revered as the First Patriarch of Zen Buddhism.

The Daoist and his pupil finally reached the flight of stone steps leading to the entrance gate of the Monastery. In front of the gate stood two stone lions, and a board hung above the gate saying 'Shaolin Monastery'. The young acolyte looked up to admire the simplicity and beauty of the architecture. 'So this is the famous Shaolin Monastery, the reputed 'Number One Monastery under Heaven'.'

The young lad's thoughts were interrupted by the Daoist. 'Shaolin is a large monastery with about 800 monks. The monastery has six main buildings. Each building is separated from the next by a courtyard. The Steles Forest is in the first courtyard. Through the courtyard, you will reach the 'mountain gate' which is the entrance to the monastery. The mountain gate opens into the first building, the Hall of Heavenly Kings, flanked by a Bell Tower and a Drum Tower. The next is the Grand Hall '*Daxiongbaodin*', then the Sutra Repository Pavilion, and the Abbot's Lodge. The monks' quarters are along the two sides of the Abbot's Lodge. Beyond the Abbot's Lodge is the Bodhidharma Pavilion. At the end of the Monastery is the Hall of the Thousand Buddhas.

There is one place you must never enter, the Stupa Forest to the west of the Monastery. This is Shaolin's holy place and no one may enter except with the permission of the Abbot.'

The Daoist pointed to the entrance gate. 'This is the mountain gate, the entrance to the Monastery. But we are not using this entrance. We will use a small path through the Steles Forest, and bypass the courtyards and halls to go directly to the Abbot's Lodge. I need to report to the Abbot at once. I will of course put in a few words for you. We will take off our Daoist habits. You can call me brother Storm and I will call you brother Speck. That's the way we address each other in the Brotherhood of River and Lake.'

The Daoist wondered what the boy had in mind for his future. 'Would you like to join the monastery? If you like, I can plead with the Abbot to allow you to become a monk. If it hadn't been for you, I would have been caught by the guards and would never have made it back to Shaolin.' He saw the hesitation on the young lad's face. 'Yes, I know I kidnapped you from the Palace and threatened you to make you lead me out. But I was seriously wounded by the guards. You could have got away many times yet you chose to stay with me. The pills and wound powder you gave me worked wonders. I am now fully recovered. Even our monastery does not have such powerful medicine for wounds. Brother Speck, I owe my life to you. Your kung fu is not brilliant. I'll teach you kung fu. You can become a monk or you could remain a lay disciple at Shaolin. I know you are a Palace eunuch, but I don't imagine you would want to spend the rest of your life in the Palace as a eunuch. This is an opportunity for you to escape and begin a new life.'

The young lad was touched. It was perhaps the longest speech Storm had ever made to him. Aware of Storm's limited education, the boy appreciated his efforts. 'I'll stay for a while at Shaolin. I will let you know what I decide to do.' He was curious. Why had Storm been at the Imperial Palace? How had he got in? He did not ask because he knew he would not get an answer. Storm and Speck entered Shaolin Monastery at the moment that the drum from the Drum Tower struck, signalling the conclusion of the day – it was 5 in the evening.

That very afternoon, the Abbot of Shaolin Monastery had received a special guest, Sir Qin, a friend of Master Fu, the Head Monk in charge of junior monks. Sir Qin had been to Shaolin several times to play chess with Master Fu, but this was the first time that he had paid a visit to the Abbot. He disclosed to the Abbot his intention of making a large donation to Shaolin monastery. In return he would ask the monastery a favour, to perform a seven-day prayer for the soul of his deceased mother.

The Abbot was embarrassed by the large sum of money offered by Sir Qin. He politely rejected Sir Qin's offer, and explained that Shaolin Monastery was an establishment for Zen

Buddhism. The monks devoted themselves to meditation with the ultimate aim of attaining 'Enlightenment'. The Abbot referred Sir Qin to other monasteries nearby which would perform prayers for the deceased. Sir Qin would not hear of it. His persistence finally swayed the Abbot's resolve, and the Abbot reluctantly agreed to discuss the matter with the other monks. As Shaolin's annual contest was to be held in the next two days, the matter of prayer for Sir Qin's deceased mother would have to wait until after the contest. Sir Qin did leave with one concession from the Abbot. He could stay at Shaolin's guest lodge together with his retainer and his stable boy until after the contest.

The Abbot had just settled the matter of Sir Qin when Storm entered. Speck waited in the antechamber as Storm wanted to speak with the Abbot in private. Storm was in the Abbot's Study for an hour. It happened that one of the Abbot's junior monks had gone home to visit his ailing parents, so when Storm explained about Speck, the Abbot arranged for Speck to live in the spare room and take charge of the Study for the time being.

Late that night, the Abbot's Study was still lit. The Abbot put down his pen, deep in thought. He went over in his mind what Storm had told him.

Storm's uncle Wang ChengEn had been a Palace eunuch. He was the last Ming Emperor Chong Zhen's most trusted confidante. When Emperor Chong Zhen hanged himself on Coal Hill, Storm's uncle had hung himself beside the Emperor. All these years Storm had assumed his uncle was dead. Then an old Palace maid who was on home leave had come to Shaolin Monastery to make incense offerings to the Buddha. Storm had recognised her because as a young boy, he had seen the maid when he had visited his uncle at the Palace. Twenty five years had elapsed since his last visit, and Storm had grown from a young boy to a burly man. Time had been kind to the maid and she had not aged beyond recognition. So it was Storm who went over to greet her.

The Palace maid was very happy to see him, and told him that his uncle was still alive. When the Capital had fallen, his uncle had been found hanging from the tree with the last Ming Emperor, but he was miraculously revived. His survival was a closely guarded secret. It was only by chance that the maid had overheard a conversation about the old eunuch, and she told Storm that his uncle was being held imprisoned in the Inner Court of the Imperial Palace.

Ming and Qing Emperors and their families resided in the Inner Court of the Palace. With the Emperor's numerous wives, concubines, and children, the imperial household was huge and generally referred to as the '*Hou Gong*' or 'Rear Palace'. The 'Rear Palace' was headed by the Empress. She had the difficult task of harmonising the complicated relationships of the Emperor's numerous consorts to ensure the Emperor's peace and quiet. She also had the authority to discipline eunuchs, maids and emperor's consorts who ranked below her, and send them to the Inner Court prison as punishment.

Storm's uncle was being kept in isolation in a cell in the innermost part of the Inner Court prison. He had been kept there initially by the rebel chief Li ZiCheng and later by the Manchu Regents, Dorgon and Oboi. Dorgon was the Regent during Emperor Shun Zhi's minority, and Oboi was one of the four regents during Emperor Kang Xi's minority.

The maid had been able to sneak into the prison to visit Storm's uncle. The old eunuch had been severely tortured but had not been allowed to die. He had begged the maid to locate Storm. The maid had very few resources of her own. The last piece of news she had was that Storm had killed someone in Yunnan and had fled. Since then, she had lost all trace of him.

The last time she had seen the old eunuch, he was very weak and close to dying. As the maid's hometown was in Dengfeng County, she decided to pay a visit to Shaolin monastery to offer incense and to pray that Heaven would take pity on the old man and enable him to see his nephew before he died. She believed her prayers had been answered when she found Storm. The maid drew Storm a map of the Palace with the location of the prison and guard arrangements.

Storm had gone to the Palace to find his uncle. He befriended a junior guard and got him drunk before he turned up for duty.

Storm dressed himself in the guard's uniform and stole the guard's identification tally. A tally was split into two halves. The guard's half-tally must match the half held by a senior officer at the entrance. Storm mingled with the procession of guards reporting for duty and succeeded in getting into the Palace. He made his way into the prison, overpowered the guards, and found his uncle's cell. It was an emotional meeting. His uncle told him a secret and made him promise to pass it on only to the rightful heir to the Ming throne. Storm wanted to take his uncle from the prison but his uncle said that he was too old and too weak to attempt an escape, and it would only risk both their lives. His uncle's last words were, 'Now that I've passed on the secret and the duty to you, I can go in peace.' He took Storm's sword and killed himself, dying in Storm's arms.

Storm lingered in the cell too long. The injured guards had raised the alarm, and there was fierce fighting. Storm was wounded and had no choice but to flee. In trying to shake off the guards, he lost his way in the Palace. He stumbled into an empty room. Hearing footsteps approaching, he leapt to the ceiling and hid behind a rafter. A group of young eunuchs entered the room, about a dozen of them between the ages of 14 and 15. They changed into wrestling robes and began to wrestle. One boy was taller than them all. The other boys called him 'Speck'. He motivated the boys, shouting encouragement to them to fight harder. He was one against several but still he came out winner. After an hour or so, the boys began to tire. When the tall boy pushed them to go on, the other boys piled on top of him, but he flung them off. They all slumped to the floor, bruised and panting for breath. The young eunuchs changed back into their clothes, and one by one they left the room, except for the tall boy.

Storm jumped down from the rafter. With a blade in his hand, he forced Speck to lead him from the Palace. Speck explained to Storm that all the exits were heavily guarded and that there was no chance of them escaping without a permit, but that he knew where the Emperor kept his seal. He took Storm to the Study, wrote out a permit in the name of the Emperor and stamped it with the Emperor's seal. As the wrestling room was inside the

Wu-Ying Palace south west of the Forbidden City, Speck suggested that they exit via the Xi-Hua Gate which was nearest. He happened to know a guard at the Gate who would let them out. With the permit, Speck and Storm escaped the Palace, but they had not gone far when the guards came in pursuit.

It was a long and difficult journey. On the way, they had taken shelter in a dilapidated temple, where they had come across a Daoist priest and his acolyte roasting a chicken for their meal. Storm overpowered them and exchanged clothes. They helped themselves to the chicken and had a rare good night's food and rest. The young eunuch Speck turned out to be an excellent rider. He also had a good knowledge of government routes and Postal Relay Stations. They were able to steal the best horses, and they swapped horses several times on the way to Shaolin.

The Abbot did not ask Storm to disclose his uncle's secret to him. Instead he turned his thoughts to Speck. The young eunuch had stood, calm and composed, with his back straight and his eyes looking straight into the Abbot's. He was taller than most boys of his age. The Abbot was impressed. He was also intrigued. Speck was polite, but the Abbot discerned something more, an air of authority and dignity. Was it because Speck was close to the Emperor that he had adopted his master's mannerisms? Or, the Abbot asked himself, had he been wrong after all in his opinion of eunuchs? Chinese opera portrayed eunuchs as pathetic creatures with fawning smiles, hunched backs and shrill female-like voices. Perhaps the operas did not do eunuchs justice.

The Abbot also noticed small pox marks on Speck's face, which must account for his nickname. The marks were hardly noticeable, and the Abbot thought that if anything, they only added to Speck's charisma.

It was nearly midnight. Tomorrow would be an even busier day for the Abbot as still more visitors were expected. But tonight he had an important task to do. He donned a black robe and tied a scarf around his face. He snuffed out the candle and slipped out from his Lodge. He leapt over a wall at the back of the monastery and headed towards the hill.

V

CLOSE ENCOUNTER

Before Storm left for Beijing, he told his friends that if they did not see him by dinner time on Flint's birthday, they should go to his hut and wait for him there. So when Flint met up with Bussie and Tobie, they set off for Storm's hut.

Storm kept his word and was back in time for the birthday celebration. Having settled Speck in the Abbot's lodge, he went back to his hut and the boys were there waiting for him. Storm had brought them delicacies from Beijing. He had even managed to get some steamed buns from the famous Riverside Inn in Kaifeng. He gave Flint a sword, the sword he had stolen from the Daoist priest in the temple where he and Speck had taken shelter on their way back to the monastery.

The boys went back to their dormitory after the party. Close to midnight, Flint lay on his bed, his eyes wide open. The other boys in his dormitory were asleep. He could recognize the breathing of each of the nineteen other boys in the room. When he had first come here, he found the snoring thunderous. Since they had started practising breathing exercises and meditation, the snoring had stopped. Breathing was faint, audible only to trained ears. Very quietly, he slipped out of his bed to the door which opened into the antechamber where the boys kept their chamber pots. Flint opened a window, climbed out, and ran to the top of a small hill. There the Abbot and Miao Shan *ShiTai* were waiting for him.

Flint started by practising the Reverse Abdominal Breathing ten times. He relaxed his body and concentrated his mind. The Abbot put his hand on Flint's abdomen and passed his *Yang* energy into Flint's *Dantian*, the energy field below the naval. His hand directed the *Qi* to flow along the Governing Vessel, up the spine to the crown of the head. The *Qi* flowed along three paths: down the nose, on each side of the face between the eyes and ears, converging at the tip of the tongue. Flint exhaled, touching his tongue to the bottom of his mouth. Miao Shan *Shi Tai* then directed the *Qi* to flow down the Conception Vessel back to the *Dantian* energy field. This completed one cycle of the 'small universe' energy flow. The cycle was repeated to enable a continuous flow of *Qi* around the Governing Vessel and Conception Vessel.

Just as they were beginning the last cycle and were close to completing the exercise, there was a loud flapping sound. A huge dark cloud came towards them. The moon rose above the mountain, and they saw that the cloud was made up of tens of dozens of vermillion finches beating their wings. Behind them walked a tall woman shrouded in a vermillion cloak.

The Abbot felt a tremor in Miao Shan *Shi Tai*'s hand. She whispered, 'That is the Vermillion Queen of Finches. What is she doing here in Shaolin? Her finches are fitted with poisonous steel tips. Just a scratch can be fatal.' The Abbot motioned to her to stay still. He hoped that the finches would fail to notice them and pass quickly by. Flint was oblivious of the threat. He was in a trance-like state. As cycles of 'small universe' *Qi* flows continued one after another, he felt his inner force grow with completion of each cycle. He had never felt so good. He was simply bursting with energy and ready to break from his trance. He knew he was near the end of the exercise.

The Abbot and Miao Shan *Shi Tai* had been careful in choosing this spot. There was just enough room for the three of them to practise the exercises, and they were well hidden behind the bushes. At the same time they could see what was happening around them.

The night was dark and still, broken only by the beating wings of the birds. In the moonlight, the woman, her long dark hair trailing behind her, followed the finches with a stick in her hand. She was soft and light on her feet and moved like an evening breeze. Her pace was swift and in an instant the woman was only a few feet from them. She wore a silver mask which covered her eyes and nose, with the nose shaped to look like the beak of a bird, sharp and pointed. Her lips were painted red, exaggerating her large mouth. Her body was completely covered by a long vermillion coloured silk cape. The occasional breeze raised her cape to reveal matching vermillion trousers and boots.

The red cloud suddenly dispersed as the finches flapped their wings wildly and flew off in all directions. Sparrowhawks zoomed in and chased after them. The sparrowhawks were well trained and executed their attacking skills with deadly precision.

The woman in red had no time to worry about her finches. Sensing something, she stopped and turned back. Sharp metal objects flew from a tree opposite, straight towards her. She bent backwards, and with her head almost touching the ground, swirled round. Her red cape whirled around her like a ring of red dust. As she moved, the metal objects fell to the ground. The woman straightened and pirouetted, leaping high in the air, her red cape opened wide like two giant wings. She was a giant red bird hovering in the sky.

The woman aimed a blow with her open palm at a tree, and the tree snapped. A shadow came out from behind it, a man clad in black from head to toe. Something long and thin, shiny green, hurtled towards the woman, a long and very fine chain attached to which was a poisonous green snake. She laughed scornfully and snapped the snake in two with her fingers. The chain continued towards her, bringing with it a single-edged blade mounted perpendicularly to a wooden handle. The blade came at great speed and force, and caught the woman by surprise. Instinctively she twisted her body and the blade missed her narrowly. When she looked up again, the man in black had gone.

The woman inclined her head and surveyed the surrounding trees. She aimed a blow at a small bush. The man emerged from the bush, but before she could aim another blow, there was a thundering sound and he vanished in a cloud of smoke. Not knowing whether the smoke was poisonous, she did not chase after him. Instead, she detached one of her long red finger nails and flung it towards the smoke cloud. There was a small muffled sound, and all went quiet. The smoke dispersed and there was no sign of the man in black. The woman flew off in the direction in which he had fled, and soon disappeared into the dark.

Flint came to the end of his 'small universe' *Qi* exercise, totally unaware of what had happened. He was bursting with energy. When he was ready to come out from his meditation, he opened his eyes. His body felt light, and when he leapt up he found himself high above the ground almost effortlessly. He leapt again and this time, landed on top of a tree. He was surprised to find himself up so high. He struck at another tree, and the tree snapped and fell. He was amazed by his own power.

The Abbot and Mao Shan *ShiTai* were smiling. The Abbot said, 'We have finally unblocked your *Qi* flow. You will feel the internal energy flooding your body like water rushing from a burst dam. You have more internal energy in your body than *Mao Shan ShiTai* and I. Yet you still will not be able to beat us in kung fu. That is because you don't yet know how to make maximum use of your internal energy. You are like a man with plenty of money but without the key to unlock the safe. You must practise hard both External and Internal Kung Fu before you can make full use of your internal energy.'

Mao Shan *ShiTai* explained, 'This means that you will need to externally train tendons, bones and muscles; and internally train the *Qi*. The Internal Kung Fu exercises help to treat and refine the *Qi* so that the *Qi* can be used more efficiently for greater power and force.'

The Abbot nodded. 'Kung fu without internal force is only good for show business. This type of kung fu is what we call 'Flowery Fist and Embroidered Leg'. A good martial artist requires the techniques of External Kung Fu and the force and power of Internal Kung Fu.'

Miao Shan *ShiTai* said to the Abbot, 'It is lucky that I had the foresight to bring my sparrowhawks with me. I have selected the two best for Flint to keep with him. Yesterday was his birthday.'

They walked to where the woman in red had been standing. The Abbot bent down, took in his fingers a piece of metal, and counted the remaining pieces on the ground. 'This is a throwing blade shaped like a four-pointed star. It is normally used as a secret weapon to attack the enemy by surprise. There are nine of these blades altogether.' Picking up the long chain with the single edged blade, he said, 'I am familiar with the kung fu styles practised by different schools, but I have not known any school to use such weapons. When I return to the monastery, I shall look in our archive for information about them.' He went over to the tree which had been snapped by the palm of the woman in red. The broken tree trunk was charred, and smoke drifted from it. 'Was this caused by the notorious Red Flaming Palm?'

Miao Shan *Shi Tai* nodded. 'Judging from the tree, the Vermillion Queen has already reached level seven of the Red Flaming Palm kung fu. If she had reached level eight, the tree would not have snapped in the middle. It would have burned inside but externally it would look as if nothing had happened. When she reaches level nine, she will be able to emit fire from her palms, and the whole tree and the surrounding area would burn in flames. I am her nemesis. The only way to combat the Red Flaming Palm is to use our Black Ice Palm.'

They all returned to the Abbot's Lodge. Miao Shan *Shi Tai* removed her veil. This was the first time Flint had seen her face, and he was pleasantly surprised at her gentle features. She was not the severe *Shi Tai* that he had imagined, but a kindly elderly woman. She said, 'I am thirteen years older than the Vermillion Queen. I have known her since she was small. She stayed with us and learned kung fu from my husband. My husband died because of her. She poisoned me and I lost my kung fu. My face was disfigured by the poison, and I had to cover my face with a veil. Without my kung fu, I could not hope for revenge. So I hid myself in a mountain cave to escape from her. There my luck turned. The mountain cave I came upon happened to contain the relic of the Ice Maiden and the manual of the Black Ice Palm. After more than 20 years, I have finally managed to regain my kung fu and my former looks.

'However I know our story will not end here. She will not let me live because I know of her past, and also because she knows well I want to avenge my husband's death. We are destined to be enemies. I am waiting for the day when we will settle our score.

Whenever I travel, I always cover my face and take my sparrowhawks with me. I was right to take these precautions. Now I have met her again, I see that her kung fu has advanced beyond my expectations, and I am at best her equal. I cannot stay here any longer. Be careful. The Vermillion Queen is an evil woman. She has a notorious reputation in the South. People fear her because she uses villagers as live targets to train her finches. She is ruthless, and has no regard for human life.'

She took out from her robes a cap and a flute, and gave them to Flint. 'This cap was made for you by your nanny. The flute is from your *Shifu*. It is an antique flute made of bamboo and it originally belonged to your *Shifu*'s father. Two sparrowhawks are in the woods waiting for your whistle. I will tell your *Shifu* about your recovery and she will be very pleased.'

Miao Shan *ShiTai* took her leave, put back the veil over her face, and walked out into the night. Flint was happy that they had all remembered his birthday. He would take the sparrowhawks to Storm's hut. It would be safer for Storm to keep the birds there.

VI

MASTER WEI'S GROOVE

Shaolin monks are also known as 'fighting monks'. In 621AD, thirteen Shaolin monks had rescued the Prince of Qin, who later became the Emperor of the Tang Dynasty. He allowed the Monastery to train 500 'fighting monks' to assist in the defence of the country. In the thousand years since, Shaolin troops had been called upon on several occasions to defend the country's borders and coastlines. As their fame spread, they attracted the best from the country to join them either as monks or lay disciples.

Junior monks and lay pupils were distinguished by the colour of their robes and the style of their hair. Junior monks wore short blue robes opened at the side, blue trousers tucked inside white leg coverings beneath the knees, and a sash around their waists. Lay pupils wore grey robes and grey trousers. Their shoes were the same, made of black cloth with thin white soles.

All monks, including junior monks, shaved their heads. Those who had taken the vow would have nine incense joist burns on their crown. The vow was usually taken after a monk reached 18 years old. The Abbot could exercise his discretion as to who was eligible. Storm and Master Wei, Head Monk in charge of lay pupils, had not taken their vows. In Storm's case, it was because of his drunken antics. In the case of Master Wei, it was because he had too much anger in his heart. Master Wei came from Yangzhou and had experienced the 'ten days' of massacre by Manchu troops which he could not forget or forgive.

The lay pupils followed the Qing hair style, but they coiled their single plait around their head when they practised kung fu. Since the Manchu Conquest, all Chinese men were required to follow the Manchu hair style by shaving their forehead and wearing their hair in a single plait at the back. The Manchus decreed, 'keep your head and lose your hair or keep your hair and lose your head'.

Occasionally babies were abandoned on the doorstep of the monastery. The babies were sent to be reared by foster families in villages around the foot of ShaoShi Hill. When these children reached the age of six, the foster families could keep the babies if they chose. Otherwise the monks would take them back to train as junior monks. Those with talent would train as 'fighting monks'. Those not selected would move to sedentary jobs, or become lay pupils for training with Master Wei.

Leo had been abandoned as a baby, and had come to the monastery to train as a junior 'fighting monk'.

Bussie was also abandoned. He had been a difficult baby, hyperactive and short fused. He proved too much to handle, and was passed from one foster family to another. By the age of four, Bussie had the height and build of a boy several years his senior. The monks could no longer find any family willing to take on the responsibility of looking after him, so they reluctantly took him back to the monastery. Normally the Head Monk in charge of junior monks would have first choice of orphans joining the monastery. It happened that the Head Monk, Master Fu, was away when Bussie arrived. His assistant was irritated by the bad tempered and hyperactive child, so passed him onto Master Wei. From the moment he saw Bussie, Master Wei knew that the child was special. When he realised Bussie's immense strength, he was ecstatic. He blessed his good luck and thanked Heaven for sending the child to him.

Tobie was the nephew of the Head Chef, a man more feared and revered than the Abbot. His vegetarian dishes were so well known that important people and martial artists travelled great distances to taste his cooking. His exalted position in the monastery was however based on very practical considerations. The Head Chef had control of the kitchen. Everyone knew what they would be given to eat if they offended the Chef. Saliva, phlegm, urine, and faeces might be mixed into their food. Tobie's mother had died in childbirth, and the Head Chef was his only relative. As was the rule at Shaolin, Tobie was first placed into foster care. Like Bussie, Tobie was moved from one foster family to another, but this time, it was not the child's fault. It was the uncle who was forever interfering. The slightest scratch on baby Tobie would set his temper flaring. Eventually no family dared to take Tobie on. The Chef could not trust anyone to care properly for Tobie, so decided to bring up Tobie himself. At the age of two, Tobie was taken to live with his uncle at Shaolin monastery.

There was bitter rivalry between the two Head Monks, Master Fu and Master Wei. The reason was simple, the annual contest between junior monks and lay pupils. The contest had begun ten years earlier when the old Abbot Tong Ti, concerned by the falling standards of the junior fighting monks, decided to encourage competition between monks and lay pupils.

Master Wei started at a disadvantage. The cream of the pupils always went to the monks' quarters. He had to be content with second choice. So he decided to beat the system by sending his scouts to scour the villages for talented boys to join the monastery as lay pupils. For a time, he had a handsome scoop of talented boys. But word reached Master Fu's ears, and he sent out scouts too. He even convinced parents that if a boy came to Shaolin, when he reached 16 years old, he would be able to choose not to become a monk but could revert to a lay disciple. The competition became stiffer and fiercer. The scouts went further and further from Henan in search of talent. There was now in Shaolin no shortage of talented young boys from places as remote as Tibet and Tianshan.

Master Wei was right. Bussie proved to be a prize asset. Although he had the strength of a lion, physical strength alone was not enough, and Bussie had to submit to External and Internal Kung Fu exercises. The limbs must be supple and flexible. The strikes and blows needed force and power. Master Wei would need to help Bussie overcome his fiery temper and restlessness or he would never make progress. But *Qi* can only be developed through breathing and meditation. The traditional form of meditation practised in Shaolin was the still form, characterised by the external stillness of the body, practised in sitting, standing or reclining positions. The sitting posture was favoured by the Shaolin monastery, passed down from Bodhidharma, founder of Shaolin kung fu. Master Wei knew that Bussie would never be able to settle down to the still form of meditation, so he devised a moving form for him which had more to do with the body and the external aspects of kung fu, with breathing serving as the link between movement and stillness. The moving form was a combination of many styles of external kung fu expressed in dance form. It was designed to flow naturally and fluidly, the rhythm regulating breathing, to bring the mind to a harmonious state. It calmed Bussie down, the body was moving but the mind was still. Bussie's kung fu improved by leaps and bounds. Bussie held the record for being the youngest person ever to take part in the annual contest when he was only ten years old. He had been the overall champion for the last two years and was odds on favourite to win the championship again this year.

Master Wei was in his mid-thirties. His motto was 'hard work and perseverance are the keys to success'. While talent was a great help, it was hard work which won out at the end of the day, and his favourite fable was the race between the tortoise and the hare. Master Wei worked harder than anyone in the monastery. There was not an ounce of fat in his body, and his cheeks were lined and craggy. His thin tight lips and stern brow were often tightly-knit with anxiety over his pupils who too often did not live up to his expectations. Each day, he pushed his pupils to work harder and harder. He could be heard crying at the top of his voice 'Hone your skills. There's no short cut in kung fu. It's just PRACTISE, PRACTISE, PRACTISE!' There was one thing Master Wei could not tolerate, SLOTH. He believed 'all illnesses could be cured except sloth'. He disliked overweight people as a matter of principle. People became fat because they were lazy. That was why Master Wei found Tobie beyond hope.

Tobie was fat and so hopelessly lazy. Master Wei had tried all kinds of ways to make him work hard on his kung fu. The carrot and stick method didn't work. The boy took the carrot, but when it came to the stick, the Chef would appear and rescue his nephew from Master Wei's wrath. Whenever Master Wei thought of Tobie, his brow locked. He had to tolerate Tobie in his camp because he could not afford to upset Tobie's uncle. If a boy failed his martial arts test three times, he would be asked to leave Shaolin or be transferred to a sedentary job. Yet every year Tobie managed to scrape through. The Head Chef must have had something to do with this. It could be the special herbs prepared by the Chef for Tobie. Or perhaps the Chef had been transferring his own energy to him. That was of course cheating. But after weighing up the pros and cons, Master Wei decided to turn a blind eye.

What Master Wei did not know was that since Tobie was a baby, the Chef had taught him breathing exercises. As soon as Tobie could walk, he had taught him the *Qingong*. The Chef's *Qingong* 'A Thousand Flying Steps' was the best in the Brotherhood of River and Lake. The Chef had once been a thief, and was nick-named the 'Shadowless Man' because when he ran, he was so fast that he left no shadow on the ground.

Tobie hated fighting and he hated kung fu. If you told him to practise his kung fu exercises, he would refuse, but if you told him it was a game, he would do it gladly and well. His uncle designed games to stimulate Tobie's interest. He played hide-and-seek with Tobie to get him use his *Qingong*. The Chef made sure that his nephew had mastered this great art of survival. 'Of the 36 strategies, the best strategy is to run away', he said. The Chef collected small round pebbles to use as marbles for Tobie to develop strength in his fingers and knuckles. He taught him to shoot using a sling and stone, and later with arrows and bows to develop his arm muscles. Dart playing and football games developed his eyesight and kept his limbs supple, along with swimming, hunting, shooting and fishing. In many ways, the Chef's methods were more ingenuous and effective than Master Wei's hard drilling.

Tobie also had a rare gift, a photographic memory. He needed only to see something once and the information would be retained. This was known only to the Chef, Storm and Tobie's two good friends. To everyone else, Tobie was a lazy boy. Shaolin was renowned for its 72 fighting skills. Not a single person in the history of Shaolin had ever mastered all 72 skills. Pupils were taught different skills according to their individual physique and talent. If someone could master even one skill, it would be sufficient for him to move about unharmed in the Brotherhood of River and Lake. Shaolin disciples usually aimed to attain perfection in several skills, but Tobie knew by heart all 72 skills. Tobie's uncle had managed to get hold of the manuals for Tobie to read and to store in his memory. But although Tobie learned the skills, he never bothered to practise them.

Because Tobie hated kung fu, when it came to kung fu tests, he never bothered to try. He had not realised that years of training under his uncle had so conditioned his body that he had acquired automatic responses and reflexes. Master Wei would like to fail him but could not. Had Master Wei known of Tobie's gift, he would have scolded Heaven for having no eyes, wasting such a precious gift on so worthless a boy.

Master Fu, who was in charge of junior monks, was almost ten years older than Master Wei. Under Master Fu, the junior monks' kung fu had greatly improved. The monks' side won the annual contests for seven consecutive years and had lost to the lay pupils only in the last two years. Master Fu was stout and jovial, and although he was an outstanding kung fu expert, he had other interests. He was over-fond of the game of chess, indeed hopelessly addicted, and more proud of his skill on the board than his kung fu. He accepted chess challenges but would ask for donations to the monastery when the challengers lost. Recently, he had met one challenger who was just too good. Master Fu refused to acknowledge defeat and asked the challenger to come back to play again and again. When Master Fu lost, the challenger never asked him for money. As a result of this obsession, Master Fu had not kept up his supervision of the junior monks. It would soon be time for the contest, and he was not confident about his side. He resolved to leave aside his chess for a while and focus on kung fu. If he did not regain his reputation as a kung fu coach, he might lose his job.

The lay pupils rose to begin their exercises at four o'clock, as they did every morning. The training ground was outside the monastery, hidden in the woods. The Shaolin Monastery, like all other martial arts schools, did not wish its training methods exposed to others. The boys started with warm-up exercises, including hand forms, punches, stances and leg stretching exercises.

When the bell tower struck five, there was still no sign of Master Wei at the training ground. The very young ones began their practice with handstands, front flips, back flips, body drops, and walking on a tightrope balancing bowls of water. Older ones stood on their heads with their feet in the air, or hung from a tree with a rope around their neck, in a sitting posture as in meditation. More advanced pupils practised their handstands on one finger tip, head down and feet up. Some practised punching or kicking at sand bags. Some broke bricks with their heads, legs, elbows or fingers. Others were working on the fire exercises. The aim was to turn fire power and steam into *Qi*. At the initial stage, the pupils tried spitting saliva onto a small stone ball until the ball could be moved by the spit. Then they would practise licking a burning hot shovel, taking in the steam and directing it to the *Dantian*, the energy field below the naval. The *Qi* was thus stored in the *Dantian*.

Some were practising palm conditioning exercises. The hand was dropped into dried peas in an urn raised to waist high. The dried peas would be mixed with stone pebbles for more advanced pupils, and the stone pebbles mixed with iron pellets for the most highly advanced pupils. Others practised finger exercises by smashing a piece of stone, or pulling the nails from a plate with their fingers. Some lifted an earthen jar with the fingers of each hand, stretching their arms horizontally. The more advanced pupils lifted jars filled with iron sand weighing more than 330 pounds. The final level would be reached when the pupil could stand with one foot on a board of nails and lift the jars of iron sand.

There were also boys practising the *Qingong* exercises, standing on long thin stakes. The stakes were set into the ground and rose to a height of eight feet with a diameter of only 2 inches. Others would tie iron sand bags around their legs and walk the edge of a large vat of water. More advanced students were given heavier iron sand bags, to walk the edge of a bamboo basket. To pass the final test for *Qingong*, Master Wei demanded that his pupils tie iron sand bags around their legs and walk along a sand path without leaving foot prints.

By mid morning, Master Wei still had not arrived. The ground was abuzz with news of his absence. Although Master Wei was a very strict *Shifu*, everyone respected him. They knew that they owed to Master Wei their achievements in kung fu.

When Master Wei still failed to appear, some boys left the training ground to enjoy a morning of relaxation. Flint and Tobie sneaked away and went to play at the mountain spring. A further absentee from the monk's training ground was Leo. He too was heading for the mountain spring. Leo was hard working and had never before missed his training exercises, but today he had a special reason for absconding. He was hoping to catch sight of the pretty Minnie.

Tobie and Leo played a game of football. The inside of a leather ball was lined with feathers and air was blown into it to make it bounce. The one rule of the game was simple. The ball must stay in the air at all times. Head, hands, feet, elbows, shoulders, chest and knees could all be used for hitting, kicking and punching the ball. The ball went up and down, forwards and backwards from Tobie to Leo and back again. At one point the ball flew right past Tobie, and a lanky boy leapt out from nowhere and stopped the ball with his head. He bounced the ball from his head to his right shoulder, from his right shoulder to his left, and rolled it down his back. He leaned forward, and with his right foot curled backwards, he flicked the ball behind him to his left foot, then high into the air, and caught it again with his head. He squatted down and lifted a leg, spinning the ball on the tip of his boot until he kicked it high up into a tree.

It was a breathtaking performance. Tobie and Leo clapped, marvelling. The performer was a thin boy of about 13 or 14. He had so much dirt on his face that his features were almost hidden. Yet he seemed quite pleasant, with lively bright eyes and a nice smile.

'Who are you?' Leo asked.

'I am Sir Qin's stable boy. My master is visiting Master Fu. My name is Qin Hai, but you can call me Haidi.' Haidi was short for 'Young Hai'

Tobie introduced himself, 'Little brother, my name is Tobie. My friend here is Leo.'

Leo looked up into the tree. 'Flint, will you please throw down our ball?'

Flint was sitting on the bough of a tree, his hands behind his head, and a cap pulled down over his eyes. He had watched idly from above the football game and was amused when he saw Haidi performing with the ball. He recognised him. This was the same boy who had tried to bump him from the carriage when he had hitched a ride back to the monastery.

The ball bounced down from the tree and Leo caught it. When he looked round to pass the ball, he saw Minnie and Greenie approaching. He dropped the ball and thought of running forward to greet them, but changed his mind.

When Minnie saw Leo and Tobie, she turned away, annoyed. Leo went forward, clasped his hands and bowed. 'Miss Minnie, we are sorry about yesterday. My little brother Tobie behaved badly. He should never have taken your shoes' He nudged Tobie to apologise.

Tobie apologised reluctantly. Although it was he who had Minnie's shoes in his hands, it had been Leo's idea to hide them. Minnie looked at Tobie and her face softened, but she was still annoyed.

Leo pulled something from inside his robe, a paper cutting of a kite in the shape of a peacock in full plumage, a beautiful blue peacock displaying a magnificent spectrum of colours. Leo knew a monk who was very skilful with his hands. He had begged the monk to make a paper cutting of a kite to give to Minnie. Minnie had had kites since she was a young child but even she had not seen one so beautiful.

'If you like, I'll put in the spars and cords and bring it back to you to-morrow.'

Minnie replied, 'You will have to do more than this. You and your friends must promise to do three things for me. Upon fulfilling your three promises, I will forgive all of you.'

Leo was cautious. 'I'll do anything for you as long as it is not against the rules of Shaolin.'

'Nothing will be against the rules. Here is my first request. Do you see that lovely red flower on the cliff top? If you can climb up and bring the flower down for me, I will accept that you have fulfilled your first promise.'

It was a very steep cliff, and it would be difficult to get to the top, but Leo would give it a try. Just as he was about to set off, Flint jumped down from the tree. The stable boy Haidi recognised him and turned away.

Flint said to Leo that he would get the flower. 'Are you sure?' Leo was a little surprised as he was not aware that Flint had achieved a 'small universe' breakthrough.

'Trust me. Today is my good day.'

Leo was a junior monk, and Flint a lay pupil. They did not train together and met only occasionally. Leo knew his own *Qingong* was not good enough to climb the cliff and was willing to let Flint take up the challenge. He introduced Flint to the girls. Greenie thought Flint the most handsome boy she had ever seen. Minnie was also impressed but said to herself, 'Jade is more stylish and he comes from a noble family.'

Flint bowed. 'Miss Minnie, would you permit me to get the flower for you on behalf of my brothers?'

Minnie did not believe for one moment that Flint would be able to do it. She had set this difficult task to shame the boys further. She pondered for a moment pretending it was a difficult decision. 'You were not involved in the incident yesterday. You do not have to volunteer. But if you insist, I will let you pick the flower for me on behalf of your brothers.'

Flint summoned his *Qi* and leapt high into the air, finding a ledge of rock on the side of the cliff. He stepped onto the ledge lightly, touching it with the tip of his toe. Breathing gently and holding his breath for as long as he could, he moved from ledge to ledge. In a moment, he had reached the top of the cliff. From below it looked as if he was flying.

He presented the red flower to Minnie who received it with a smile. He kept his other hand behind his back, in it a white flower. He walked over to Greenie and gave the flower to her. She was overwhelmed by his act of kindness, and put the flower into her hair. Minnie was astonished that Flint would pay attention to a maid, especially such a plain one.

The stable boy Haidi protested that it was unfair. He wanted a flower too. Minnie scoffed, 'You're a boy, what do you want a flower for?'

'I have a sister. I want to give the flower to my sister.'

Without a word, Flint went back up the cliff, and returned with a red flower like Minnie's. Minnie saw that Haidi's red flower was even prettier than hers. She said to Greenie, 'Look, why don't you let me put the red flower in your hair too. You'll look prettier with both flowers. I have so many pretty flowers in our garden at home, I don't really need this one.'

Leo wished he could impress Minnie as Flint had done, but he was not jealous. He was shrewd enough to know that his real rival for Minnie's attention was the wealthy scion Jade. He asked, 'What is the second thing you like us to do?' But Minnie was no longer in the mood. 'I can't think of a task for you at the moment. I'll let you know when I come up with something.'

At lunch time, the boys returned to the monastery. Some senior monks were ascetics and ate only one meal a day, but this did not apply to lay pupils, junior monks or the fighting monks. They had three meals to provide the nutrition they required for their kung fu training. After lunch, the boys were pleased to see Master Wei back in the training ground. The young eunuch Speck asked Master Wei for permission to watch the training. He stood quietly, paying close attention to the Shaolin fighting skills.

Master Wei began his routine testing of fitness and skills. Tobie hid behind the tall boys hoping Master Wei would not notice him. But Master Wei asked him to perform a horse-riding stance. Master Wei would not normally pick on Tobie, but he was in a foul mood.

The other boys stopped their exercises to watch. Tobie spread out his legs and squatted as though he was riding a horse. Master Wei gave a kick at his leg and Tobie fell. The boys covered their mouths with their hands not to laugh too loud. Master Wei shouted at Tobie, 'If you had practised, you would not have fallen so easily.' More and more angry, Master Wei tested Tobie's knowledge. 'Tell me how you would perform a horse-riding stance.'

Tobie replied, 'The toes must not point sideways. The feet should be parallel and about two shoulders' width apart, the body must be upright, and the thighs must be parallel to the ground.'

'What else?'

'The mind must focus on the abdomen.'

'Why?'

'So that the *Qi* can be stored in the *Dantian*.'

Master Wei tested him on Shaolin kung fu. 'What is the essence of Shaolin kung fu?'

'Stand like a Pine, Sit like a Bell; Move like Lightning, Walk like the Wind; Defend like a Virgin, Attack like a Ferocious Lion.'

'And…'

'Soft as Cotton, Light as Swallow, Hard as Steel.'

'Ok! Show us how you can be 'light as a swallow'. See that branch hanging from the tree? Jump up to that branch.' said Master Wei. The bough was thirty feet from the ground.

Tobie looked at the height of the bough and made up his mind that he could not do it. Master Wei sent Tobie up to the bough with a flick of his sleeve. 'Now jump down.' Tobie looked down and was scared. He closed his eyes and jumped. He hit the ground hard and wailed, so pitifully that a bystander would have imagined the worst possible tragedy.

Tobie had learned *Qingong* from his uncle. He had often leapt up and down from heights. But then he had been playing games and not practising kung fu. When it came to kung fu exercises, he shut down his body and mind, and refused to put in the slightest effort. Although Tobie's fall had been clumsy, he was not hurt. His body had responded automatically and his *Qi* regulated itself, cushioning the fall and reducing the impact.

Master Wei raised his hand. 'Get up and stop complaining, you useless good-for-nothing …' But someone ran onto the training ground, a machete raised high in his hand. 'Tobie, my precious boy, are you hurt?' The Head Chef was coming to the rescue once again. He embraced his nephew. When he saw Master Wei's outstretched hand he asked, 'My boy, did Master Wei slap you?' Tobie shook his head. The Chef, unconvinced, gave Master Wei an ugly stare. Master Wei walked away muttering enough curses to drown the whole of mankind.

The bell of the monastery began to chime. It was an alarm warning. Something had happened. A young monk came running onto the training ground and shouted, 'Soldiers, lots of soldiers, surrounding the monastery. You must all return at once.'

VII

HUNT FOR THE THIRD PRINCE

The monks gathered at the Hall of the Thousand Buddhas and were told that the soldiers were searching for a killer. A Shaolin monk had been killed in an inn at the foot of Mount Song. The dead man had been identified as a disciple of Master Zheng, Shaolin's Senior Master of Discipline.

Eye witnesses confirmed that two Shaolin monks had been drinking and became involved in a fight. One of them ended up dead. The incriminating evidence was a red palm print left on the dead man's body. The body tissue around the palm print was charred. It could only have been caused by someone who had practised the Shaolin Iron Palm. The force of the blow was consistent with that of a senior practitioner of the Iron Palm Kung Fu.

The killer had been wounded by a soldier as he escaped from the scene of crime. Soldiers pursued him until he leapt over the walls of the monastery and disappeared, and the military commander had obtained a warrant to search the monastery until the killer was found. As it was beyond doubt that the monk was a grown man, all those below the age of 16 were exempt from the search.

The Commander in charge of the search operation heard that Master Wei had been absent from the training ground that morning. He was anxious to question him.

In the early hours of the morning, Master Wei had staggered into the Abbot's room and collapsed, a poisonous dart piercing his shoulder. The Abbot extracted the dart and sucked the poison from the wound. The blood that flowed was black. The Abbot continued to suck until the blood turned red to be sure that the poison was gone. He told Master Wei to go to the Study to get some medicine for his wound.

The Abbot focused his mind in meditation. He circulated the *Qi* around his body to get rid of any poison from his contact with Master Wei's wound, and waited for Master Wei to explain to him what had happened.

In the Study, Master Wei found Speck, and he was surprised to see a new face. Speck brought some powder and applied it to the wound, and gave Master Wei a red pill to take to prevent infection spreading. He told him that the wound would heal in a couple of hours. Master Wei was astonished to learn that he would need only one application of medicine. He had not known that the Abbot had in his possession such a potion. Normally even the most effective medicine would require at least three applications and three days to work. But there was no time to ask questions. He had a more pressing matter which had to be reported to the Abbot immediately.

Master Wei explained to the Abbot that after dinner the previous evening, he had gone to Vinaya Hall to pay a visit to Master Zheng. Vinaya Hall lies next to the monks' quarters and is Shaolin's disciplinary centre. Master Wei and Master Zheng had been talking when they realised that someone was eavesdropping outside the window. They signalled to each other to continue their conversation until they heard the eavesdropper leave. Covering his face with a piece of cloth torn from his sash, Master Wei jumped from the window and quietly followed.

The man led him to an inn at the foot of Mount Song. Master Wei followed him through the courtyard to a small lodge at the back of the inn. There was light in one of the rooms. When the man went into the lodge, Master Wei hid under the window. He poked a small hole through the rice papered lattice and looked in. In the reception area, there was a round table where sat two men, one wearing the uniform of a Regimental Commander. A bordered yellow banner in the corner of the room told Master Wei that this man must be an officer under the command of Regent Oboi.

Master Wei, like all Han Chinese, was aware that although Kang Xi was the emperor in name, Oboi was the de facto ruler of China. He could not understand why Oboi would be so interested in Shaolin Monastery that he would send his officer here.

The other man at the table appeared to be a retainer, a man in his fifties with a goatee beard. A third man knelt with his head to the ground. The Commander demanded, 'Have you seen Prince Zhu San?'

'Commander, there have been no sightings of Prince Zhu San at Shaolin monastery.'

Master Wei had heard the rumour that Prince Zhu San was the third son of the last Ming Emperor Chong Zhen. He had also heard that Prince Zhu San had recently surfaced in the Brotherhood of River and Lake, rallying support for his claim as the rightful heir to the throne.

When the kneeling man lifted his head, Master Wei recognised him as the third disciple of the Senior Master of Discipline. He was shocked at this betrayal by the disciple.

The Commander banged his fist on the table. 'You useless slave! We've spent a fortune keeping you lot in Shaolin. We have maintained your families for you, kept them fed and clothed. But what have you done for us? All these years, the only report I have had is 'no signs of subversion at Shaolin Monastery'. Is that all you can tell me? If what you say is true, tell me why Shaolin keeps 800 fighting monks? I'll be damned if I believe that Shaolin is not involved in the 'Overthrow the Qing and Restore the Ming' movement. We've finally got credible information that Shaolin is in contact with a new Ming Pretender to the throne. Yet you come back again with a negative report.'

So there was more than one traitor in the monastery. Master Wei listened carefully. The Shaolin monk repeatedly kowtowed. The retainer asked, 'Tell us again about visitors to Shaolin over the last two days. You may have failed to notice something when you made your report.'

'There was only Sir Qin, his retainer and a stable boy,' the monk answered. 'They arrived yesterday afternoon. Sir Qin is in his late-thirties and is not the right age to be Prince Zhu San. He has been to Shaolin several times over the last few months. He likes to play chess with Master Fu, the Head Monk in charge of junior monks.'

'There's something strange about Sir Qin,' said the retainer.

'Nobody had heard of him two years ago. Then suddenly he is mingling with elite society in Beijing. His wealth is apparently impressive. He attends society functions and arrives in style, always impeccably dressed and adorned with the finest jewels. His carriage is the most magnificent in Beijing, inlayed with gold and encrusted with precious gems. No one knows how and where he has made his money. He is always surrounded by ladies who are curious to find out more about him, especially whether he is in need of a wife.'

'What else do you know about him?' the Commander asked.

'He is extremely generous, it seems, fond of giving gifts, especially to the ladies. Apparently, he bought his title. He is called 'Captain of the Imperial Guards, Fifth Rank'. The title is only honorary. Nobody expects him to carry out any official duties.'

The Commander turned to the monk again, 'Who else has been to Shaolin?'

'We have information that a number of guests arrived last night and have dropped their calling cards to call on the Abbot tomorrow morning. At the moment they are all staying here at this inn.'

The retainer said, 'I have a list of those who arrived here last night. They include the godson of Prince Geng JiMou and his attendants. Apart from this godson, the others do not fit the age description.'

'Is Prince Geng's godson around 25 years old? If the rumours are correct, that should be the age of Prince Zhu San,' said the Commander.

'We have had Prince Geng, his sons and his godson under surveillance for some time. The godson's natural father is a retainer and a close confidante of Prince Geng. There is no doubt that the retainer's wife was pregnant at the time and gave birth to a boy. Young Master Jade is a precious child, an only son. Prince Geng is very fond of him. He is one of those pampered rich boys, spends his days on wine, women and song. He frequents brothels, very much a ladies' man. You must have heard that Young Master Jade is handsome, and with his wealth and status, his reputation as one of the country's most eligible bachelors is not without cause.'

'Is he a martial arts practitioner?'

'He knows a bit of kung fu but he is not brilliant. There is nothing to worry about.'

'There's something strange going on here,' said the Commander. 'We have seen the Vermillion Queen of Finches in the Shaolin hills.'

'That's not surprising. Whenever you see Young Master Jade, the Vermillion Queen is always nearby. The story of how they met is well known. About eight years ago, before Prince Geng and his family moved to Fujian, the Vermillion Queen captured Young Master Jade. She was going to use him as a live target for her finches but when she saw how beautiful he was, she changed her mind. Young Master Jade was a smart boy. He asked the Vermillion Queen to accept him as her pupil. He promised heaven and earth if she would only spare his life.'

'So has Young Master Jade learned kung fu from her?'

'I don't think so. Her type of kung fu seems to have come from the west and is not compatible with our traditional kung fu styles. I would say she is more of a bodyguard to Young Master Jade. She lives in a house in the grounds of Young Master Jade's mansion and is treated like a real queen.'

The Commander turned to the monk, 'Who else has arrived?'

'Chief Armed Escort Ma QingLing, head of Four Seas Armed Escort Delivery, and his daughter, his third disciple, and a number of maids and servants. They arrived last night and have not yet called on the Abbot. In any case, they have no choice but to stay at the inn because Shaolin Monastery would never allow female visitors at their guest lodges.'

The Commander said, 'We know Chief Armed Escort Ma. There is nothing to connect him to Prince Zhu San. But why have all these people gathered here now?'

'They are probably hoping to attend the annual Shaolin contest between junior monks and lay pupils. Shaolin annual contests are strictly an internal matter. Guests are generally not invited, and no other martial arts schools have ever taken part in the contests. Our old Abbot, before he retired into seclusion, made it clear that he did not wish Shaolin annual contests to be used as open competitions for Championship to the Martial Arts Fellowship.'

'When is this year's contest?'

'It is supposed to take place in two days time. But I'm not sure now. I know for a fact that the Abbot is seriously considering postponing the contest because of the unexpected arrival of so many guests.'

Master Wei decided that he had heard enough, and slipped away quietly. His foot caught a fallen twig, and although the sound was barely audible to normal ears, the Commander and the retainer were both adept martial artists and they jumped from their chairs shouting, 'Who's out there?' The window opened and a dart flew out hitting Master Wei in the left shoulder. The guards chased after him, and saw him disappear through the walls of Shaolin Monastery.

Master Wei finished his report to the Abbot. The Abbot told him to return to his quarters and make sure he recovered completely before the soldiers arrived.

When Master Wei fled the inn, the retainer had raised his palm and killed the traitor monk instantly. 'The monk's identity has been exposed. He is of no more use to us. Do you see we can now kill two birds with one stone? We can say that the killer is another Shaolin monk. This will give us a pretext to raid the monastery. According to our information, Prince Zhu San is meeting someone there.'

'Are you sure your information is accurate?'

'We paid a large sum for it. We heard it from no one other than the omniscient Mr Know.'

Mr Know was another mystical figure in the Brotherhood of River and Lake. He charged a huge fee for information, and his clients were never disappointed. The information always proved reliable.

`Contact this Mr Know and ask him for confirmation.'

'Nobody knows his whereabouts. He is always the one who makes contact when he wants to sell information. We have had his middlemen followed many times without success. The middleman could be a hawker in the street, a shopkeeper, a waiter, or somebody you meet everyday. Even the middlemen know nothing about Mr Know. Their only involvement is passing on messages and receiving payment for their services.'

'In that case, we shall proceed with your plan. But first I must find some reinforcements.' That afternoon, reinforcements arrived. The soldiers surrounded Shaolin Monastery. All routes to the monastery were closed. A soldier rode ahead to the monastery to inform the Abbot of the impending arrival of the Regimental Commander and the reason for his visit.

In recent days, the Abbot had had a strange sense of foreboding. First there was Storm's return with the eunuch Speck. Then there was the sighting of the Vermillion Queen and the man in black who had attacked her in the woods. This was followed by the arrival of Sir Qin and the news of more unexpected guests. And then this morning Master Wei had told him about the traitor. And now in a matter of minutes, soldiers would march into the monastery.

The Abbot did not for one moment believe that Master Wei or any other of the monks would have the wickedness to kill a Shaolin monk. Master Wei would never lie to him. But the Abbot could not help wondering why he had gone to see Master Zheng in the middle of the night. Master Wei must have had his reasons for keeping quiet. He was a person of integrity.

The Reception Monk announced the arrival of the Regimental Commander and the retainer. With his right hand raised, thumb to the chest, palm upward in the Buddhist fashion, the Abbot saluted the Commander. 'Amida Buddha! What can I do for you, Commander?'

The Commander faced the Abbot arrogantly, 'Two Shaolin monks were engaged in a fight in the early hours of this morning. One was killed and the other has fled. The deceased was killed by Shaolin's Iron Palm, and so the murderer must be someone senior in your monastery. Only a person skilled in the Iron Palm would be able to penetrate so deep and kill the monk with one blow.'

The Abbot clasped his hands. 'Amida Buddha! Shaolin monks are forbidden to kill. I would like to examine the body to see the wound for myself.'

The commander called to his soldiers to bring the body to the courtyard outside the Abbot's Lodge. The Abbot examined the Iron

Palm mark. 'Amida Buddha! This monk was not killed by Shaolin's Iron Palm. You can see, his clothes have been torn and there is a red palm print on his back. It looks similar to the Iron Palm because the rib case is undamaged but the heart has been broken. Anyone who practises the Shaolin Iron Palm would know that the Iron Palm can go through stacks of bricks, yet damage only the target brick. If he had aimed at the heart, only the heart would be touched. The clothes, the rib case and the surrounding tissue would have remained intact. No palm print would be visible.'

The Commander was not convinced. 'We have witnesses who saw the killer disappear into your monastery. It will be easy to identify him because he has been wounded by our soldiers. We have obtained an order from the court to search your monastery, and to body search everyone over the age of sixteen.'

The Abbot again clasped his hands. 'Amida Buddha! We have nothing to hide. You may conduct your search if you so wish. All the senior monks are here. The other monks are waiting in the Hall of the Thousand Buddhas.'

The first to be searched was Master Wei. When the soldiers stripped off his monk's clothing, they found not a single mark on his body. Master Wei and the Abbot were relieved. Neither had expected the wound to heal so completely.

The commander asked, 'Master Wei, I'm told that you were absent from the training ground this morning. Have you been ill?'

Master Wei replied, 'Indeed, commander, I had an upset stomach. I'm much better now.'

There was no evidence against Master Wei. The Commander ordered the soldiers to continue body searching the other monks. Other soldiers conducted a search of the monastery and all its lands, including the courtyards, training grounds and farmlands. In the meantime, the younger boys were discharged. The more disciplined ones continued their exercises in the training ground. Other boys were glad to have an afternoon free and went off to enjoy some free time.

A group of soldiers searched the main kitchen next to the monks' quarters. They found there a young cook poking at the fire, his face black with charcoal dust. He looked no older than 16, and the soldiers ignored him. They searched the stove, cupboards, water vats, large rice containers and any places which might provide a hiding place. They looked up into the ceiling and tested the rafters. The search was thorough and efficient and they left, satisfied that the killer was not there.

Tobie came into the kitchen and saw the young man wearing the chef's head wrap and apron. He recognised him as the newcomer who had been at the training ground. 'Who are you?'

'You may call me Speck. I am boiling some hot water for tea.'

'I haven't seen you in here before. Are you our new cook?'

'No, I am the Abbot's new assistant in charge of the Study,'

'Where is the junior monk Moonie? He is supposed to be in charge of the Study.'

'He went on home leave, so the Abbot asked me to take charge of the Study during Moonie's absence.'

'But you are not a monk. I saw you at the training ground this morning. You were wearing a plait. It's most unusual for the Abbot to allow a lay person to work in his Lodge.'

'Storm brought me to see the Abbot. Moonie happened to be away, so I took his place. It is only a temporary arrangement,' said Speck. 'By the way, do you have any idea how to tell whether the water is hot enough for tea?'

Tobie shrugged.

'But your uncle is the Head Chef. I thought you would know.'

'Whenever I go into the kitchen, my uncle pushes me out. He says accidents happen too often in the kitchen and it is not a safe place for boys. Hey, if you are the Abbot's personal assistant, how come you don't know how to make tea?'

'I have never needed to know. I am only in charge of the Study.'

Speck and Tobie watched the pot, trying to figure out when the water was hot enough. The water bubbled and steam rose from the pot. They were still watching when Flint appeared at the kitchen door. Flint removed the pot from the stove, pointing out to his foolish friends that when the water bubbled, it was ready for tea.

A loud voice called out for Tobie and Flint, and Bussie burst into the room. He too was trying his luck in the kitchen, and he was surprised to see Speck there. Flint explained that Speck was a friend of Storm and had been brought in to help out during the absence of Moonie. That was good enough for Bussie. Anyone who was a friend of Storm, Tobie or Flint was his friend as well.

A junior cook returned to the kitchen after the body search and began the job of preparing tea for the soldiers and the visitors. The eunuch Speck suggested paying Storm a visit at his farm.

'I want to come too,' Bussie told them. But Tobie reminded him, 'Since that time when you broke someone's arm, Master Wei said you were not to go out without permission. We can't take you with us.'

'Look, Master Wei and the senior monks are all busy with so many soldiers around. I promise I'll not cause trouble. We'll be back before anyone notices.'

Flint and Tobie did not really want to leave Bussie behind. A promise of good behaviour from Bussie was necessary if there was to be any hope of keeping him in check.

They set off for Storm's farm. Flint, Bussie and Tobie were impressed by Speck's fine manners and his wealth of knowledge. He fascinated his listeners with anecdotes of Manchu and Mongol warriors, especially the Mongol wrestling skills. The boys had never met anyone like him. Even Bussie listened attentively as Speck spoke. They were curious about Speck's background, but Speck quickly changed the subject.

In Storm's hut, there were only the basic essentials: a bed, a table, some chairs, a stove, some cooking utensils and farming tools. He was happy to have visitors. Only Flint, Bussie and Tobie came to visit him. Other boys avoided him. They had been scared off by the Shaolin monks, who led them to believe that Storm was a child-eating ogre. Storm's appearance certainly did not help to improve this image. He was toweringly tall, and his round dark eyes, large mouth, bushy eyebrows and messy beard made him look fearful. His drunken antics had been exaggerated to such an extent that stories about him often ended with him not only injuring the monks but eating them too. Storm struck such fear in the hearts of the younger boys that the mere mention of his name would be sufficient to keep them well behaved.

It was Flint who had first come across Storm's hut. Later he brought Bussie and Tobie with him. Soon the hut became something close to a home for them. They could relax in Storm's company, enjoying fresh fruit from the farm, and the candies and cakes that Storm kept for them. They loved to listen to Storm's stories about how he used to be a guard at a magistrate's court. They were fascinated to hear how he had fought and punished evil, and how he had rescued the weak and oppressed. They asked to hear again and again the story of how Storm killed the nephew of the traitor Wu SanGui with one blow of his fist. The boys were loyal to Storm and they never told others the story of how Storm had become a fugitive and ended up at Shaolin. They resolved that when they grew up, they would become heroes like Storm: fighting evil, protecting the weak.

Flint could no longer contain his curiosity, and he asked how Storm and Speck had met. Storm thought for a while, then decided that he could trust his young friends. Over the years the boys had proved their loyalty. He made the boys promise that they would never disclose Speck's identity as this would put both his and Speck's lives in danger. Young as they were, their word was their bond. They were going to be the future heroes of Shaolin. Loyalty to a friend is the first golden rule in the Brotherhood of River and Lake. Not even the threat of death would make them betray a friend.

The boys simply could not believe it when Storm explained that Speck was a palace eunuch. Remembering the stories Storm had told them about eunuchs, Tobie asked, 'Is your penis preserved in a bottle then?' It was an embarrassing question but Speck felt he had to answer it. 'After castration, eunuchs preserve their penises in alcohol and put them in bottles labelled with their names. The bottles are kept in a room in the eunuchs' quarters called the 'Treasure Room' because these bottles are the eunuchs' most treasured possessions. When a eunuch dies, his penis will be taken out from the bottle and buried with his body. Eunuchs believe that in this way, if they are reborn as a human, they will return to the next life as a complete man.'

They bombarded Speck with questions about life in the palace. Speck told them that the Emperor was fifteen years old. He had ascended the throne at the age of six when his father died, and two years later, his mother died too. He became close to his grandmother who was the Grand Empress Dowager. He liked hunting and shooting but he was also very fond of Chinese culture. He was a great admirer of Confucian philosophy and Chinese literature and poetry, and was learning Chinese language and practising Chinese calligraphy.

Speck was preparing himself for more questions from the boys, wondering how much he should tell them. Then to his relief there was a loud knocking at the door.

VIII

HEROES AND VILLAINS

'Haidi, come in and meet my young friends,' said Storm.

Haidi asked, 'Uncle Storm, can I please wait here for Uncle Toga. He is Sir Qin's retainer, and he will come here to collect me.'

'Why don't you ask your Uncle Toga to come in and take a cup of tea with us?'

'He is chasing after a lama who snatched a woman and carried her away. Uncle Toga has followed the lama to Shaolin Monastery. This lama has killed many women'

Unknown to Storm and the boys, the lama was wanted by his monastery. He had been held in isolation at a remote cliff top to meditate and repent for his deeds, but he had escaped. While on the run, he met Master Wan who persuaded him to join the anti-Manchu resistance movement. The lama knew Tibet wanted independence from Qing rule and he thought that if he could help 'overthrow the Qing', he might be pardoned and regain his position in his monastery.

Tobie asked Haidi, 'Why did the lama kill so many women?'

'Uncle Toga said that the lama wanted to extract the *Yin* out of the women.'

In martial arts terms, this is known as 'Extracting the *Yin* to Nourish the *Yang*' for a male, or 'Extracting the *Yang* to Nourish the *Yin*' for a female, and can be achieved through sexual intercourse. The stronger partner is able to boost his or her own internal energy by extracting the *Yin* or *Yang* from the weaker partner, who then dies from energy depletion.

Only Storm and Speck fully understood the extraction of *Yin* or *Yang*. Flint, Bussie and Tobie had learned about *Yin* and *Yang* in their kung fu training, but they had only a vague idea of the process. When it came to discussion of sex, the monks brushed the subject aside. Haidi knew even less.

The act of extracting *Yin* or *Yang* from a weaker partner is greatly despised in the Brotherhood. There is a clear demarcation in the world of 'River and Lake' between righteous people and those who are despised as villains. It was a rule strictly adhered to in the Brotherhood that 'righteousness and evil do not stand together'. If a righteous man is seen in the company of villains, he is a fallen soul and shunned. In the world of 'River and Lake', heroes do not mix with villains. But in reality the line between the two is often blurred.

Tobie was pleased to find someone younger than himself. He addressed Haidi as 'little brother'. Haidi said he preferred to be addressed as 'big brother'. Bussie overheard them. 'If you want me to call you 'big brother', you have to fight for your title.'

Haidi accepted the challenge. He drew a circle on the floor. 'I will let you hit me three times in the chest. If I fall out of the circle, I lose. If I remain standing, you must address me as 'big brother'.'

Haidi was rather thin. He looked as though he had no muscle at all. There was no chance that Haidi could withstand three blows from Bussie. Bussie did not want to hurt Haidi and so used only 10 percent of his strength in the first punch. Haidi remained steadfast in the circle and did not budge at all. For his second blow, Bussie increased his strength to 30 percent. Still Haidi did not move. 'Try using your full strength,' he said. But Bussie could not bring himself to use all his power, so the third blow used 70 per cent of his strength. Haidi swayed slightly but otherwise stood unharmed. Bussie was wide-eyed with disbelief. How could Haidi withstand his power?

Haidi turned to Tobie, 'How about you? Do you want to challenge me? What is your special fighting skill?'

Without thinking, Tobie replied, '*Qingong*.'

'I'll set the rules.'

'Ok,' Tobie said confidently. Running was his particular talent, and no one could beat him at that.

'Instead of using our feet, we will use our hands. Whoever reaches that tree over there first is the winner.'

Tobie had never before tried running on his hands. He too lost to Haidi.

Flint was sitting on a chair, quietly watching. He could not suppress a smile. Haidi said, annoyed. 'Do you want to challenge me too?'

'No. Because I might lose, and anyway I don't want to call you 'big brother'!' replied Flint.

'All right, we will fight for something else. What about that flute on your sash?'

The flute was a birthday present to Flint from his *Shifu* and he would not have given it away for anything in the world. But for some reason he liked Haidi. The boy's eyes reminded him of his *Shifu*. He would probably lose, but if Haidi really wanted the flute, he would give it to him.

Haidi asked Flint to take a sword and pierce him in the chest. Flint borrowed Storm's sword and aimed at Haidi, increasing his strength slowly. The sword pierced Haidi's clothes but went no further. Was Haidi wearing a chainmail beneath his clothes? Flint wondered, but he said nothing and gave his flute to Haidi.

When it came to Speck's turn, he chose wrestling. 'But,' he said, 'I will not call you 'big brother'. If I lose, I will owe you a favour.'

'A favour? What good is that? If I asked you to get me the moon from the sky, could you do it?'

'No, but a favour from me may well come in useful to you some day.'

A promise was still something and Haidi was persuaded. He asked Speck to step into the circle he had drawn. 'The first to fall down loses. Do you agree?'

'Of course,' replied Speck.

Haidi began by running the circumference of the circle. He ran so fast that all Speck could see was a grey ring spinning around him. Speck's kung fu was not strong. He was dazzled by the ring and lost all sense of direction. Haidi leapt on to his shoulders from behind, his legs curled around Speck's neck, his body dropped backwards, and with his hands he pulled at Speck's legs from behind. They both fell down, Haidi on top of Speck. Speck had fallen first, so Haidi won again.

There were no hard feelings and the boys relaxed and began to chat. Although Haidi was the youngest, he seemed to know more about the Brotherhood of River and Lake than the others. He knew about the rescue of Scholar Gu YanWu, the emergence of the Third Prince and the appearance of the Vermillion Queen. 'I've never met the Vermillion Queen. From what uncle Toga tells me, she is very tall. She always wears a long red cape, and a mask over her eyes and nose. She commands a fleet of vermillion finches fitted with poisonous metal blades on their claws and beaks. Uncle Toga also said that whenever anyone saw Jade, the godson of Prince Geng, the Vermillion Queen would always be near at hand. It looks as though she has been hired as a retainer.'

The boys remembered meeting Jade by the stream on his way to Shaolin. Haidi continued, 'Last night Uncle Toga was following the tracks of a woman who died of *Yin* depletion and he came to a hilltop in Shaolin. He was looking for the killer, and instead he encountered the Vermillion Queen. She hit a hundred year old cypress tree and the tree snapped into two. Her finger nails can be detached and used as weapons. Uncle Toga was injured by one of her nails, but luckily he was able to get away.'

Flint realized then that the man in black who had attacked the Vermillion Queen in the woods was Uncle Toga. Storm asked, 'What does Uncle Toga say about her kung fu?'

'According to Uncle Toga, only two other people in the Martial Arts Fellowship can match her. One of them is a man called the White Tiger from the West.

Storm knew of the White Tiger as he himself was from the Western Region. 'The White Tiger is a bodyguard of the traitor Wu SanGui. Over the years, many brave men have tried to assassinate Wu without success. Not only does Wu have an army of soldiers and bodyguards to protect him, but the White Tiger never leaves his side. No one can get near Wu without first killing the White Tiger. The White Tiger's kung fu originated from Shaolin, but I doubt that the Shaolin monks are anywhere near his level. He is a potential champion of the Martial Arts Fellowship.'

Haidi disagreed. 'I don't know much about the White Tiger, but I do know about the Green Dragon of the East. He too has kung fu skills as good as the Vermillion Queen.'

'Yes, I've heard of him. He is greatly respected by the Brotherhood,' said Storm.

Haidi beamed. 'You are so right. The Green Dragon has saved many from the clutches of evil. He is a wandering knight. No one knows when he is going to appear. He leaves behind no trace. As the saying goes, he is 'a mystic dragon whose head and tail are hidden and invisible to the human eye'.'

Flint piped up, 'There is someone else whose kung fu is as good as that of the Vermillion Queen. Miao Shan *Shi Tai*, my *Shifu*'s *Shifu*. She is a Daoist, and the successor to the Ice Maiden. Her Black Ice Palm is the nemesis of the Vermillion Queen's Red Flaming Palm.'

The door flew open, and a man staggered in. Haidi screamed, 'Uncle Toga! What happened?'

Storm laid Toga down on his bed and examined his injuries. A green palm print marked his back. Toga told them not to touch the wound because it was poisonous. He had pressed his own energy points to prevent the poison from spreading to his heart and his vital organs. 'I was following the lama but lost sight of him. I searched everywhere and then spotted him in the brambles. He had just finished with a woman and was about to throw her down the slope. He turned and saw me. I ran as fast as I could because I knew I was not his match in kung fu. He struck my back with his palm.'

While the flesh around Uncle Toga's wound was burned, the wound itself was icy cold. His face was a pale green. He asked the boys to carry him to Sir Qin, who was staying at Shaolin's guest lodge.

Sir Qin told them, 'Toga has been wounded by the Green Demon Palm which has emitted a deadly poison. This type of kung fu originates from the western region near Tian Shan, and it takes at least 20 years of practice to be effective. Toga is lucky to be alive. The Tibetan lama has used only seventy per cent of his internal force. People who practise this type of poisonous palm need to be cautious because if an opponent has more powerful internal force, the poison can rebound to the person who delivers the blow.'

Storm asked, 'Is the lama not immune from his own poison?'

'To train for the Green Demon Palm, you must soak your palms in small doses of poisonous solution every day. The poison is absorbed into the body and turned into Qi, which is circulated through the Qi channels and finally stored in the Qi centres ready for use. The poisons in the dosage are increased gradually over the years. But at the end of the day, it is the power of the internal force that matters. If an opponent has more powerful internal force and the poison rebounds, the deliverer of the Green Devil Palm will be poisoned just like his victims. The poison can only be turned slowly into Qi. The deliverer would not be able to cope with a sudden influx of poison.'

Sir Qin had no antidote for the poison. Because Flint had been immune to poison ever since he had drunk the blood of the Sea Serpent, he offered his blood as an antidote. Sir Qin explained, 'The poison used by the Tibetan lama is no ordinary poison. It contains the venom of many different poisonous insects from western regions mixed with poisonous herbs. Unless the type of insect or herb used in the poison is known, you cannot produce an effective antidote. If the wrong antidote is used, it will kill the victim immediately. I can cure his wound injury, but before I do, the poison in the wound must be removed, and we cannot risk trying Flint's blood.'

Flint asked, 'How much time do we have to find the antidote?'

'Toga is an expert user of poison himself and his body has developed a tolerance for poisons. But without the antidote, he could die in hours. I believe that the Tibetan lama carries the antidote with him in case he needs it himself.'

They stood silent as the seriousness of Toga's condition sunk in. Then Flint spoke up, 'Haidi, could you withstand a poisonous blow from the lama?' Just as Flint had suspected, Haidi admitted that he was wearing chainmail under his clothes. Flint outlined his plan. He and Haidi then covered themselves in black clothing from head to toe, and set off to look for the Tibetan lama.

The lama was part of Jade's entourage. He was fuming. He had lost sight of the man in black who had found him with the woman. Reluctant to give up the search, he scoured the hillside. He thought he saw a black shadow through the trees, so he turned back to chase after it. Sure enough there was a man clad in black. The lama raised his palm, using his full strength, ready to strike, but then realised that this was not the man he was seeking. At the last moment he withdrew most of his internal force, and the blow was much weakened. When the lama went over to the man, he saw to his dismay that he had hit Jade's Chief Steward who was wearing a dark coloured robe and trousers. The Steward was collapsed on the ground, writhing with pain. Beside him stood his master Jade, in an exquisite long white robe. They both reeked of alcohol. Jade was bent over his steward and looked up angrily at the lama. The lama ran forward to help, but again he caught sight of a man in black through the trees. It was essential that he kill this man to prevent his secret being leaked to the Brotherhood. The Chief Steward's wound was not serious. It was the poison that came with the blow that was fatal. He thrust into Jade's hand a small vial of green powder, telling him to sprinkle the powder onto the wound, and ran back through the trees after the black figure. He saw a black flash to his right, and then left, but the figure never stayed long in one spot for him to aim his palm.

Jade and his Chief Steward headed straight for Shaolin's guest lodge. The Steward ran excitedly into Sir Qin's room shouting, 'We've got the antidote!'

Storm smiled, 'Well done, Bussie and Speck.'

Speck's impersonation of Jade had been perfect. He had the arrogance, the regal manner, the exquisite robe, and the smell of alcohol which helped to fool the lama. Haidi was the make-up artist, and Speck and Bussie were transformed into Jade and his steward. Bussie had been able to withstand the poisonous blow because he was wearing Haidi's chainmail, an exquisite piece which could not be pierced by the sharpest sword. It was light as feather and thin as paper, and could fit any shape of body. It was made from silk spun by rare spiders, stronger than steel and more elastic than rubber. The wearer was protected from cuts, kicks, blows, fire, acid and poison. It was indestructible, and its existence was legendary.

Flint and Haidi, each dressed in black, had been responsible for luring the lama away. Although the lama's kung fu was superior, he had not worked out that he was dealing with two different shadows.

Toga's poison cleared when the antidote was applied but he would need time to recover completely. Everyone waited anxiously for Flint and Haidi to return safely from their mission to lure away the lama. Speck offered to go and look for them. Tobie volunteered to go too. Bussie wanted to accompany them but Storm insisted that he stay behind and help look after Uncle Toga. They could never be sure about Bussie and the trouble he might make.

Speck and Tobie decided to look for their friends first in the Stupa Forest. Stupa is a pagoda-style structure which houses the remains of a Shaolin elder. The structures, over 200 of them, vary in height and size. It was Shaolin's holy place. No one was to enter without the permission of the Abbot. Senior monks took turns to patrol the Stupa Forest day and night.

The black clothing Flint and Haidi wore made them almost invisible in the dark, so it was Flint who found Speck and Tobie. The boys kept very quiet and moved quickly to get out of the Stupa Forest, because they knew Master Wei was on patrol tonight. Suddenly Flint signalled to the others to hide behind a tree and keep still. Footsteps approached a tall stupa. There were two men, but their faces could not be seen in the dark. A man with a southern accent said,

'All our people have arrived. The soldiers are leaving tomorrow. We can have our gathering tomorrow night.'

'Have you decided on the venue?'

The moment the second man opened his mouth, the boys realised he was Master Wei. His familiar Yangzhou accent could not be mistaken.

'Do you have any suggestions?'

'The Five Breast Peak behind the monastery. Go up to the plateau at the middle peak. There is a flat piece of land bigger than our training ground. It is well hidden by trees.'

'What time?'

'Nine o'clock. Most of the monks will be in bed by then.'

'We'll be there at nine.'

The speaker left and Master Wei continued his patrol.

The boys agreed that they too would go to Five Breast Peak tomorrow evening to find out what was going on. But they would not tell the others because they did not want Bussie involved. It was just too risky. They returned to Shaolin's guest lodge. Bussie was pleased to see them back safe. He returned the chainmail to Haidi and urged him to put it on immediately for his own safety.

Sir Qin had already returned. The boys sat quietly waiting for him to tell them what had happened.

IX

A TEST OF STRENGTH

While the boys were tricking the lama into handing over the antidote, Sir Qin's task had been to keep Jade and his steward out of the way.

It would have been awkward to call on Jade when they had barely met, apart from the altercation they had had at the brothel in Beijing over a sing-song girl. He would have to arrange to meet Jade through a third party. He remembered that Ma QingLing, head of Four Seas Armed Escort Delivery, was staying at the same inn. They had met each other on several social occasions, but were no more than acquaintances.

Chief Armed Escort Ma opened the door. 'Sir Qin, I did not realise you were at Shaolin.'

'Nor I you. Otherwise I would have called on you earlier.'

'What wind blows you here?'

'I have an unfinished chess game with Master Fu. The annual Shaolin contest will be held over the next two days. I am thinking that if I concede the game to Master Fu, I might have a chance of being invited as an onlooker. Have you also come for the Shaolin contest?'

'I came at my little girl's request. I was fetching her home from E-mei School of Martial Arts for a summer holiday break. She has never visited Shaolin and wanted to pay a visit to the monastery. My daughter will be thrilled to hear about the annual contest, and no doubt she will want to stay to watch.'

'I'm sure that will not be a problem. You know so many eminent people in the Brotherhood of River and Lake. The Shaolin annual contests are normally a strictly internal affair, but all rules have exceptions.'

Ma QingLing had been born into a wealthy family. His father

had been able to provide his family with a comfortable lifestyle from a successful armed escort business even during the war-torn periods. Ma QingLing had had his share of wild days when he was a young man. After his marriage he settled down and became a family man. Marriage and responsibility as head of the largest armed escort service had changed him.

As well as being a great martial artist, Ma QingLing was also a 'licentiate', an official title awarded to scholars who had passed examinations at both county and prefecture level. His Confucian outlook, scholarly manner and good judgment had earned him the acclaim of 'a righteous man of noble character and moral integrity'. He had helped to solve a number of disputes within the Brotherhood, and his sound judgment and fairness had gained him respect and admiration. As his reputation grew, he had increasing influence in the Brotherhood. He was surrounded by disciples who promoted him as a future leader. There was only one thing stopping him from claiming the crown. He had yet to prove that he was a champion in martial arts. The time was drawing near for a formal contest to determine who would lead the Brotherhood.

Chief Armed Escort Ma asked courteously, 'What can I do for you, Sir Qin?'

'We have met socially in Beijing, but we have never had the time to get better acquainted. As there is nothing much happening at Shaolin tonight, I thought it would be a great pity to miss again the chance of making a good friend. Would you do me the honour of joining me for a drink? There is a tavern not far from here which has good wine and food.'

Chief Armed Escort Ma was flattered by the respect shown by Sir Qin. He readily accepted the invitation. Sir Qin was about to propose the inclusion of Jade in their drinking party when there was a knock at the door. It was Sir Qin's lucky day. At the door stood Jade and his Chief Steward. Jade had met Chief Armed Escort Ma on the first day of his arrival at Shaolin. It was he who had found Ma's daughter Minnie on the way to Shaolin and had taken her back to the inn in his carriage. Jade had promised then that he would call on the Chief Armed Escort again.

Jade and Ma exchanged pleasantries. Jade was surprised to see Sir Qin. Chief Armed Escort Ma was proud to show off his rich and famous friends, and gladly made the introductions. Jade presented his steward as 'Chief Steward Zhu'.

Jade had come to invite Chief Armed Escort Ma to join him and a group of friends for a drink at the very same tavern that Sir Qin had suggested. But Ma had already accepted Sir Qin's invitation. To save Ma from embarrassment, Sir Qin offered to play host to Jade and all his friends. Reluctantly Jade accepted.

Jade's friends had already booked a private room in the tavern, with a large round table. Jade introduced his friends, Wan YunLong, the 'Praying Mantis' kung fu expert, and the five men who had rescued Scholar Gu YunWu.

Annoyed at first by Sir Qin's presence, on reflection Jade's friends concluded that this meeting might not be such a bad idea. Sir Qin had a reputation as a fun loving, idle rich man with no known political alliance. His wealth appealed to them.

They sat around the table. Sir Qin took the seat opposite the door. At his right hand was Jade, and at his left was Chief Armed Escort Ma. Next to Jade were Master Wan YunLong, and then the fisherman, the butcher, the horse trader, the hunter and the 'iron-fan' scholar who ended up with Chief Armed Escort Ma on his right. Steward Zhu stood behind Jade to attend to his master. On the table were two large jugs of rice wine and many small dishes of food, stewed beef, glazed ham, drunken chicken, smoked fish and shrimp dishes, pickled vegetables, nuts, cakes and fruit.

Master Wan watched Jade, Ma QingLing and Sir Qin. Jade's beauty was effeminate, with fair, smooth skin and long shapely eyebrows. He was wearing a long white robe in the Han Style, with wide sleeves, buttoned at the side with a sash around the waist. The robe was of the finest silk, and on his sash hung a large piece of rare jade. Ma QingLing was a handsome and elegant man, confident and self-assured, but inclined to be a little aloof. Sir Qin wore a small moustache. He was a charming man with easy manners, and more approachable than Ma QingLing. Both Sir Qin and Ma wore the Qing Style of clothing, a narrow cuffed short jacket over a long robe. Ma wore a maroon coloured jacket of excellent tailoring and taste, and Sir Qin a light green jacket with exquisite embroidery, rich in design and elegant in style. Sir Qin's attire, like his personality, was more flamboyant than Ma's.

Master Wan knew nothing of Sir Qin's kung fu, but he knew that Chief Armed Escort Ma was an expert in Taijiquan and Taiji Sword, which originated from the Wudang style of martial arts.

Sir Qin stood up and expressed his delight in meeting so many good and brave men of the Brotherhood. He proposed a toast. They all stood to drink a bowl of wine. Then it was Master Wan's turn. He used his internal force to cause the jug of wine to rise from the table. The jug went round the table of its own accord, pouring wine into everyone's bowl. The bowls were filled to the brim and yet not a drop was spilled, powered solely by the internal force of Master Wan. All stood again to return the toast to Sir Qin and they thanked him for his generosity.

Not to be outdone, Chief Armed Escort Ma used his internal force to move the bowls from their places and line up before him. The jug rose from the table to fill every bowl. As the jug touched down, the bowls floated through the air to their rightful places before the drinkers. Ma's performance was more stylish, but everyone at the table was an Internal Kung Fu expert, and recognised it as a clever trick. Ma had used the rapid movements of his palms to cause the bowls to move.

The jugs were soon emptied. Master Wan asked the waiter to bring in a large vat of wine. He summoned his internal force to make the vat rise and float towards Chief Armed Escort Ma. The Chief Armed Escort knew that Master Wan was testing his internal force and so raised his palm to slow down the vat. When the vat came near, it tilted for Ma to take a mouthful of wine. Again not a drop fell to the table. Chief Armed Escort Ma had fully demonstrated the essence of Taijiquan characterized by a slow and continuous flow of *Qi*. The *Qi* from Ma was continuous as the waves of the Yangzijiang river flowing to the sea, the palm 'soft as cotton', the *Qi* 'hard as steel'. Master Wan realised that Ma's Internal Kung Fu was in no way inferior to his.

Chief Armed Escort Ma then decided to test Jade's Internal Kung Fu, and caused the vat to float towards him. Master Wan knew that Jade's Internal Kung Fu was far inferior and he placed his palm behind Jade's back. The *Qi* flowed from Master Wan's palm to Jade's palm and Jade was able to slow down the vat and take his gulp of wine.

Master Wan now wanted to test Sir Qin. The vat floated towards Sir Qin. Everyone was curious about Sir Qin's level of kung fu. When Sir Qin saw the vat coming, he hastened to catch it with his hands. The force was so powerful that he fell backwards and would have been knocked from his chair had Chief Escort Ma not intervened, putting his palm behind Sir Qin's back to send the *Qi* forward and stop the vat. Sir Qin covered his embarrassment with a smile, and graciously took his mouthful of wine.

Chief Armed Escort Ma pressed forward his *Qi,* and the vat moved from Sir Qin's hands to the fisherman who sat next to Master Wan. The fisherman used his blade to steady the vat. He took his mouthful of wine and passed the vat to his neighbour, the butcher. The butcher used his axe to keep the vat still and after drinking, passed the vat onto the horse trader. The horse trader used his whip, then the hunter his metal arrow container, and the scholar his iron fan.

Each person's level of Internal Kung Fu was plain to all. Chief Armed Escort Ma and Master Wan were at the highest level because they could make the vat move without touching it. After them were the five brave men who needed an article to steady the vat. Jade and Sir Qin had exposed their mediocrity in kung fu. Nobody had expected otherwise. Jade and Sir Qin were known for their wealth, their social status and their success with women. They did not rely on kung fu for a living.

Master Wan was secretly pleased that Sir Qin was no expert in martial arts. He liked the idle rich because they were easy to handle. He hoped that he could get Sir Qin on side as they would need funding for what they were about to do.

Master Wan stood up and again toasted Sir Qin and Chief Armed Escort Ma. 'I must apologise for our childish display. I hope this has not affected our evening of entertainment. Brother Ma, you have my admiration. As the saying goes, 'Meeting you in person is better than hearing your name'. Your Taijiquan is second to none in the Brotherhood.' Toasting everyone again, Master Wan said, 'Now, let's forget kung fu and enjoy our food and wine.'

Master Wan sounded out Chief Armed Escort Ma and Sir Qin on their political views. He rose to make a special toast to his five friends, 'My brothers, let's drink to the five brave men who rescued Scholar Gu YunWu from the evil Tartar barbarian Oboi.' After downing the wine, he continued, 'One month ago was the 25th death anniversary of Emperor Chong Zhen. On the date of the Emperor's death, my brothers and I held a memorial service in remembrance of the Emperor and to remind ourselves that we are Han Chinese.'

Jade and his friends applauded, and toasted the deceased Emperor Chong Zhen. There was no response from Chief Armed Escort Ma or Sir Qin. They were surprised at Master Wan and Jade's open support of the Ming dynasty.

Master Wan continued, 'After the death of Emperor Chong Zhen, Ming princes set up kingdoms in the south. But instead of uniting to 'overthrow the Qing and restore the Ming', they fought against each other over succession to the Ming throne. The cities in the south fell one by one to the Tartar barbarians. The Ming princes were all killed. Their supporters turned to support their heirs and their battle continues to this day. If only we could find one rightful heir to the Ming throne and unite all Han Chinese behind him. Then history could be rewritten.'

The scholar waved his fan. 'It was Wu SanGui who had the Prince of Gui executed. He was responsible for bringing down the Ming Empire.' The mention of Wu SanGui gave rise to a surge of curses.

Master Wan ignored the interruptions. 'When Koxinga was alive, he swore allegiance to the Ming cause. He was supported by all Ming loyalists as the leader of the resistance movement. Unfortunately he died not long after the Prince of Gui was executed. He was succeeded by his son Zheng Jing, who promised to carry on the resistance movement initiated by his father. But in the seven years since the death of the Prince of Gui, no single claimant to the Ming throne has had strong support. I fear that enthusiasm for the Ming cause will fade in Taiwan if we cannot come up with a rightful heir to the Ming throne.'

As if he had finally made up his mind, Master Wan said solemnly, 'My brothers, I entrust my life to all of you here. I have something to tell you all. We have found the rightful heir to the Ming throne.'

Sir Qin asked, surprised, 'Who?'

'Prince Zhu San, Emperor Chong Zhen's third son by his Imperial Honoured Consort Lady Li Shen of the Western Palace. When Beijing was besieged by the rebels, Lady Li Shen fled to Yunnan and there she gave birth to a son who is the Third Prince.'

Chief Armed Escort Ma was sceptical. 'Do you have any proof that this claim is genuine?'

Master Wan smiled. 'Yes, I have. The Third Prince has produced two precious swords as proof of his identity. The two swords, 'Peachwood-red Sword of the Loyal Ministers' and 'Sword of the Two Dragons Fighting for the Pearl', belonged to Emperor Chong Zhen. The swords are imperial treasures and could only pass down the line of Ming Emperors. When Lady Li fled the Palace, she took the swords with her. Anyone who can produce the two precious swords, I will accept as the rightful heir to the Ming throne.'

Chief Armed Escort Ma and Sir Qin were too shrewd to express an opinion. While both scorned Wu SanGui, they did not openly oppose the Manchus, nor declare enthusiasm for the restoration of the Ming Dynasty. Jade's friends were clearly anti-Manchu activists, but why was Jade, the godson of Prince Geng involved with these men? Was Prince Geng planning a rebellion against the Qing government? Sir Qin was puzzled also by the relationship between Master Wan and Jade. This was not an equal relationship, more like a master and servant. Master Wan, a well-known personality in the Brotherhood of River and Lake, subservient to Jade? Unthinkable. The meeting turned out to be more interesting than Sir Qin had expected.

Master Wan began to wonder about Sir Qin. Perhaps there was more to him than wealth. By the end of the dinner, he knew nothing more about him than before. He had already researched

Chief Armed Escort Ma's background and was confident that they would be able to enlist Ma to their cause.

Jade's vassal came in with an urgent message from Prince Geng for Jade to return home immediately. Jade took his leave and apologised to his host Sir Qin and the other guests. Jade had wished to stay on to see Shaolin Monastery join the anti-manchu resistance force, but with the soldiers now surrounding Shaolin, it would be prudent for him not to be associated with Master Wan. He was still known as the godson of Prince Geng. It was not the right time for him to reveal his identity as the Third Prince. Apart from Prince Geng, only a handful of people, including Master Wan and Master Zheng, knew. Before he could emerge as the rightful heir to the Ming throne, he needed to rally sufficient support. Shaolin Monastery was one of his targets and he had gained the support of Master Zheng, the second most important person at the monastery. Taiwan was his next target. Zheng Jing's support was crucial. Jade was a clever man, it had not taken him long to figure out why Prince Geng had kept him alive and held on to the secret of his identity. He was Prince Geng's safety net against the Qing, and also against Wu SanGui, whose power and ambition became more evident every day.

Shortly afterwards Chief Escort Ma's pupil Madaha came to the tavern. He broke the news that Ma's mother was seriously ill and required him back home immediately. Chief Armed Escort Ma too apologised and took his leave. After Jade and Ma QingLing had left, the party broke up and Sir Qin returned to his Shaolin guest lodge to tell the boys what had happened.

When Sir Qin described Jade's friends, Storm and Speck realised that they had met them all on the road to Shaolin. Sir Qin did not mention the anti-Manchu stance taken by Jade's friends. It was the ethics of the Brotherhood that one should not put fellow brothers' lives at risk. He mentioned only the kung fu tests, touching briefly on the common hatred of Wu SanGui by all those there. Speck remembered Storm telling him that the five men who had rescued Scholar Gu were followers of Zheng ChengGong of Taiwan, and Master Wan appeared to be their leader. Why was Jade, the godson of Prince Geng, in the company of anti-Manchu activists?

X

A STRANGER COMES BEARING GIFTS

The following morning, the soldiers began to relax their surveillance. They surrounded the monastery but allowed people to go in and out. The senior monks including Master Wei still did not attend training sessions.

The boys had an extra day off. Leo took a kite and went to the mountain spring hoping to catch sight of Minnie. She was there with Greenie. Leo gave Minnie the kite with cord and reel. He had fitted a special gadget to the kite so that the peacock's plumage would open up as the kite soared to the sky. Minnie was truly impressed with the craftsmanship. Leo helped her to launch the kite and sort out the cord when it became caught in the trees.

After a while, Minnie grew tired. 'I've heard so much about Shaolin Monastery but I've still not been inside,' she complained. She had been reluctant to go through the protocol of being formally received by Shaolin's Reception Monks. In any case, this would take time, particularly now with all the soldiers around. It could be days before Minnie was received formally. She told Leo how disappointed she was, so Leo volunteered to take her and Greenie on a guided tour of the monastery, disguising them as lay Shaolin pupils. Minnie lingered outside the Abbot's Study, disappointed that the study was out of bounds to visitors. After the tour, Minnie was happy. She promised to come back in the afternoon bringing cakes and delicacies to thank Leo for his guided tour.

While Leo and the girls were touring the monastery, Tobie spent the morning studying a book given to him by Sir Qin. After lunch, he was taken by Sir Qin to see Master Fu, to challenge Master Fu to a game of chess.

This morning, with no training exercises, Master Fu had gone through every step of the earlier games he had had with Sir Qin, and he was confident he could beat him. So when Sir Qin called in the afternoon, he gladly agreed to a game. But Sir Qin said, 'Master Fu, you have a new challenger today. I have discovered that our young Tobie is good at chess. I bet you that you cannot defeat him.'

Master Fu thought at first that the bet was a joke. Even if Tobie had learned to play, how could he beat the Top Master? Master Fu always referred to himself as the Top Master, forgetting momentarily that he had been beaten many times by Sir Qin. He laid out the chess board and set out the pieces. 'Shall I concede any pieces before we start?'

'No,' said Sir Qin.

'How much do you want to wager then?'

'20 taels of silver.'

'That's a lot of money.'

'Are you worried that you might lose?'

Master Fu accepted the challenge, though even with 20 taels of silver it would not give him any satisfaction to defeat Tobie, who was a newcomer to the game. Sir Qin reminded him, 'But I warn you that if you lose, you have to give me 20 taels of silver.'

Master Fu did not believe for one moment that he would lose the game to Tobie. He wondered whether Sir Qin was planning to communicate with Tobie using a signal. 'Is there a trick? Am I playing with Tobie or with you?'

Sir Qin laughed, 'You are playing with Tobie. Don't worry. There's no trick. I'll sit with my back to the chess board and I will not make a sound.'

To Master Fu's surprise and annoyance, he was checkmated by Tobie's pawn. The pawn was the weakest piece and most players sacrificed their pawns early in the game. Master Fu blamed himself for being careless. Perhaps he had underestimated Tobie's ability. He demanded another game and doubled the bet. After five games, Master Fu had lost a total of 620 taels of silver. This was embarrassing because he did not have the money to pay. He could not understand how Tobie had managed to win and he pressed Sir Qin to explain. Sir Qin offered to waive the bet. He would tell Master Fu the secret of Tobie's success. Not only that, he would make Master Fu the greatest chess player in the world.

Master Fu was not so naïve as to think that this would come for free. 'What do you want of me then?'

Sir Qin said, 'I am a devout Buddhist. I have heard that your monastery has the largest collection of the original Sanskrit scriptures brought back by the Tang monk, Xuan Zhuang, from India. I have a small collection myself, and it is my greatest wish to see what is missing from my collection.'

Master Ma was suspicious. 'Are you sure you are not after Shaolin's secret kung fu manual, 'Tendon Transformation and Marrow Cleansing'? You must have known that the manual is kept in the same place as the sutras.'

The 'Tendon Transformation and Marrow Cleansing' manual is the most precious manual of Shaolin kung fu. This kung fu was created by Bodhidharma, founder of Shaolin kung fu, and is taught only to Shaolin's select few disciples. Even then, the teaching is in oral form passed from teacher to pupil. Apart from the Abbot, no one was allowed to read the written manual. Over the years, the monastery had been subject to numerous break-ins. The intruders had only one thought, to lay their hands on the secret manual. The old Abbot had at one point thought of having it destroyed, and to pass down the kung fu orally to the disciples. But he could not bring himself to destroy this great treasure of Shaolin. So the manual was still hidden in the Monastery.

Sir Qin assured Master Fu that he had no designs on the manual. 'I won't even look at the manual. I will look only at the sutras.'

'Even if I agree to help you, you will still need to persuade Master Wei and Master Zheng. The sutras and the manual are kept in a room with steel walls, and the door to the room is made of heavy cast iron. The door can be unlocked only by three keys turning at the same time. The keys are held separately by three senior monks. I am one keyholder and the two others are Master Wei and Master Zheng.'

'I have already contacted Master Wei and Master Zheng. They have promised to meet me at dinner time outside the guest lodge.'

If Master Wei and Master Zheng trusted Sir Qin, Master Fu could not see why he should refuse. Even in the possibility that Sir Qin had fooled them all, Master Fu could not believe that Sir Qin would be able to defeat the three of them fighting together. 'OK, so what's your secret with the chess game?'

Sir Qin withdrew from his breast pocket a book. This book had been written two hundred years earlier by an expert in chess, who had analysed hundreds of chess games and noted in detail every step of each game. He wrote of every possible combination of steps in attack and defence. He explained strategic moves, how to avoid the pitfalls, and how to plan steps ahead of each move.

'If you study this book carefully, you will become the greatest master in chess.'

Master Fu fingered the book excitedly, and agreed to meet Sir Qin at dinner time outside the guest lodge. Tobie must have a photographic memory, Master Fu thought. How else could he have memorised all the moves in such a short time?

Sir Qin was not lying when he said he had arranged things with Master Wei. This morning, he had sent Flint to ask Master Wei to meet him at his guest lodge, saying he had something very important to show him. Master Wei knew of Sir Qin as Master Fu's chess partner. He also heard that Sir Qin was a very wealthy man who had promised a large donation to the monastery. Soon Master Wei was knocking on the door of Sir Qin's room. 'What can I do for you, Sir Qin?'

'I have something interesting to show you, Master Wei. I bought this sword from a pawn shop in Beijing because I recognised it. Master Fu once showed it to me and asked me to give an opinion on whether or not the sword was authentic.'

'So what do you know about the sword?'

'The sword is ninety years old and once belonged to the famous Ming General Qi JiGuang.' General Qi was a national hero, renowned for driving away the Japanese pirates from the south-eastern coasts of China. General Qi's sword was much sought after by antique collectors.

Sir Qin showed Master Wei the small print on the sword which read, *'Tenth Year of Wan Li Dengzhou Qi'*, and explained,

'General Qi's father was an official in Dengzhou. The sword was made in the tenth year of the reign of Emperor Wan Li. The sword is genuine. This is your sword, isn't it? How much did you sell it for?'

Master Wei looked embarrassed. The sword had been given to him by the Abbot after his team had won an annual contest. 'I got 200 taels of silver for it. Quite a large sum of money.'

Sir Qin looked surprised, 'Do you know how much I paid the pawn shop for this sword? 1,000 taels of silver.' Master Wei was annoyed. He should have sold the sword direct to Sir Qin. He had allowed middlemen to get in the way of profit.

'Are you in need of money, Master Wei? If money is your worry, I may be able to help.'

Master Wei knew Sir Qin was a very wealthy man. And Master Wei had money problems. He was shrewd enough to know that if he asked Sir Qin for money, there would be a price. It occurred to him too, that Sir Qin might be after the kung fu manual. Sir Qin assured him that he only wanted to see the original Buddhist scriptures in the Sanskrit language which had been brought back from India. He had no interest at all in Shaolin's secret kung fu manual. The three keyholders specialised in different kung fu skills. Master Wei, like Master Fu, was confident they could use Shaolin kung fu to protect the manual. Master Fu specialised in the Shaolin Qin-Na, a 'grabbing and controlling' technique, enabling him to 'grab and control' the opponent's joints, muscles and tendons. Pressure is applied to the opponent's vital energy points to immobilise him. The Qin-Na techniques could tear muscles and tendons, displace bones, seal breath, and block the *Qi* flow.

Senior Master Zheng specialised in the Five Animal Set, also known as the *Wuxing Quan*, the Five Styles of Pugilism. These styles imitate the movement of the Dragon, the Tiger, the Panther, the Snake and the Crane. Master Zheng was best known for his White Crane Fist, which emphasised unification of Internal Kung Fu and External Kung Fu. The Crane techniques depend on the 'Flapping and the Quivering Hands'. 'Flapping' is soft and 'Quivering' is hard. This requires withdrawing hands as soft as cotton, and shooting out hands as the bow sends out arrows. Traditional Shaolin White Crane kung fu usually uses kicking skills. However, Master Zheng had placed greater emphasis on the hands. As he had long and strong arms, he could use the Flapping and Quivering Hand technique to his advantage.

Master Wei himself specialized in Shaolin Long Fist Sword. He used a double-edged, narrow-blade sword. The techniques of the sword are difficult to master. In order to make the sword an effective weapon, the user must project his power into the weapon, requiring muscle power and internal energy. A practitioner must have a solid foundation in both External and Internal Kung Fu before moving on to the use of sword. Master Wei was also an expert in 'Qi Men Jian', the Qi family's long sword sequence. Learning the sequence is a slow and painful process. Only someone with Master Wei's determination could master such a skill. 'Qi Men Jian' was created by General Qi JiGuang. The antique sword which the Abbot had given to Master Wei was of great sentimental value to him as it had originally belonged to General Qi. Master Wei would not have parted with it in normal circumstances. But he had needed money desperately and so had been forced to sell it.

Master Zheng, Master Fu and Master Wei, had never fought together against a common enemy, but Master Wei was confident that no one could defeat them. With this in mind, Master Wei accepted Sir Qin's offer. 'I need 12,000 taels of silver.'

Sir Qin readily took out a bundle of notes and handed them to Master Wei. 'These notes are issued by the largest money exchanger in the country. You can take the notes to any of its branches and get the money any time you want.'

In a show of generosity, Sir Qin returned the antique sword to Master Wei. Master Wei was overwhelmed, and immediately took him to meet Senior Master Zheng in his room at Vinaya Hall. He left them to speak in private and agreed to meet up at dinner time outside the guest lodge.

Master Zheng was surprised to see Sir Qin. They had never met before. After an exchange of salutations, he invited Sir Qin into his room for tea. Sir Qin opened the conversation. 'I have long heard of your name, Master Zheng. Your fame is spread far and wide but 'meeting you in person is better than hearing your name'.'

This was more than flattery. Master Zheng was actually better known than the Abbot in the Brotherhood of River and Lake. While the Abbot was a modest man, Master Zheng had a more forceful personality. He was known not only for his superior kung fu but also for his high moral standing and his strict disciplinary control of the monks.

Master Zheng was older than the present Abbot, and had been the old Abbot's first disciple. Whether by seniority or age, he had expected to succeed the old Abbot when he retired. He had therefore been disappointed when he was by-passed by the present Abbot. As Head of Discipline, he now occupied the second most important position in Shaolin. He had tried to ignore worldly desires of power and status. But time and again he wondered why he had been passed over, why he had not been appointed Abbot of Shaolin. His kung fu was in no way inferior to that of this Abbot. If anything, it was better.

The fact is that the old Abbot had found Master Zheng narrow-minded. He had tried to help Master Zheng to take a broader view of things and to become more tolerant, emphasising the importance of the development of the 'mind and spirit' in order to reach the highest level in martial arts. But while Master Zheng had concentrated on the development of his '*jing*' and '*qi*', he had overlooked the '*shen*'. He had failed to realise that only a person with the right 'mind and spirit' could reach the top in martial arts. There is a saying, 'It is easier to change the course of a river or the shape of a mountain than to change a person's character.' The old Abbot had little success in reforming Master Zheng's approach to life.

The present Abbot was the old Abbot's second disciple. The old Abbot found in his second disciple those qualities of wisdom, compassion and magnanimity he was looking for. In his heart, he knew that his second disciple would make a good abbot and would in time become a top master in martial arts. He decided to break with tradition. Before he retired, he had appointed his second disciple, Xuan Kui, to succeed him.

Master Zheng was flattered by Sir Qin's visit. A person of Sir Qin's eminence and wealth had shown him deference. 'Do sit down and have a cup of tea.' Master Zheng waited for Sir Qin to tell him the purpose of his visit.

Sir Qin took a sip of tea. 'Master Zheng, I know that you are a connoisseur of herbs, and that you collect all kinds of rare and precious species. Which herb would you say is 'the master of all herbs'?'

Master Zheng had relied on herbs to enhance his energy level, and certainly knew a great deal about them. He replied without hesitation. 'I would say the thousand-year ginseng',' The Chinese characters for 'ginseng' are '*Ren-Shen*' meaning 'man-root'. The name suggests that ginseng is a plant with long roots and the shape of a man.

'Have you ever seen one?' asked Sir Qin.

'I nearly had one once, but it slipped through my fingers.' Master Zheng could not conceal his disappointment.

Master Zheng had once gone to Long White Mountain in Liaoning Province, and there he had spent days and nights looking for the thousand-year ginseng. Then one night when the moon was full, he saw a small child-like figure. It was a 'thousand year old ginseng', which had already assumed a human shape, with a head, a body, and very long limbs. It began to run and dance under the moonlight. Master Zheng held his breath. He flew up into the air like a crane and caught the ginseng in his hand. The ginseng cried like a small child. In his exhilaration, Master Zheng forgot to watch his step, and he was bitten by a poisonous snake. The sudden sharp pain made him loosen his grip. The ginseng slipped through his fingers and disappeared into the field. He spent another three weeks there, watching and hoping that the ginseng would re-emerge. But it never did. After all his years of collecting, he should have remembered that precious and rare herbs were protected by Heaven.

Sir Qin said, 'I gather you were at Long White Mountain.'

'How do you know?'

'There must be dozens of ginseng poachers at Long White Mountain. If you have heard about the ginseng in Henan Province, how many more people must have known of it. We all know ginseng is a state monopoly, but that does not put a stop to poachers, particularly when most of them are experts in kung fu.'

Master Zheng agreed. 'A thousand-year ginseng can add ten years to a person's internal energy. It is the dream of every kung fu practitioner to possess one.'

Sir Qin took out a box with a glass top wrapped in red silk. Inside the box was a thousand-year ginseng, a red thread around its neck.

'Master Zheng,' said Sir Qin, 'did you forget the tale about a Buddhist monk and the ginseng? You must always tie a red thread around the neck of the ginseng so that it will not escape. Of course, you must also beware of dangerous creatures protecting the precious herb.'

Master Zheng envied Sir Qin's good luck in finding the thousand-year ginseng. He could not believe his ears when Sir Qin offered the ginseng to him as a gift. He asked cautiously, 'Is there anything I can do for you, Sir Qin?'

Sir Qin told him what he had told Master Wei. Again he said that he was only interested in the original scriptures written in Sanskrit language which had been brought back from India by the Tang monk Xuan Zhuang.

Master Zheng followed the same thought process as Master Wei. He had an additional reason to believe Sir Qin because no martial artist would give away a thousand-year ginseng, and relinquish the chance of enhancing his own internal energy by ten years. He too agreed to meet Sir Qin at dinner time outside the guest lodge.

Sir Qin had long heard of Shaolin Monastery's vast collection of Buddhist sutras. His retainer Toga was a Ninja from Japan, skilled in the art of spying. Before Sir Qin arrived at Shaolin Monastery, he had sent Toga on secret visits to the monastery. Toga could not find the sutras but he had brought back some useful information, which included Master Fu's addiction to the game of chess, and Tobie's astonishing memory.

Sir Qin suspected that the sutras were kept with Shaolin's treasured kung fu manual in the same secret location. He began his acquaintance with Master Fu by challenging him at chess. During the chess games, Sir Qin would casually pose questions. On one occasion, in a slip of the tongue, Master Fu told him about the secret chamber. On another occasion, Master Fu had revealed the names of the three keyholders to the secret chamber. What remained to be done was to get the three keyholders to co-operate. Toga had found out about Master Wei's selling of the antique sword for money, and Master Zheng's use of precious herbs to enhance his internal energy. Every man had a price, and religious men were no exception.

Sir Qin returned to the guest lodge. He found himself thinking about Haidi's mother. She was such a beautiful woman but she had died so young. He had vowed to avenge her death, and he felt he had now taken a step closer to this goal.

XI

THE SECRET UNDERGROUND CHAMBER

In the afternoon, when Tobie was playing chess with Master Fu, Flint and Leo went to the mountain spring. Leo waited there for Minnie. Finally he saw her, Greenie walking behind carrying a basket. The girls greeted Leo and they all sat under the shade of a tree. Minnie opened the basket. Inside were pieces of chestnut cake coated with cassia-flavoured sugar, walnut, caltrop, green bean and rose-flavoured cakes, cream rolls stuffed with pine-kernels, dried peach, honeyed lychees and red dates. Minnie said, 'Try some. They came all the way from the south. My father got them for me.' Leo had never seen such a rich assortment of delicacies.

Other junior monks and lay pupils saw them picnicking and flocked towards Minnie like bees to flowers. Minnie was a pretty girl and she was generous. She invited everyone to share in the snacks. Leo sneaked plates and dishes from the main kitchen, collected spring water, and helped to dish out cakes to Minnie's crowd of admirers. Minnie had led a cosseted life. She had been sent to an all female martial arts school. Apart from her kung fu brothers, she had had no contact with boys of her own age. She enjoyed being showered with attention from the opposite sex, although of course they were only junior monks and lay pupils from poor families. She was learning very quickly the power a girl has over boys.

Minnie was wondering where Flint was when she saw him with the stable boy Haidi. Flint was chatting with Haidi and did not notice Minnie and the crowd surrounding her. Minnie stole glances at Flint, but Flint did not look her way. She could not understand why Flint would befriend a lowly stable boy and ignore a pretty girl like her. She was growing restless when Speck came over with Flint and Haidi. Leo and Minnie had not met Speck, so Flint made the introductions.

Speck was not the handsomest of boys, yet he commanded attention. Minnie thought Speck had a regal air. There was an arrogance and authority in him, most unusual in someone who worked in the monastery. Was Speck really the Abbot's assistant in charge of the Study? Minnie offered him the delicacies she had brought and not surprisingly Speck could name every one of them and even knew from which special shops they had been bought. Speck explained that before he came to Shaolin he had been working for a noble household in Beijing. He was on leave and as the Abbot was short of an assistant, he was helping out for a while.

Minnie was curious. 'My father knows many important people in Beijing. What is the name of your master?'

'Aixin Gioro.'

'But that's the surname of the Imperial family? Do you work for an Imperial Prince? Have you met the Emperor? Has he really got 3000 concubines?'

Speck laughed. 'Far from it. I don't know about the Ming Emperors, but the Qing Emperors have only a couple of concubines. You must have been influenced by the Tang poet Bai JuYi who wrote that 'the Tang Emperor had 3000 beautiful concubines, but he lavished all his love and attention on one woman, the Honoured Consort Lady Yang'.'

'How I would like to be a Princess,' Minnie said wistfully.

'Why do you want to be a Princess?'

'Think of all the attendants that would be at my beck and call.'

'You can't be a Princess unless your father is the Emperor or a Prince. But I may be able to present you to the Emperor, who could make you his Honoured Consort.'

Minnie was offended. 'Who said I wanted to be a consort?' It was insulting to suggest that other women could rank above her, even in an Imperial Household.

Speck thought, 'Silly girl, she has no idea that the Palace is a gilded cage. A Princess has no freedom, her life is not her own, and when she grows up, she will be married off for political reasons. She could be sent to some remote place to marry an old tribal chief. Minnie doesn't know how lucky she is.'

Minnie interrupted his thoughts. 'Do you know, before I came to Shaolin, I thought Shaolin was the number one martial arts school under Heaven. Now that I have come here and seen your Shaolin kung fu, honestly, I think 'it's better to hear the name than to see it in person'. With no disrespect, my school, the E-Mei School of Martial Arts, is better. Our kung fu is superior. I can prove it to you. I'll perform three acts of kung fu. If any one of you can do the same or better, then I'll admit that Shaolin kung fu is superior to E-Mei. If I lose, I'll give you a big basket of delicacies, the nicest you will ever taste. If I win, I want Speck to take me to the Abbot's Study because I've heard the Abbot has a large collection of sutras. I want to see whether Shaolin has as many sutras as we have in E-Mei. My *Shifu* said E-Mei had the largest collection of sutras anywhere, and I want to tell her when I go back that she is right.'

The challenge was accepted. The first kung fu act was fire swallowing. Minnie lit a torch, swallowed the fire, and then blew flames from her mouth. This was impressive. In Shaolin, only the very advanced student could lick a hot shovel and produce hot steam to heal wounds. The boys had not seen anyone who could actually swallow fire and blow it out again.

The second act was breaking bricks. Each stack consisted of twenty-one solid bricks. Minnie said she would break the middle brick of any pile they designated. She hit her palm on the pile of bricks, and then removed them one by one. The top ten and the bottom ten remained intact, and only the middle brick was broken. None of the boys was able to do this.

The third act was a *Qingong* test. She challenged Flint to race her to the top of the hill and down again. She said that she had placed a red box on top of the hill. Whoever came down with the box would be the winner. The route up the hill was tricky, a maze of thick bushes. Flint ran as fast as he could. He was about to reach the top, when to his surprise, he found Minnie ahead of him. When he returned, Minnie had already arrived, the box in her hand. Flint's *Qingong* was the best among the boys, so if Flint could not beat Minnie, none of the others would be able to.

A bet was a bet and the loser had to pay the forfeit. Speck agreed to meet Minnie under the gingko tree in the Steles Forest at dinner time. He would show her the Abbot's Study and Minnie was to disguise herself as a lay Shaolin pupil.

Speck, Flint, and Haidi had seen through Minnie's tricks. Speck had seen magicians performing fire-swallowing. Any one who knew the trick would be able to do it. For breaking of the bricks, it was obvious that Leo had been in cohorts with Minnie by preparing the bricks beforehand. The third task could not have been simpler. It reminded the boys of their own trick, fooling the Tibetan monk. They had all noticed the disappearance of Greenie. When Minnie went into the bushes and was out of sight, Greenie was waiting ahead of Flint, wearing the same dress and hair style. The two of them took part in the same race. The boys were curious as to her motive, but went along with her game for the moment. Flint whispered to Speck. 'Take care!'

The Study was adjacent to the Abbot's bedroom on one side, and to Speck's bedroom on the other. There was no access to the Study except through the bedrooms. Inside, there were long, high narrow windows to let in air and light. Not even a child could squeeze through them. Below the windows were rows and rows of shelves filled with books and sutras. The Study was not left unguarded at any time. Tonight, the Abbot was giving a farewell dinner for the Commander and the soldiers, and he instructed Speck not to leave the Study. But at dinner time, Speck left his post and waited for Minnie under the gingko tree. He had been there for some time when he sensed someone nearby, and before he could turn around he felt a prick to the vital energy point to his back. He was instantly immobilised, and hands reached around him to tie on a blindfold and a gag to his mouth. He glimpsed no more than a flash of green sleeve before he was thrown into the undergrowth. He did not see his attacker but knew that it was not Minnie. It was a woman, he thought, but someone taller.

Minnie, dressed in Shaolin lay pupil's clothing, went through Speck's bedroom to the Abbot's Study and started searching. When she heard footsteps approaching, she jumped up to the ceiling and hid behind a rafter.

The three keyholders, Master Zheng, Master Fu and Master Wei, had excused themselves from the Abbot's dinner reception for the soldiers. They met up with Sir Qin outside the guest lodge, and together they walked over to the Abbot's Lodge. 'So the secret chamber is actually inside the Abbot's Lodge,' thought Sir Qin. They went through Speck's bedroom to the Study. They were surprised not to find Speck there. Master Wei grumbled, 'These days you just can't trust the youngsters. The moment your back is turned, they go off somewhere. I will speak to the Abbot to make sure that this does not happen again. The Study must never be left unattended.'

Master Zheng moved aside the desk in the Study. Then he removed the carpet from the floor under the desk. He lifted the floorboards to reveal a flight of stone steps. He and his companions carried torches as they went down the steps one by one into a long, dark narrow corridor. At the end of the corridor was a heavy cast-iron door. They left two of the torches on the walls of the corridor. Master Zheng, Master Fu and Master Wei each used their key to open the door. With his torch Sir Qin saw a small room with steel walls, and shelves stuffed full of sutras. On one wall hung a painting of Bodhidharma, founder of Shaolin kung fu.

A writing desk faced the door. On it sat a wooden box with a glass lid. The box was sealed. Master Zheng took up the box and was pleased to see that Shaolin's treasured manual, 'Tendon Changing and Marrow Cleansing', written in the Chinese language, was safely inside. He clutched the box to his chest and sat on a chair. Master Fu and Master Wei sat on each side of him to protect the box from being snatched by Sir Qin.

Sir Qin did not even glance at the kung fu manual. He went straight to the shelves to look at the Sanskrit sutras. He had been granted 15 minutes for his search. After five minutes had passed he turned, and in a flash he pressed the energy points of Master

Zheng, Master Fu and Master Wei so that they fell into a deep sleep. He removed a sutra from one of the shelves and hid it in his sleeve, replacing it with another that he had brought with him. He then released the energy points of the monks and went back to the shelves, flipping casually through the pages of a sutra. The monks were not aware that they had dozed off. Master Zheng was still clutching the box containing the kung fu manual. The seal was still unbroken.

Master Zheng said, 'Time's up, Sir Qin, we must leave now.' The monks closed the iron door behind them. On their way back up the steps, they collected their torches from the wall. They closed the floorboards, put back the carpet and desk, and left the Study. After they had gone, Minnie leapt down from the rafter, went out of the Study to Speck's room, opened a window, and climbed out.

Half an hour later, Speck's vital energy point relaxed and he could move again. He tore the gag from his mouth and pulled the cloth from his eyes. He looked around for Minnie but could not see her. He ran back to the Study and was relieved to see that nothing was missing. But he noticed that the window of his room was unlatched, and he sensed that someone had been in the Abbot's Study. Why had Minnie not turned up for their meeting?

The dinner reception for the commander and the soldiers which had started at five o'clock finished at eight, and the soldiers left Shaolin Monastery. The monks retired to their rooms after the disruption of the past two days.

In the lay pupil's dormitory, Flint lay wide awake, ready to sneak out when the other boys had fallen asleep.

XII

THE HEAVEN AND EARTH
TRIAD SOCIETY

'By Heaven, my father, by earth my mother, we swear we will overthrow the Qing and restore the Ming,' the men chanted in chorus. The place was lit by rows and rows of torches. Hundreds had gathered on the hilltop of Five Breast Peak.

A platform had been erected, with an altar-like table in the middle, and on it stood two spirit tablets. The central tablet was the spirit tablet of the last Ming Emperor Chong Zhen, and beside it was the spirit tablet of Marshall Zheng ChengGong. In front of the tablets were the offerings, a grain bushel containing the five grains (millet, glutinous millet, wheat and barley, legumes and hemp seeds), five fruits (pear, banana, sunflower seeds, taro and tangerine), five bowls of wine, three cups of tea, a horse head representing Heaven, an ox head representing Earth, and a pig's head. Right in front and in the middle of the altar was a large incense burner holding seven burning incense sticks, inscribed with the characters '*Fan Qing Fu Ming*', 'Overthrow the Qing and Restore the Ming'.

On the right side of the altar was a row of five seats. The first seat was empty, and in the next seats were Master Wan YunLong, Master Zheng, Scholar Gu YanWu and Master Wei. On the left side of the altar, there was another row of five seats, occupied by the five brave men who had rescued Scholar Gu. There was the fisherman dressed in black with a black flag hoisted beside him; next sat the butcher in red with a red flag; then was the horse trader dressed in vermillion with a vermillion coloured flag; next, the hunter in white with a white flag; and the last seat was taken up by the scholar in green with a green flag hoisted beside him.

Those sitting on the ground were divided into five groups of black, red, vermillion, white and green distinguished by the colour of their clothing. Each held a matching flag in his hand. All the men wore Ming style clothing and hair.

Gongs and drums sounded to signify the start of the ceremony. Those on seats rose and moved towards the altar, Master Wan leading the procession. With three burning joist sticks clasped in both hands, they bowed three times before the altar, and placed the joist sticks into the incense burner. They then kowtowed three times, their heads to the ground, and returned to their seats.

Master Wan rose and moved to the front of the platform to speak. He had powerful internal force and his words were heard clearly by everyone on the hilltop. 'Brothers, I am Wan YunLong, your Incense Master. The empty chair on my right is reserved for our Grand Lodge Master, Chen YongHua, who unfortunately could not attend our ceremony tonight. For the benefit of our many new members who have joined our Society in the last few months, I shall begin with a short history of our Society. Seven years ago, our Heaven and Earth Society was established. Our Society has only one goal, to 'overthrow the Qing and Restore the Ming'.' The crowd responded, 'Overthrow the Qing and Restore the Ming'.

Master Wan continued, 'Koxinga was our leader in the resistance movement but sadly he died soon after he had defeated the 'red hairy devils' in Taiwan. It was left to his military adviser Chen YongHua to establish the Heaven and Earth Society.

'We regard Koxinga and, after his death, his son, the Prince of Yanping, as leaders of the anti-Manchu resistance movement in China. We look to Chen YongHua as the Grand Lodge Master of our Heaven and Earth Society. As your Incense Master, I am responsible for initiation ceremonies. I also assist the Grand Lodge Master in overseeing Society affairs.

'Our Society achieved little during the first few years after Koxinga's death. The change of power in Taiwan consumed much of our Grand Lodge Master's time. But we continued to work slowly and steadily. Then with the help of our Grand Lodge

Master, we have established five lodges in different parts of China, and appointed five Lodge Masters.

'Some of you may wish to know more about our five Lodge Masters. I'll tell you now. These are the five brave men who rescued our best known scholar Gu YanWu from the Tartar barbarians in Kaifeng. They are now seated on the left hand side of the altar. The Master of the Green Lotus Lodge is in charge of our affairs in Fujian; the Master of the Hong Compliance Lodge is in charge of Guangdong and Guangxi; the Master of the Family Posterity Lodge is in charge of Yunnan and Xichuan; the Master of the Great Reach Lodge is in charge of Hunan and Hubei; and the Master of the Grand Sublimity Lodge is in charge of Zhejiang.' As Master Wan read out the names, each Lodge Master rose from his seat, clasped his hands and bowed to the applause of the crowd.

'After the death of Emperor Chong Zhen, several Ming Princes were supported by Ming loyalists in their claims to the Ming throne. Instead of fighting the Manchus, the Ming loyalists fought amongst themselves over the question of succession. You all know the outcome. Every one of the Ming Princes was killed by the Tartar barbarians. Yet factional fighting continues to this day among Ming supporters. It now falls on our Heaven and Earth Society to unite every Han Chinese in the struggle against the barbarians, and to put an end to factional fighting.

'We have been looking for the rightful heir to the Ming throne to unite us in our movement to 'Overthrow the Qing and Restore the Ming.' Master Wan paused, then said slowly and carefully, 'Brothers, tonight I have exciting news to tell you. We have found the rightful heir to the Ming throne, Prince Zhu San, the third son of Emperor Chong Zhen. He is the only surviving heir to Emperor Chong Zhen. No one can dispute his claim to the Ming throne. Many of you may wonder, is there any proof that he is the real Prince Zhu San? I don't blame you for thinking this way. He has produced proof which I cannot refute.'

Master Wan signalled for a follower to bring to him two swords. He raised the swords high in the air. 'Brothers, these two precious swords are the 'Peachwood-red Sword of the Loyal

Ministers' and the 'Sword of the Two Dragons Fighting for the Pearl'. These swords were worn personally by Ming emperors and could only be passed down to the rightful heir. I can assure you that the swords have been authenticated.

'Prince Zhu San is the son by the Honoured Consort Lady Li of the Western Palaces, who was pregnant with the prince when Beijing fell into the hands of the rebel chief, Li ZiCheng. She escaped from the Imperial Palace and took with her the two precious swords which could prove the identity of her child. However, we do not rely solely on the two swords. We have other evidence which has convinced us that this is indeed the genuine Prince Zhu San, the third son of Emperor Chong Zhen. Prince Zhu San has promised to meet with us at our next meeting. You will be notified of the date and place nearer the time. It will be the greatest event ever of our Society.'

Master Wan then introduced Scholar Gu YanWu. Scholar Gu spoke eloquently, reminding the crowd of the atrocities of the Manchu barbarians especially in 'The Ten Days of Yangzhou' and 'The Three Slaughters of Jiading' where hundreds of thousands of Han Chinese were killed. He gave a harrowing account of the literary inquisitions. He told the story of the Zhuang family, 'The only crime of the Zhuang family was to publish a book on Ming history, originally written by a Ming Grand Chancellor. This book on Ming history is a great work and highly regarded by all scholars. Yet because of a few errors in the reign years, many innocent people were persecuted and executed. Of the Zhuang family, all the males over the age of sixteen were executed, and the women and children were either sold to whore houses or taken into slavery.'

The listeners called out angrily. 'Down with the Manchu dogs! We want to drink their blood and eat their flesh.'

When the crowd had calmed down, Master Wan introduced Master Zheng. 'Brothers, we are honoured to-night with the presence of Master Zheng from Shaolin Monastery. Some of you might already have heard of Master Zheng who is a highly regarded member of the Brotherhood of River and Lake. Not only is Master Zheng a kung fu master, he is also a Ming Loyalist. He is the second senior person at Shaolin. With his help, we will bring Shaolin Monastery into our fold, which would lend great force to our resistance movement. You all know that Shaolin is the foremost monastery in the country and a leading force in the Brotherhood. I cannot emphasis more how important Shaolin's support is to our cause.' Master Zheng rose from his seat and bowed.

Gongs and drums signified the start of the initiation ceremony. Master Wan addressed the crowd, 'I want to introduce a very special new member to our brotherhood, Master Wei from Shaolin Monastery. He has not taken his monk's vow. The Abbot will not ordain Master Wei until he is ready to get rid of the anger and hatred in his heart. But Master Wei cannot forget or forgive what the Tartar barbarians have done to his family. Master Wei comes from Yangzhou. He was a victim of the 10 days of massacre there when he was a young boy of ten years old. He saw his father killed, and his mother and sisters raped before his very eyes. His own life was saved by the old Abbot who took him into Shaolin Monastery. But the scenes of his parents' and sisters' deaths have been etched in his mind. Every time he closes his eyes, he can see them crying out to him. He wants their deaths avenged. In our Society, he has found people who share his anger. He has vowed to kill every single Tartar barbarian. He will fight for our cause with his life. After his initiation to our Society, Master Wei will leave Shaolin to become fully involved in our activities. 'Wei' is his Buddhist name. From now on, Master Wei will be known by his own name, Yang Quan.

'Tonight we bind ourselves together as blood brothers, forever after of one heart. When we were born, we did not share our father or come from one womb. From tonight onwards we must see each other as family. Our family surname is 'Hong' taken from the reign name of the Founding Emperor of the Ming Dynasty, 'Hong Wu'. Once we enter into a blood covenant, we become blood brothers of the Hong family. From tonight, you will join us as brothers of one womb.'

Master Wan read out a list of names. 'This night, we swear by oath our loyalty to the Heaven and Earth Society.' The crowd repeated after him.

'We swear by oath our loyalty to our brothers,' the crowd repeated.

'We swear by oath our loyalty to our Society's mission to 'Overthrow the Qing and Restore the Ming'.' The crowd repeated and cheered.

'It is important that you keep the secrecy of our Society. Everything you see tonight and everything you know of our Society must be kept to yourselves. You must not divulge any information even to persons closest to you. What we have entered into is a blood covenant which binds us for the rest of our lives. He who leaks information or betrays a brother will pay with his own blood.'

Master Wan took from the folds of his clothing a piece of paper. He read the 36 Oaths and the 10 Prohibitions and 10 Penalties. Depending on the seriousness of the offence, the severity of penalties ranged from flogging to beheading or slicing the body into eight pieces. In the most severe case, an entire family could be eliminated to serve as a warning to others.

To the side of the platform was a large container of wine. The paper on which was written the 36 Oaths was burned into ashes, and the ashes mixed into the wine. Master Wei led the procession of new members up to the platform. Each new member cut his middle finger and let his blood drip into the wine. The wine was then distributed and drunk by everyone.

Gongs and drums signalled the end of the meeting. 'From tonight's blood covenant, if any brother has had ill feelings or sought revenge from another brother, these thoughts should now be cast into the rivers and the seas. We are now of one family. If there is good fortune, we shall all share in the good fortune; if there is danger, we shall …

Before Master Wan could finish the sentence, 'run to each other's rescue', an explosion pierced the air. Everyone thought the Qing Army had attacked. Then came a vile smell. Master Wan realised it was not a bomb but someone breaking wind. But this was no ordinary flatulence. These sounds could only be made by someone with immense *Qi* in his body.

107

Master Wan raised his voice to calm the crowd. 'Brothers, keep calm. There is no attack.' He concluded the meeting and hurried to follow the odour still drifting in the air. In the darkness, he saw the figure of a large man carrying a sack on his back. Master Wan gave chase with Master Zheng and Master Wei close behind.

XIII

TO CATCH A SPY

When the boys in the dormitory were asleep, Flint began to creep out, but Bussie heard him and insisted he come too. Otherwise, he said, he would wake the whole dormitory. Reluctantly Flint agreed.

Speck and Haidi were outside. Tobie was waiting outside his uncle's hut which they would pass on their way to Five Breast Peak. They were all clad in black. Flint asked Speck how his meeting with Minnie went. Speck just said that she had not turned up.

The boys climbed up Five Breast Peak. They quickly found a tree both big enough to hide them all and high enough to give them a good view of things below. When Master Wan began to address his followers, the boys recognised him as the person who had been with Master Wei at the Stupa Forest the previous night. The strong southern accent was so distinct, it could not be anyone else.

At dinner Tobie had drunk a bowl of ginseng soup prepared by his uncle. While the other boys were listening to Master Wan, he was struggling with the *Qi* flow in his body. He felt the *Qi* running amok and his body began to swell. He vowed that he would never touch a bowl of ginseng soup again. He did not know that it had been a thousand-year ginseng soup, the most sought after treatment for every martial artist.

Martial artists frequently use herbs to enhance their internal energy. The preparation of herbs was a time consuming process. The timing, water temperature, type of water, and the proportion of herbs in the mixture must be exactly right. Master Zheng always enlisted the help of the Head Chef in preparing his herbal soup. What he did not know was that there was another beneficiary of the Chef's preparations. The Head Chef always managed to save a small bowl for Tobie. In fact, Tobie usually got the best bits. This was one reason why Tobie had such strong internal force without the hard drilling which other boys had to undergo.

The Head Chef was knowledgeable about the properties of herbs. Master Zheng always erred in calculating the proportions, and tended to put in more herbs than was necessary. This did not mean that he would benefit more. If the herbs were not in the right proportion, it could cause more harm to the body than good. If Master Zheng asked the Chef to boil down the liquid to one bowl of soup, it would be just right for two bowls. The other bowl of course went to Tobie. Master Zheng trusted the Chef, and would not allow any one else to prepare his soup.

When Tobie was small, the Chef diluted his soup. As he grew, Tobie's soup became more concentrated. Herbal soup was not the only source of Tobie's energy. Kung fu experts from all over the country came to Shaolin to taste the Chef's famous vegetarian dishes. The Chef always managed to manipulate the experts to transfer some of their own energies to Tobie, in order to help his precious nephew to move up in Shaolin. The experts could not get away without teaching Tobie a few fighting poses. When Tobie was a child, the experts demonstrated their fighting poses more for fun than to teach him. To impress the cook, they selected the most deadly manoeuvres to teach Tobie. How could they have guessed that everything they taught was stored in Tobie's memory and would one day come back to haunt them? By now Tobie had learned so many different styles that he could have become a master in kung fu. But he had no such ambition, and never bothered to practise.

The Chef had prepared the thousand-year ginseng soup. He gave half a bowl of concentrated ginseng soup to Tobie and diluted the other half for Master Zheng. He had never before prepared 'thousand-year ginseng' soup. Both he and Master Zheng greatly underestimated its potency. In diluting Master Zheng's soup, the Chef had unwittingly got the proportions right for him. But Tobie was not so lucky. He drank his bowl of concentrated ginseng soup. As he was climbing the hill with the other boys, his face and body became increasingly warm. There was a burning sensation inside him, and his body became bloated. The *Qi* was building rapidly and he began to expand like a balloon. Tobie had immense internal energy in his body, but had never done the exercises necessary to help him channel the *Qi* to the right places. His *Qi* reservoirs were already full. With the new influx of *Qi* generated by the ginseng soup, the reservoirs began to overflow, looking for an outlet. While the others were watching what was happening on the platform below, Tobie struggled to cope with the excess *Qi*. Just as the initiation ceremony was about to finish, he could no longer control himself and he released a loud, long and pungent wind. The *Qi* began to build up again. By then Master Wan was running towards them.

The boys jumped from the tree and ran. Tobie's body had grown so swollen that he could barely walk, so Bussie carried him on his back. Speck's *qingong* was not good, so Flint took his right hand and Haidi his left and the three of them ran together. Haidi's *qingong* was surprisingly good and he could keep pace with Flint. Soon, the three of them were running ahead of Bussie and Tobie, and they disappeared into a small narrow path hidden by bushes.

Master Wan, Master Zheng and Master Wei caught up with Bussie and Tobie. In the dark, it looked as though Bussie was carrying a large sack on his back. Master Wan summoned his full internal force and raised his palm. He struck at the figure, expecting to fell him. The blow fell on Tobie's back. Tobie's body was on the verge of exploding when the blow hit. Instead of killing Tobie, the blow saved his life by channelling his *Qi* to the *Qi* channels. The release of pressure was instant and Tobie immediately felt better.

Master Zheng was beginning to feel the benefit of his share of the ginseng soup. His body was light and he was full of energy. He too struck a blow at Tobie. Master Wei followed suit, though his internal force was weaker than that of Master Wan or Master Zheng.

The blows all had the same effect. Every blow made Tobie feel better. The three great masters had no idea that they were helping Tobie to achieve 'a small universe' breakthrough. Each of their blows assisted the *Qi* circulation in his body. Each circulation helped to treat and refine the *Qi* and to channel the *Qi* to the right places.

Master Wan and Master Zheng were dumbfounded. Instead of killing the intruder, the blows seemed only to move the intruder forward. When they caught up with him, they struck again. Every time they punched out, the human football moved further on. They chased after Bussie and Tobie, raining blow after blow upon them, until Bussie, with Tobie on his back, leapt sideways down the side of the hill.

Flint, Speck and Haidi did not have such a lucky escape. The Tibetan lama had also been in hiding, watching the meeting below. When he saw the boys leap down from the tree, he thought of the men in black who had cheated him of the poison antidote. There is a saying, 'when the enemies meet, their eyes turn red'. The lama's eyes flamed with rage. He was determined to catch them, and he followed them into the small bushy path.

Flint saw a cave ahead in the side of the mountain. The entrance to the cave was very small, and the boys just managed to squeeze in. There was no way that the lama could get through the entrance. He cursed the boys from outside.

He wanted to use fire to smoke out the boys but heavy rain had started and he could not light a fire. A poisonous snake was coiled around a tree trunk. The lama snatched it and threw it into the cave. Almost instantly the snake flew back at him. He threw stones into the cave but they too were thrown back.

The lama had a hidden weapon, a weapon he wanted only to use as a last resort. Reluctantly, he flicked his sleeve, and small needles coated with poison flew into the cave. He heard nothing. He was about to congratulate himself when the needles came flying back, hitting him in the face and body. As a practitioner of Green Demon Palm, the lama was immune to many types of poison, including the poison on the needles. These needles were effective in killing his enemies but there were plenty of antidotes, so they were less deadly than the specially manufactured poison that he had used to injure Toga. Such poisons took time to process and he used them only sparingly.

He was at his wit's end when an idea struck him. He inserted a tube into the entrance to the cave and blew in poisonous fumes. Inside the cave was a passage with twists and turns, which was why the stones, the snake, and the poisonous needles had missed their targets. But the lama's poisonous fumes were odourless, and before anyone was aware of the danger, Speck and Haidi had collapsed, their faces turning blue. Flint realised that his friends had been poisoned, so he pulled them further back into the cave. There he saw another exit and pulled his friends out.

Flint was immune to poison after drinking the blood of the sea serpent, but Speck and Haidi had no such immunity. In desperation, Flint decided to use his own blood as an antidote. He slashed both his wrists, summoned his internal force, and pulsed blood from his wrists into the mouths of Speck and Haidi.

Master Wan, Master Zheng and Master Wei continued their search for the man with the sack. They stumbled into a muddy swamp and Master Wei almost drowned. They walked into a pit full of poisonous snakes. Master Zheng urged them to retreat. 'We are in the Chef's territory. The Chef is protective of his recipes and he has built his hut within a maze to keep out intruders. This place is full of swamps, bogs, reptiles, poisonous insects and poisonous plants. Let's go to Master Wan's room to discuss what to do next.' Whoever was spying on them could not have survived their blows.

Back in his room, Master Wan said, 'Let's forget about the intruder and get back to important business. We'll go to see the Abbot tomorrow morning as planned, and lay down our cards.'

Master Wei was not optimistic. 'I don't think the Abbot will support the resistance movement. He and the old Abbot have always been against the monastery becoming involved in political activity. He'll say that Shaolin is devoted to Buddhism, and that the monks must extricate their minds from all worldly affairs.'

Master Zheng was irritated at the mention of the Abbot. 'It's not up to him. We must remind him that he is a Han Chinese and that China is our country. The Tartar barbarians are invaders.'

'We are in a win-win situation.' Master Wan reminded them. 'We are to set up a Southern Shaolin Monastery. If the Abbot agrees to support us, then he can continue to be the Abbot of Northern Shaolin, and Master Zheng the Abbot of Southern Shaolin. If the Abbot refuses our proposal, we'll take the monastery by force. I have gathered my men at Five Breast Peak. At my command, they will move in and take the monastery. Master Zheng will then take over as Abbot of Shaolin. We will hold the Abbot hostage until the Shaolin monks come over to our side. If they don't, they will be eliminated.'

Master Wei was cautious. 'What will we do if our men fail to take the monastery?'

'We'll retreat and set up Southern Shaolin in direct competition,' Master Wan said. 'I have seen Master Zheng's kung fu tonight. I can tell you that it is already superior to the Abbot's. We will have to deal with Master Fu, but this will not be a problem. There is really no need to worry. We are in a very strong position. If we take over the monastery, things will continue as normal. Apart from a few senior monks, no one will even be aware there has been a change in regime. The tactic will be to strike like lightning and to shroud everything in secrecy. Shaolin Monastery will appear the same as before.'

Master Wei was concerned about the strategy for overthrowing the Manchus. 'Are we going to assassinate the Tartar Emperor?'

Master Wan chuckled. 'What's the point? The Tartar Emperor is only a boy. He is heavily guarded by Oboi's men and his every movement is closely monitored. The real power is in the hands of the Regent Oboi. If we kill the young Emperor, Oboi will just install another young Manchu prince as emperor, and he too will be completely under his control.'

'What about that filthy traitor, Wu SanGui? Are we going to finish him off?'

'Let's take one step at a time. If we finish off that turtle egg Wu SanGui, the Tartar barbarians will only send another official to fill the position. Wu is rumoured to have amassed an army of over 100,000 men. The other two, Shang and Geng have about 20,000 men each. The military forces controlled by these three cost the Qing court 20 million taels of silver each year, half of the country's entire expenditure. The three traitors' incessant demands for money and their expanding military might are already threatening the Tartar barbarians. Soon there will be a show down. We don't want to do the Tartars' job for them. Let them fight it out amongst themselves. We will just sit back and reap the benefit.'

Master Zheng added, 'There is a saying, 'in the fight between the snipe and the clam, it is the fisherman who benefits'.'

'So are we just going to sit back and do nothing?'

Master Wan laughed at Master Wei's lack of political insight. 'Master Wei, you're a master in kung fu but you're no strategist and no politician. I ask you, who is the centre of Manchu power?'

'You mean the Regent Oboi?'

'You've got it. We'll get rid of Oboi first. His hands are covered with the blood of Han Chinese. We are not the only ones after his life. The families of those he has killed all want to avenge the deaths of their dear ones, but I want our Society to be the one to kill Oboi. Can you imagine the glory if we succeed? We will be hailed as national heroes. Every Han Chinese will look up to us because we can deliver.' Master Wan's eyes lit up. 'We, the Heaven and Earth Society, must kill Oboi to maintain our leadership of the resistance movement.'

Master Wei was still not fully convinced. 'What if we get rid of Oboi and that traitor Wu proclaims himself emperor?'

'Wu's best chance is to help Prince Zhu San reclaim the Ming throne. Wu has betrayed the country once. No Han Chinese will trust him again. Once you have lost the hearts and minds of the people, you have lost the battle forever.'

They went on to discuss other matters in relation to the Heaven and Earth Society. Master Wan was pleased that Master Wei had raised funds for financing five more lodges. Master Wei did not tell him that the money was a gift from Sir Qin.

They arranged to meet first thing in the morning outside the Abbot's lodge. Then they would go together to see the Abbot.

XIV

THE SECRET MANUAL OF 'TENDON TRANSFORMATION'

The stable boy Haidi could taste blood in his mouth. He opened his eyes, and when he realised what had happened he jumped up quickly to stem the flow of blood from Flint's wrists. Soon after, Speck came round. He too struggled to his feet and together with Haidi, helped Flint to stand. With Speck taking most of Flint's weight, they limped from the cave. Haidi had with him a gourd of water, and he made Flint drink regularly to keep him awake. Eventually they emerged from the wood into pouring rain. Drenched and completely exhausted, they collapsed to the ground.

Flint remained in a deep sleep. He dreamed that he was being fed soups tasting of beef or pig's liver, and a concoction from tree bark. When eventually he woke, he looked around to find found himself in a hut. Sunlight was streaming in through the small window. He felt his energies returning and looked up to see the old Abbot Tong Ti.

The old Abbot told Flint how he had found them all, on the ground near his hut. He told Flint that Speck and Haidi had fully recovered, and he had sent them back to the monastery. He said that he wanted Flint to visit the three Elders of Shaolin before he met up with his friends again.

The three elders had lived in seclusion in a grotto for thirty years. They were all close to a hundred years old. One of them was a former Abbot of Shaolin Monastery. He was also the *Shifu* of the old Abbot. The other two elders were his *Shi-Dis*[6].

When Flint arrived he kowtowed to the three elders. 'Shaolin

---

[6] Younger kung fu brothers

pupil Flint comes to pay respect to *Tai Shi-Gong*[7] Qing Wang, *Tai Shi-Shu Gong*[8] Qing Zhi, and *Tai Shi-Shu Gong* Qing Xin.'

'You may sit.' The words came from the yellow-faced elder in the middle. His voice was not strong, but he spoke clearly and kindly.

The three elders sat upright on the ground, their legs crossed in the lotus Buddha pose, the Shaolin meditation posture. Flint sat as they did, his upper body straight and relaxed.

Apart from their complexions, the elders looked very much alike. Each had a long white beard and long white eyebrows. Flint guessed that the monk in the middle must be the former Abbot Qing Wang. The monk on the right with the ruddy features, Flint guessed to be Qing Zhi. The monk on the left with the dark complexion was Qing Xin.

Shaolin Monastery keeps a family tree which consists of 70 Chinese characters, each character representing one generation. The family tree begins with Abbot 'Fu Yu' in the early Yuan Dynasty. 'Fu' therefore became the first character in the family tree. Monks in the same generation share the same first character in their religious names. Thus when a Shaolin monk gives his religious name, he discloses his generation. The three elders belonged to the 'Qing' generation, the 17th character in the family tree. The old Abbot, being the disciple of Qing Wang, belonged to the next generation, the 'Tong' generation, and his religious name was 'Tong Ti'. The present Abbot and Master Zheng as disciples of the old Abbot belonged to the 'Xuan' generation. The present Abbot's religious name was 'Xuan Kui' and Master Zheng was 'Xuan Zheng'.

Elder Qing Wang said, 'I understand that when you were six years old, you were attacked by a sea serpent. You killed it by biting into its neck and drinking its blood. The sea serpent contained tremendous *Yin* energy. You were kept alive by the Golden Pearl of Elixir until you reached Shaolin Monastery. You were given *Qi* transfers by Shaolin's senior monks and were taught the Yang style kung fu in order to generate *Yang* energy in

---

[7] Great Grand kung fu teacher
[8] Great Grand kung fu Uncle

117

your body to combat your excess *Yin* energy. But these alone could not have restored the *Yin-Yang* balance in your body. However, I see that your face no longer displays two shades of colour, one side paler than the other. You must have achieved a 'small universe' breakthrough. This could only have been done with the help of experts equal in their levels of kung fu, one specialising in the *Yin* style and the other specialising in the *Yang* style.'

Flint nodded. 'Yes, *Tai Shi-Gong*. Abbot Tong Ti and Miao Shan *Shi-Tai* helped me achieve a 'small universe' breakthrough.'

The elder nodded. 'I don't want to disappoint you, but you must know that the root of your illness has not been eradicated. As time goes on, the *Yin* energy will regenerate much faster and with greater power than your *Yang* energy and you will be back to square one.'

'*Tai Shi-Gong*, is there any cure at all?'

'It is the will of Heaven that you drank the blood of a sea serpent. It is the will of Heaven that you have come to see us at a point when, after thirty years of meditation, we have finally achieved a breakthrough in our understanding of the 'Tendon Transformation and Marrow Cleansing' kung fu.'

Seeing the bewilderment on Flint's face, the elder explained, 'The secret manual of 'Tendon Transformation and Marrow Cleansing' is the most sought after treasure in the Brotherhood. The kung fu in this manual is so powerful that whoever acquires the skills can achieve invincibility and become the champion in martial arts. Martial artists will pay any price to get hold of the manual. But if Shaolin is in possession of such a powerful kung fu manual, why has Shaolin not yet produced the greatest kung fu master? If Shaolin does have such a champion, why call for an open contest in the Martial Arts Fellowship?'

Flint could see the logic in this. The elder continued, 'The 'Tendon Transformation and Marrow Cleansing' kung fu was created by the First Patriarch, Bodhidharma, more than a thousand years ago. The Bodhidharma Cave at the Five Breast Peak is where the First Patriarch practised his meditation. You have been there?'

'Yes, *Tai Shi-Gong*. I have been there several times.'

'The First Patriarch practised meditation for nine years facing the wall in the cave. Have you seen that wall?'

'Yes, *Tai Shi-Gong*. The surface of the wall appears even but actually it is uneven. It appears clean but is actually marked. The stone wall is rough. The strange thing is that when you step back from the wall a little, you can see the shadow of a man on the wall. And when you step back a little further, you can see the First Patriarch in meditation as though you were looking at a reflection in a mirror. Many people believe that the First Patriarch has left his image on the wall after sitting in meditation for so many years.'

'Before the First Patriarch died, he wrote the 'Tendon Transformation and Marrow Cleansing' kung fu and put the manual in a stone box. He dug a hole in the wall to hide the box, and then filled the wall in again. The box remained there until it was discovered 300 years later in the Tang Dynasty. The manual is written in Sanskrit and consists of two volumes. Volume I deals with 'Tendon Transformation' and Volume II deals with 'Marrow Transformation'. The Chinese translations of the two volumes were finally completed in the fourth year of the reign of the Tang Emperor Wu Zong. Unfortunately, the Tang Emperor preferred Daoism, and in that very year, he abolished Buddhism. Many Buddhist monasteries were destroyed and the monks and nuns fled their monasteries. It was during this period that Shaolin Monastery hid its sutras. After Emperor Wu Zong died, Buddhism again became popular. The monastery recovered most of its sutras but some had been lost. Amongst those still not recovered are the original Sanskrit version of 'Tendon Transformation and Marrow Cleansing' kung fu, and the Chinese translated version of the 'Marrow Cleansing' kung fu. In other words, Shaolin Monastery has in its possession only the Chinese translated version of the 'Tendon Transformation' kung fu.

'The 'Tendon Transformation' kung fu trains the *Jing* and *Qi*. The tendons, muscles and bones can be transformed to become soft and malleable, so that the body is completely flexible. The manual contains many extraordinary skills.' The elder paused and asked Flint, 'On a stone monument in the Steles Forest, there is a carving of the First Patriarch crossing a river. Have you seen it?'

'Yes, *Tai Shi-Gong*. The name of the sculpted painting is 'Crossing the River on a Reed'.'

'You will know that it tells the story of how the First Patriarch came to Shaolin Monastery, which was part of the Kingdom of Northern Wei at the time. The carving depicts the First Patriarch crossing the river to the Kingdom of Northern Wei, stepping onto a floating reed.'

'To be able to step onto a floating reed, a person's body must be lighter than the reed. Is that possible, *Tai Shi-Gong*?'

'Many martial artists believe it is possible. They have even convinced themselves that the particular *Qingong* skill of the First Patriarch in crossing the river on a reed is the secret kung fu of Shaolin, and is depicted in the 'Tendon Transformation' manual. You asked me whether this was humanly possible. I think that if a person reaches the highest level in *Shen*, many things are possible. While the 'Tendon Transformation' kung fu deals with the physical side, the 'Marrow Cleansing' kung fu deals with the spiritual side, the *Shen*. The development of the 'Mind and Spirit' can raise levels of consciousness, creativity and insight, and can accelerate the path to 'enlightenment'. When that level of spiritual fulfilment is reached, a person can acquire occult powers, walking over water, soaring through the sky, in two places at the same time, raising the dead, and other extraordinary abilities.

'Over the years, the original Sanskrit version was gradually forgotten. It was the Chinese version that was relied upon and which gained importance. However, there is a problem with the Chinese translation. The 'Tendon Transformation' manual consists of two parts. Part 1 deals with External Kung Fu and Part 2 deals with Internal Kung Fu. The two parts must be practised together because the skills in Part 1 need the *Qi* deployment set out in Part 2 to produce the power and force. The problem lies with Part 2 of the manual. There are paragraphs which are incomprehensible, perhaps the result of translation errors or omissions. To make sense of the paragraphs, some abbots have attempted their own interpretations and improvisations.

Inevitably there have developed contradictions and discrepancies. Unlike External Kung Fu skills, the *Qi* exercises need to be accurate and cannot be determined by trial and error. A wrong turn in *Qi* flow can cause the *Qi* to backfire, resulting in serious damage to the body. This is why *Qi* exercises have always been practised by a pupil under the supervision of his *Shifu*.

'Our Shaolin kung fu was passed down orally from the First Patriarch. Many kung fu styles which have learned by oral tradition are also included in Part 1 of the manual. After combing through the manual, it was found that some of the *Qi* exercises in Part 2 could be adapted. Over the years, Shaolin developed 72 skills by combining oral teachings with the 'Tendon Transformation' manual. These 72 skills have been written down and the manuals are kept at Shaolin Monastery.

'Many powerful kung fu styles in the 'Tendon Transformation' manual cannot be practised without an accurate understanding of the *Qi* deployment. It is for the protection of Shaolin disciples that the monastery rules that only the Abbot is allowed to read the written version of the manual.'

The elder sighed. 'It would be fine if the story stopped here. But something happened two hundred years ago. A Shaolin monk escaped from the monastery taking with him the only Chinese translated copy of the 'Tendon Transformation' Manual. No one had paid attention to him because he occupied the lowest position in the monastery, in charge of the stoves in the kitchen. When he was discovered stealing the manual, he displayed such amazing feats of kung fu that no one could prevent his escape. He was a martial arts expert who had disguised himself to gain entry to Shaolin for the very purpose of stealing the 'Tendon Transformation' manual.

'At the time, the Abbot of Shaolin was a monk by the name of Yuan Sheng, a genius in martial arts. He rewrote the manual entirely from memory. It was an accurate reproduction, but when he went over what he had written he realised that the problem with Part 2 of the manual on Internal Kung Fu was that the *Qi* flow was wrongly described. This was why some of the more powerful kung fu could not be practised. He spent days and nights going through the possibilities. He finally came up with a version which created the most powerful kung fu imaginable. He named the kung fu style 'True Tenets of Yang Supremacy'. But before Abbot Yuan Sheng died, he asked his disciple to destroy the manual he had written. The kung fu he had created could cause great harm. After the Abbot's death, his disciple could not bring himself to destroy the manual, and so he hid it.

'When I became the Abbot of Shaolin, I had access to the 'Tendon Transformation' manual. When I came to Part 2 of the manual, like others before me, I could not understand the *Qi* flow. I refused to give up. I went frequently to the Bodhidharma Cave to seek inspiration. I sat down before the same stone wall and meditated, legs crossed, in the same spot and in the same manner as the First Patriarch. I prayed fervently to the First Patriarch to guide me to his kung fu secrets. My prayers may have moved his spirit, because one day, when I had meditated until the dark of night, the full moon rose in the sky and shone into the cave. A moon beam pointed like an arrow to the stone wall. As if guided by the Spirit of the First Patriarch, I opened my eyes to see what looked like an opening in the wall. I took a closer look. An area of the wall appeared to be slightly different in colour from the rest. I chipped away the surface of the wall, and found hidden in the crevice a manual, 'True Tenets of Yang Supremacy', that had been created by Abbot Yuan Sheng. I removed the manual, and filled in the wall again.

'The 'True Tenets of Yang Supremacy' had incorporated and perfected the 'Tendon Transformation' kung fu. This kung fu created by Abbot Yuan Sheng was so powerful that once I started practising, I could not stop. I could feel the *Qi* in my body growing from strength to strength. How could this be a bad thing, I asked myself? I practised day and night and my internal force grew rapidly. One day, fire flew from my palms, setting the trees ablaze and reducing everything around me to ashes. This is *Yang* kung fu at its zenith.

'The sensation of being invincible was simply overwhelming. I did not notice the side effects. The first indication was the pains from the 'Supporting Fullness' and 'Slippery Flesh' energy points on the upper abdomen. In the beginning the pain attacks came intermittently and were not too serious. After some time, the 'Stone Gate' energy point located on the lower abdomen started to feel numb and a lump appeared about the size of a small finger. As days went by, the pain became more poignant, and the pain attacks came several times a day. The lump grew to the size of a tea cup. The pain was ceaseless. It was a living hell.

'Your *Tai Shi-Shu Gong* Qing Zhi was at that time Shaolin's physician. At first he thought the problem was 'hot illness' because the *Yang Qi* was too strong. He prescribed herbs and medicines to lower the heat in my body. I tried everything, rhino horn, cow and water-buffalo gall stones, antelope horn and special herbs. But none of them were any use. The *Yin* energies they produced had no effect because my illness was not caused by *Yin–Yang* imbalance.

'The great misfortune was that I did not detect the illness early enough. Once I started practising the 'True Tenets of Yang Supremacy' kung fu, I was like an addict. I could not stop. Eventually I suffered a massive stroke, and all the tendons in my body snapped. I became paralysed from my neck down. I destroyed that kung fu manual so that no one else would suffer the same fate. I retired and went into seclusion. My two *Shi-Di*s followed me to take care of me. And so we have been here for thirty years. We did not bring with us the manual of 'Tendon Transformation' because it belongs to the monastery.

'I began to devote my time to Buddhist teachings and Buddhist sutras. I have had time to reflect. In my pursuit to reach the best in kung fu, I deviated from the Buddhist path. I was carried away by my ego-self. I was blind to the dangers facing me.'

As the elder Qing Wang explained to Flint what had happened to him, it was as if he was speaking about someone else. He expressed no sadness. 'When the First Patriarch created the kung fu exercises, they were meant to improve the physical well being of the monks so that they would have the health and longevity to withstand long hours of meditation. Kung fu was designed as a means to an end, the end being 'enlightenment'. But soon kung fu came to be seen as a fighting skill. When the means becomes the end, the consequence is disastrous. Amida Buddha!'

Elder Qing Wang lowered his head in shame. 'External kung fu trains the *jing*, that is, the muscles, the tendons and the bones, so the person becomes physically strong. Even if harm sometimes results from the training, the damage is not serious and the body is more than able to cope with any injury. But *Qi* training is an entirely different matter. The power and force projected by *Qi* is lethal. It can rebound, injuring the bowel and viscera. The damage to the body is a hundred times more serious than any external injury. It is only by emulating the compassion of Buddha that a practitioner can neutralize the lethal effect of the *Qi* and prevent it from rebounding.'

'*Tai Shi-Gong*, 'compassion' is the teaching of Buddha', pondered Flint, 'and *Qi* is the training of Internal Kung Fu. I cannot understand the connection between the two.'

'All things in the universe are bound by cycles of creation and cycles of destruction. Fire burns to ashes creating earth but is destroyed by water. The *Qi* is designed to kill, whereas the compassion of Buddha aims at salvation of all sentient beings. 'Killing' and 'salvation' are opposites. Only by practising Buddhist compassion can one neutralise the lethal effect of the *Qi*.

'Like most Martial artists, I made the mistake of concentrating on the physical side, the strengthening of the '*Jing*' and *Qi*', and overlooked the development of *Shen,* 'mind and spirit'. I forgot that the ultimate aim of kung fu is to achieve spiritual fulfilment and attain 'enlightenment'. The realization came after I devoted myself to the teachings of Buddha. It was as if a dark cloud had been lifted, and I could clearly see myself. When I was a child, I liked to blow bubbles from soapy water. The bubbles were so pretty in the sunlight, but soon they vanished into the air. Obsession with kung fu was like chasing after a bubble. Amida Buddha! 'Form is Emptiness; Emptiness is Form'. Since the awakening, I am slowly regaining some of my kung fu.

'I finally realise that the way to develop the *Shen* is to keep the Mind and Spirit pure. The way to keep the Mind and Spirit pure is to follow the teachings of the Buddha and follow the Buddhist eightfold path.'

'*Tai Shi-Gong*, what causes the *Qi* to rebound?', asked Flint.

The dark-faced elder Qing Xin spoke up, 'Nothing in the universe is permanent. After Spring comes Summer, after Summer comes Autumn, after Autumn, Winter, and after Winter comes Spring again. Change is the only immutable law in the universe. When *Yang* is at its strongest, the *Yin* begins; and when *Yin* is at its strongest, the *Yang* begins. After the pinnacle, is the descent. When kung fu is at its most lethal, it begins to rebound on the practitioner and force the downward spiral.'

The ruddy-faced elder Qing Zhi, a former Shaolin physician, took a scientific approach. 'To neutralize the lethal effect of kung fu, one must cultivate a Buddha's mind. This leads to the development of the *Shen*. Let me explain in medical terms. When the mind is in a state of tranquillity, *Qi* is led to the brain and it stimulates the dormant cells, enabling the brain to function more fully. The brain keeps the *Qi* circulating in the marrow and keeps the marrow clean and healthy. Bone marrow manufactures blood cells which provide nourishment to the internal organs, and take away the waste products. When the blood is healthy, the body grows stronger, develops greater immunity and becomes more resistant to the lethal effects of kung fu. This is what we mean by development of *Shen*.'

Elder Qing Wang said, 'While we have been in seclusion, we have been thinking about the title of Volume II, 'Marrow Cleansing'. It has dawned on us that this volume deals with the development of the mind and spirit. Our First Patriarch must have intended the two volumes to be practised together. He hid the manual to prevent disciples practising the kung fu on their own.'

Flint now understood. '*Tai Shi-Gong*, I am most grateful for this guidance.'

Elder Qing Wang said, 'You have not been able to cure the root of your illness because the *Yin* energy in your body came from a sea monster. The *Yin* energy from the sea monster is too strong for any Yang style of kung fu. The only kung fu that will generate equally powerful *Yang* energy is the 'True Tenets of Yang Supremacy'. We will teach it to you and you will then be cured of the root of your illness. But do not think for one moment that the immense *Yin* energy in your body will neutralise the lethal effects of the *Yang* energy you are about to acquire. When you reach the pinnacle in kung fu, you will face the same problem that I encountered. You must adhere to the Buddhist path and simulate the compassion of Buddha.

'I have memorised the manual by heart. We will teach you the techniques. After that it will depend on you how you apply the skills.'

The elder encouraged Flint to memorise the manual. 'What you are learning is very powerful kung fu. Don't hope to take it all in at once. Your understanding will increase with time and experience.'

After Flint had gained an understanding of the basic concepts, he began the Qi exercises. He started with several rounds of 'Small Universe' breathing. He relaxed his body and concentrated his mind on the *Qi* flow. The elders soon found that Flint could manage on his own, and they left him alone to practise his kung fu skills.

XV

MUTINY AT SHAOLIN

In the early morning, Master Wan, Master Zheng and Master Wei met at the entrance of the Abbot's Lodge and asked to speak to the Abbot. A junior monk told them that the Abbot was at the Grand Hall '*Daxiongbaidin*', performing a seven-day prayer for the late mother of Sir Qin. He had given instructions not to be disturbed for seven days.

They were mystified by the Abbot's commitment to seven days of prayer. They thought he had turned down Sir Qin's offer of a donation to the monastery. In fact Sir Qin had offered 14,000 taels of silver to the monastery for performing prayers for his deceased mother. It was too great a sum to decline.

Master Zheng reminded Master Wan, 'It's not an inconvenience that the Abbot is engaged in prayer. Now we can take control of the monastery without alerting him. When we come to lay down our cards, the Abbot will have few options open to him. The important thing is to strike while the iron is hot. We must seize the monastery now. Whether the Abbot agrees to our terms or not is immaterial. We can replace the Abbot and any who oppose us.'

Master Wan could see the sense in this. 'Is Sir Qin at the prayer sessions too?'

'Sir Qin was there during the morning session.' Master Wei replied. 'He had to leave because of a personal matter, but he promised to return as soon as possible. His retainer will attend the prayer sessions on Sir Qin's behalf.'

Master Wan gave instructions for the plan to proceed. His followers disguised themselves as Shaolin monks or lay disciples and successfully found their way into the monastery. The Reception Monks were replaced by Master Wan's men. Everyone who arrived would be thoroughly checked. Even the delivery men would have their carts, their baskets and their goods searched.

The kitchen was also staffed by Master Wan's men, although they retained the Head Chef. He was forced to stay in the monks' quarters and was not to go back to his own hut. Master Wan had designs for the Chef. He was to lure important people to the monastery with his famous vegetarian dishes.

The junior monks and lay pupils were prevented from using their training grounds. If they wanted to practise, they would have to use the Hall of the Thousand Buddhas at the back of the monastery. A curfew was imposed and no one was to leave his room at night. Everyone in the monastery had to be accounted for. There were Master Wan's men in all the living quarters, and the grounds were patrolled.

Master Zheng had always liked Leo, a capable and hard working boy who could be very useful to the Society. He asked Leo to take responsibility for head counting the junior monks and lay pupils twice a day, in the morning before breakfast and again in the evening after dinner. Leo found his task somewhat strange, but Master Zheng said only that something extraordinary would soon happen, and that special measures needed to be taken.

Leo noted that Flint was missing from the monastery, and was told that Flint had been taken ill the night before and so had been sent away for medical treatment. He duly reported Flint's absence to Master Zheng. Master Zheng had many things on his mind, and he did not bother himself with the absence of a pupil who would be of no use to him.

But what had been responsible for the Abbot's change of mind in relation to Sir Qin's offer of a donation for the seven-day prayer sessions for his late mother?

The previous evening, after the initiation ceremony of the Triad Society at Five Breast Peak, when Master Wan, Master Zheng and Master Wei had returned to Master Wan's room to discuss their plan to enlist Shaolin Monastery to their cause, someone was listening to their conversation. Toga had been looking for Sir Qin's stable boy, but was drawn to the window when he saw the light in Master Wan's room. He did not want to get too close because the masters were experts who could detect the slightest sound. But Toga was no ordinary eavesdropper. He was a master spy himself. He climbed onto the rooftop of the guest lodge and used a listening device, a long tube with ear-like tips at each end. He lowered his pipe to the window of Master Wan's room and listened.

What Toga heard was important. He crept into the boys' dormitory where he found Bussie and Tobie. They went together to the Abbot's room to wake him. Toga told the Abbot what he had overheard and Tobie filled him in on what they had learned about the Heaven and Earth Society. They explained that they were worried because Flint, Speck and Sir Qin's stable boy had still not returned to the monastery.

The Abbot wanted to discuss the matter first with Master Fu. Together they decided to make an excuse to delay the Abbot's meeting with Master Wan until they could consult the old Abbot Tong Ti. They sent Tobie and Bussie to inform the old Abbot of the danger facing the monastery. If they found Flint and Speck on the way, they were to bring them back to the monastery. They were specifically instructed to return before six o'clock in the morning.

Tobie and Bussie returned just before six as planned, and brought with them Speck and Haidi, but not Flint. They had briefed the old Abbot Tong Ti about the threats to Shaolin, and he had written his advice on a scroll to deliver to the present Abbot. After reading the message, the Abbot looked relieved. The plan was that he was to delay the meeting with Master Wan until Flint's return to the monastery in seven days' time. The best way to do this would be to accept Sir Qin's offer of a donation, and commence the seven-day prayer for his late mother.

Master Zheng continued with relocation of the monks and lay pupils in the monastery. Speck was sent from the Abbot's Study to stay with Storm. Tobie and Bussie were given permission to stay there too. The boys were pleased to be able to stay in Storm's hut. Although they were watched by Master Wan's men and were not able to leave, they were happy to be with their friends.

While they were confined there, Bussie and Tobie practised their kung fu. Since the night at Five Breast Peak, Tobie understood that he would have to practise his breathing to direct his *Qi* flow, to prevent his body from bloating.

Some five years earlier, a master in martial arts had come to visit Shaolin. Tobie was then already nine but because he was short and chubby, he had looked much younger. The Chef had said to the kung fu master that his nephew could not understand Internal Kung Fu and *Qi*. The kung fu master, a kindly old soul, produced a book from his breast pocket and showed it to Tobie. The book contained sketches of naked men in different poses. Black and red lines were drawn through their bodies, and tiny arrows marked on the lines. The old man explained to Tobie that the black lines represented the *Yin* energies and the red lines represented the *Yang* energies. He flipped through the book to show him, 'Look, this is a black line, this is a red line, and this is a black line again, and this is a red line again.' He was not intending to teach Tobie the *Qi* flow, and did not bother to explain the meaning of the arrows and the lines. That kung fu master was a direct descendant of the last king of Dali, a kingdom destroyed by the Mongol armies under Kublai Khan. The kung fu style of Dali was a family secret of the royal household and closely resembled the Shaolin style. The most famous of their kung fu styles was the 'One-Finger Zen' where the *Qi* shot through the forward-pointing index finger. The great master had gone on to show Tobie the manual of 'One-Finger Zen' to impress the child with the way the *Qi* could come from the finger. He had inadvertently passed on the Duan family's kung fu secret to Tobie.

While practising his *Qi* exercises, Tobie's mind flashed back to the sketches. He thought of the arrows on the lines and the directions in which they were pointing. He felt his *Qi* following the directions of the arrows. His mind moved from one sketch to another, and his *Qi* flow followed. He finally understood what Master Wei had meant about training the body to be 'light as swallow'. After the first round of exercises, the *Qi* began to flow faster and faster following the paths indicated by the arrows. He practised his *Qi* exercises every day. If he failed to practise, he would begin to feel bloated again.

While Tobie and Bussie practised, Speck showed Storm the Mongolian art of wrestling. They tested themselves against each other. Although Storm was an expert in kung fu, wrestling had more to do with skill than with the strength of internal force, so they were equally matched.

During the lunch period, Leo escorted the Chef to the hut, bringing specially cooked meals for his nephew Tobie and his friends. When Leo saw Speck, he went over to chat to him. He found Speck different from the other boys at Shaolin. Most boys were not interested in anything except kung fu. Leo sometimes felt an outsider in the world of martial arts. He liked kung fu but was also interested in other things. In his spare time, he studied the Four Books and Five Classics. His favourite was 'The Art of War by Sun Zi', which he had read many times. He discussed Sun Zi's war strategies with Speck and was surprised by Speck's knowledge of the book.

Leo explained to Speck, 'I was abandoned by my parents on the doorstep of the monastery when I was only a few days old. I don't know who my parents are. The monks sent me to live with a foster family. At the age of six, I was taken back by the monastery to be trained as a monk. I like the monastery. I have had the opportunity to learn kung fu and how to read and write. If I had stayed on with the foster family, I would probably have ended up a farmer.'

'Are you going to be ordained as a monk?'

'I have never seen the outside world. I have a desire to make something of my life. I have even thought of having a family of my own. I can't extricate worldly desires from my mind. I can't lead the life of a monk. I don't really know what I will do after my graduation. There is a saying, 'A bird picks the best branch to build its nest; a good horse chooses its own master'. When I meet my master, I will know what to do.' Leo was surprised to find himself telling Speck, a stranger, something which he had held secret to himself. He had never discussed his ambitions with anyone, even his good friends, Flint, Tobie or Bussie.

After lunch, the boys played cards, eating cakes and candies and telling stories. They had nothing else to do. They were virtually under house arrest.

XVI

HIDDEN DRAGON

Eventually the light in Storm's hut went out. Every one was deeply asleep. Two people outside were speaking in a whisper.

'Sire, we lost track of you last night. I neglected my duty. Please punish your humble servant.'

'It was not your fault. Rise, Songgotu. For the time being, you are to dispense with formal court etiquette.'

Songgotu was the third son of the late Regent Soni. He had been appointed a Vice Minister to the Board of Civil Office, but aware of the dangers surrounding the Emperor in the Palace, he asked to return to duty as 'Imperial Guard of the First Rank'. Songgotu was one of Emperor Kang Xi's most trusted confidantes.

The emperor Kang Xi and Storm had met in the wrestling room of Wu-Ying Palace. The young Emperor was unhappy with Oboi's dictatorial manner, and he planned to seize back power. He could not count on the Imperial Guards or military commanders as most were under Oboi's control. The Emperor had to rely on his own resources, and so he started by training a group of young eunuchs in the art of wrestling. He did not want the eunuchs to know who he was. It happened that a young eunuch by the name of Speck was about to join the service. Kang Xi secretly arranged for the young eunuch to be transferred elsewhere in the Palace, and he joined the eunuchs in the wrestling room posing as Speck.

As a child, Kang Xi had lived with his grandmother in her palace, the Ci-Ning Palace. When he became Emperor at the age of six, he continued to live there with her. He began to rule in person when he turned thirteen. Oboi's role as 'Regent' then lapsed, and he was made duke of first rank. But Kang Xi kept a low profile, and only those in the inner circle of politics were aware of his personal rule.

When Kang Xi reached fifteen years, the Grand Empress Dowager announced that it was time for him to leave her palace and move to his own palace, the Qian-Qing Palace. Qian-Qing Palace required extensive renovation, so the Emperor moved temporarily to Wu-Ying Palace, outside the central palace compound, to the south-west near the offices of the Imperial Household. It was in Wu-Ying Palace that Kang Xi set up the wrestling room. It was there that, posing as a young eunuch wrestler, he had been kidnapped by Storm, escaped from the Palace, and arrived at Shaolin Monastery to become a junior assistant to the Abbot. No-one knew that Speck was actually the young emperor Kang Xi.

Kang Xi and Storm had been able to escape from the Palace because they produced a permit stamped with the Seal of the Emperor. The permit was in fact an edict from Kang Xi to Songgotu written in Manchurian. The Guard on duty that night was a trusted aide of Songgotu. Kang Xi instructed Songgotu to allow them out of the Palace and to follow until further instruction. This was an opportunity to see for himself what the outside world was like. Songgotu and his men were waiting at the government Postal Relay Station when Kang Xi and Storm arrived, and had prepared horses for them. When they reached Shaolin, Songgotu and his men stayed in cottages at the foot of ShaoShi Hill, living with farmers' families and posing as farm hands. Kang Xi and Songgotu kept in touch every day. Songgotu kept Kang Xi informed of what was happening at the Palace.

Songgotu had arranged to meet Kang Xi outside Storm's hut after the others had gone to sleep. He had an urgent message from the Grand Empress Dowager.

'The Grand Empress Dowager has sent her retainer Samara and Princess Jian Ning to Shaolin Monastery to bring you back to the Palace as soon as possible.'

'Has Oboi realised that I am not in the Palace?'

'No, not yet. The Grand Empress Dowager announced to the court that you were ill with influenza but she is finding it increasingly difficult to deflect the prying eyes of Lord Oboi's men. Every day Lord Oboi sends someone to give his regards and to find out how you are getting on. The latest information from the Palace is that Lord Oboi came personally to pay his respects. He marched into your bedroom and insisted that the bed curtain be opened. The young actor taking your place was brilliant. He asked croakily in your distinct Manchurian accent, 'Who is it?' Even the Grand Empress Dowager could not tell the difference.'

'It will not take long for Oboi to find out the truth.'

'The Grand Empress Dowager is worried that she will not be able to cover for you much longer. She needs you back immediately. Samara and Princess Jian Ning pretended that they were going to NanShan Temple at the Five Terraces Mountain to fulfil a promise the Grand Empress Dowager made many years ago. They are now on their way to Shaolin.'

Samara had been a personal maid to the Grand Empress Dowager, a Mongolian princess, before her marriage to Abahai at the age of twelve. Samara was devoted to Kang Xi and had taught him the Manchu language as well as kung fu.

'When will Samara and the Princess get here?'

'About three day's time.'

'Let me know as soon as they arrive.' Kang Xi nodded towards the men keeping watch over Storm's hut. 'Are they your men?'

'Yes. We heard that the Heaven and Earth Triad Society were recruiting members, so we posed as anti-Manchu activists. Early this morning, we were assigned to guard buildings in the monastery. Storm's hut was rated as low security risk. The men assigned to it were new recruits like us, so we took them drinking, made them an offer, and they swapped jobs with us.'

It was now clear that anti-Manchu activists were planning a revolt. Kang Xi remembered that on the road to Shaolin, Master Wan was riding behind Jade's carriage as if he was a servant. That was very odd. 'Is Jade still in Shaolin?'

'No, he left when the soldiers arrived.'

Kang Xi continued to practise wresting with Storm every day. Storm had a solid foundation in kung fu, and he used this to help Kang Xi improve his wrestling skills. When Kang Xi had some free time, he explored the surrounding farmland with Storm. He was curious about farming techniques from the sowing and ploughing to the harvest. The Manchu bannermen, while they were good on horse-back, had little farming knowledge. Fertile lands which had been seized from Chinese farmers soon became wastelands. The bannermen had resorted to contracting out land to Chinese farmers, paying them meagre wages and reducing them to serfdom. Those who tried to escape faced harsh punishments. This caused great discontent among the Han Chinese. Kang Xi recognised that such practices needed to stop as stability of the peasant class was essential if Qing rule were to be maintained. Bannermen needed to learn farming from the Chinese, become more self-sufficient and less reliant on government support.

Kang Xi's thoughts turned to Haidi. He wished Haidi had been able to stay longer at the monastery, so that they could become better acquainted, but Haidi had left with Sir Qin soon after returning from the old Abbot's hut. Haidi was such good company and he would miss him. He would seek out Sir Qin when he was back in Beijing and maybe he would be able to get to know Haidi better there.

On the fifth day after the Triad besiege of Shaolin Monastery, Speck suddenly got up and left the hut. Minutes later, three visitors arrived, the retainer Samara, the Princess and Songgotu. Samara was dressed as a Palace maid and the Princess as a junior eunuch, the disguises they had adopted to fool Oboi's soldiers on the route to Shaolin.

Tobie was bored and he stood up to go after Speck. He had just opened the door when the Princess arrived, and he bumped right into her, almost knocking her over. The Princess slapped him across the face. 'You clumsy boy!'

Tobie was shocked. For a moment, he did not know how to react. He put a hand to his reddening cheek. 'Who are you?'

The Princess replied, 'Why should I tell you?'

Tobie did not normally fight with the boys in the monastery. Everyone knew who his uncle was and no one would lay a finger on him. But this little boy in strange clothing had dared to slap him. He raised his hand to return the slap. The Princess pulled a face at him, and skipped around him singing,

'*Fat little boy,*
Fat little face,
Small little eyes,
Round face, round body,
JUST LIKE A BALL!'

She stretched out a leg and kicked at Tobie as if he were a football. With a slight twist of his body, employing the *Qingong* steps, Tobie slipped behind the Princess. He was about to grab the visitor by the scruff of his neck, when someone forced back his hand. He looked up to see a handsome elderly woman. She said, 'My name is Samara and I am a Palace maid. Songgotu here is an Imperial Guard. The boy who has behaved badly is a junior eunuch, Huang Ding. We have come for Speck. Can you tell us where he is?'

'He left the hut just a short while ago.'

The Princess said, 'Take me to find him.'

'Why should I?'

'Because I said so.' She pulled Tobie by his sleeve. He shook her off, but followed her outside. The guards were crowded around someone. The Princess pushed her way through. 'So here you are.'

'Hi, Ding-Dong, nice to see you.' Kang Xi pulled her away from the group so that they could talk more freely. Ding-Dong was Kang-Xi's nickname for the Princess. When she was a child, she had worn hand and leg bracelets with little bells. When she moved, the bells chimed 'ding-dong, ding-dong.' It was a device to keep track of her. She was a mischievous child who kept her nannies and maids running after her all over the Palace.

'Grandmother wants you back immediately. You must come with us at once.'

'You and Samara go back now, and I will come soon after. I have things I need to do here.'

'No, Grandmother said that we had to return together with you.'

'I am the Emperor. You return first and I will follow.'

'If you don't come with me, I will expose your identity.'

Kang Xi was quiet for a moment. 'Give me two days. I have soldiers looking out for Oboi's men. The moment they arrive at the foot of Mount Song, we will leave.'

Shaolin was under threat from the Triad Society. He had to wait to see what would happen to the monastery. He was confident that Shaolin would survive the attack, but if the worst were to happen, he was prepared to take the three boys, Flint, Bussie and Tobie, with him to Beijing.

★★★

Flint was in the elders' grotto, practising the kung fu 'True Tenets of Yang Supremacy'. When he was hungry, he ate whatever was put before him. He was oblivious to what was going on around him. He forgot the time, and was unaware of day and night.

He felt the *Qi* inside his body trying to pass through the *Qi* channels. The *Qi* flowed down the three *Yin* Channels of the hand to the finger tips, then up the three *Yang* Channels of the hand to the head. Then it flowed from the head through the body along the three *Yang* Channels of the leg to the toes, and along the three *Yin* Channels of the leg from the toes up through the body to the chest, where the *Qi* continued back into the three *Yin* Channels of the hand. This completed the *Qi* cycle. The *Qi* flowed in torrents along all the twelve primary channels from head to toe and from toe to head again, circulating faster and faster through the cycle an endless number of times. He spun round, he leapt up and down. Sometimes he moved so fast that he could be seen only as a hazy ring.

Still trance-like, he began to practise the fighting poses he had learnt, from the elementary 'Black Tiger Steals Heart' to 'Dragon Rises from the Sea' or 'Poisonous Snake Spits Venom'. He struck out at will, without thinking about the pose, until he gave a cry and woke from his trance. He felt his body light as feather, refreshed and full of energy. The feeling was even better than when he had had a 'small universe' breakthrough. When he first came to the grotto, he had thought it dark. Now he saw everything clearly. He was dismayed to see cracks in the walls. The force had been so powerful when Flint was exercising that the walls had cracked.

The three elders were there, smiling. Elder Qing Wang said, 'You have not only achieved a 'big universe' break through in the *Qi* flow, you have also mastered the 'True Tenets of Yang Supremacy' kung fu.'

The elder Qing Wang asked Flint to strike at a sturdy cypress tree thirty yards distant. He hit out softly, but the tree stood still. The old Abbot Tong Ti went to the tree, gave it a light push, and the tree fell. It had been destroyed by the force from Flint's palm.

Elder Qing Wang told Flint, 'You have grasped the essence of Shaolin kung-fu: 'Light as Sparrow, Soft as Cotton, Hard as Steel'. The *Yin–Yang* in your body is now balanced. But because this is still early days, you may find that your right hand emits *Yin* energy and your left hand emits *Yang* energy. As you continue with your *Qi* exercises, the *Yin* energy and the *Yang* energy will merge and you will be able to emit *Yin* and *Yang* energy from either hand.'

The old Abbot Tong Ti said, 'You have been here for seven days and seven nights. You may take leave of the elders.'

Flint had not realised that seven days had passed. He kowtowed three times to each of the elders, deeply grateful to them. They had taught him everything they knew and had cured the root of his illness. In addition, they had taught him two kung fu skills; the 'Bone Shrinking' kung fu in which bones, muscles and tendons could be shrunk to pass through narrow openings, and 'Shifting Energy Points' kung fu in which energy points could be slightly moved from their original location before being attacked by an enemy.

Flint took his leave from the elders. The old Abbot Tong Ti explained what had happened at the monastery and asked him to return at once.

XVII

THE SHOWDOWN

The Abbot finished the seven-day prayer sessions and was at last ready to meet with Master Wan. He waited in the reception room inside the Abbot's Lodge with Master Fu and the remaining five senior monks.

So as not to be outnumbered, Master Wan brought with him Master Zheng, Master Wei and the five Lodge Masters. The five Lodge Masters took guard at the four corners of the room and the entrance door. Outside, Master Wan's men surrounded the Abbot's Lodge. Master Wan was confident that none of the monks, including the Abbot, could match him or Master Zheng in kung fu skills.

Master Wan came straight to the point. He asked the Abbot to show his support for the Triad Society's resistance movement by allowing them to use Shaolin Monastery as a base of operation. The Abbot flatly refused. Shaolin Monastery was a Buddhist institution and the monks devoted themselves to meditation and attaining 'enlightenment'. The Abbot clasped his hands. 'Amida Buddha! Form is Emptiness and Emptiness is Form. The change of Dynasty is predestined. It is difficult for we humans to understand the inscrutable workings of Providence.'

'You have no choice in this matter.' Master Wan threatened. 'Either you agree to our request or you'll be removed. Think it over.'

'I don't need to think it over. Shaolin Monastery is a Zen establishment. We do not get involved in worldly matters.'

Master Wan responded angrily, 'Shaolin could have been ten times bigger if you had not been so stubborn. The monastery needs a more radical man at the helm. Step aside and let Master Zheng take over as Abbot.'

The Abbot remained calm. 'I am afraid you will need the old Abbot's and the three elders' approval to replace me.'

'The three elders? They must be nearly a hundred years old. No one has seen them for a very long time. Are they still alive? Ha, ha….As for the old Abbot, we are not worried about him.'

Master Zheng told the Abbot, 'You see, *Shi-di*[9], during your seven-day prayer sessions, we have taken control of the monastery.'

The door to the room flung open, and Flint, Bussie and Tobie marched in.

Master Zheng shouted, 'Who gave you permission to enter?'

'I gave them permission,' the Abbot said.

Master Zheng stepped forward and adopted the fighting pose 'White Crane Raises Its Beak' to target the throat of the Abbot, his right arm outstretched and his fingers and thumb closed to form the beak of a crane. The Abbot moved one leg back to block the attack by 'Beauty Looks In a Mirror'. Master Zheng quickly changed to 'White Crane Stretches Its Neck', bending his fingers, and turning his 'crane beak' into a 'hook hand' to put the Abbot off balance. He relinquished his attack when a powerful force came towards him from Bussie who punched out 'Black Tiger Steals Heart'. This was an elementary fighting pose of Shaolin kung fu, but when the punch came from Bussie, the force was tremendous, and Master Zheng had to withdraw and face his new opponent.

Someone shouted, 'Stop, everybody. Stop!' It was the old Abbot Tong Ti. He had summoned his internal force to make a 'Lion's Roar', penetrating the eardrums of all those in the room. While those with stronger internal force summoned their *Qi* to combat the sound, the others covered their ears with their sleeves.

The old Abbot looked straight at Master Zheng. 'Xuan Zheng, what are you trying to do?' Master Zheng lowered his head. The old Abbot then said to Master Wan. 'Before you try to take over our monastery, we shall have a kung fu contest. Each side will nominate three contestants, and we will play three matches. If your side wins, we will allow your people run the monastery. If you lose, you will leave this place immediately, never to return.'

---

[9] Younger kung fu brother

Master Wan agreed, and nominated himself, Master Zheng and Master Wei to fight. To his surprise, the old Abbot nominated three pupils, Flint, Bussie and Tobie. The old Abbot had no doubt about Flint's supremacy in kung fu as he had witnessed Flint's transformation under the guidance of the three elders. As regards Bussie, the old Abbot was confident that his attacking skills and his tactic of 'dying together with the enemy' was the perfect antidote for Master Zheng's White Crane kung fu, which concentrated on defensive skills. He had observed the change in Tobie. Tobie was vibrant and light on his feet, his eyes clear and bright, his face radiant, all of which signalled a person with immense *Qi* in his body. Tobie's kung fu skills and lack of combat experience were a gamble, but there was no better candidate.

The old Abbot stated the rules of the contest. 'This is not life-or-death combat. When one party surrenders, the other party must stop immediately.'

The match took place in the courtyard outside the Abbot's Lodge and began with Tobie against Master Wei. This was an opportunity Master Wei had been waiting for, to give Tobie a good thrashing without interference from the Chef.

For Tobie, it was a nightmare moment. Not only had he to fight like a martial artist, he had to fight none other than his teacher, Master Wei, and in the full glare of so many people. He wished the ground under his feet would open and swallow him up. He could not bear the thought of what would happen if they lost the contest.

Tobie began with the Shaolin greeting pose. His hands together with fingertips pointing upwards, he bowed low to Master Wei, in deference to his former teacher.

Master Wei expected to dispose of Tobie in three rounds, and began his attack by deploying 'Black Tiger Steals Heart', the most elementary Shaolin fighting pose. Since Tobie had no actual fighting experience, he decided that the best thing to do was to imitate Master Wei's movements. With a slight twist of his body and deploying his *Qingong* footwork, he evaded the fist blow from Master Wei and quickly adopted the same 'Black Tiger Steals

Heart'. The two poses were identical, but the force that came from Tobie was more powerful, and his movements were faster. The evasion and the delivery of the attack were almost simultaneous.

Master Wei was surprised. Tobie's *Qingong* footwork was definitely not a Shaolin style. Master Wei guessed that Tobie's *Qingong* had been taught to him by the Chef. But what he could not figure out was how Tobie had acquired such powerful internal force. As he was attacked by 'Black Tiger Steals Heart', he responded with 'Raging Tiger Emerges From Its Lair' followed by 'Poisonous Snake Spits Venom', targeting Tobie's throat.

Tobie deployed the same fanciful footwork, avoided the attack and at the same time he counter-attacked with the same 'Poisonous Snake Spits Venom'. Master Wei defended with 'Beauty Looks In a Mirror'.

Master Wei adopted further poses to confuse Tobie. He used in sequence 'Mischievous Monkey Kicks Tree', 'Roving Dragon Plays In Water', 'Wild Swan Glides Through Lotus', 'False-Leg Stance[10] and Hand Sweep', 'Chirpy Bird Hops Up Branch', 'Lohan Beats Drum' and 'Poisonous Snake Spits Venom'. Tobie followed suit. To onlookers, it looked like a training session with the *Shifu* teaching his pupil kung fu skills. But Tobie moved faster, and it was Master Wei who was finding it difficult to follow.

Master Wei tried reversing the order of the sequences. Having been through the sequences once, Tobie understood how to counter-attack. Relying on his memory and sharp observation, he was able to anticipate Master Wei's poses and respond accordingly. He quickly learned how to link the fighting poses into sequences, and he varied them as he went. He recalled from memory poses he had seen or read of and added them into the sequences, throwing Master Wei into total confusion. They fought over a hundred rounds. Tobie was no longer imitating Master Wei. As the combat continued, Tobie felt more and more at ease, and his movements became more fluid. He moved seamlessly from one sequence to another.

Tobie had the match under his control and Master Wei knew

---

[10] The body weight leans on the back leg.

that he would have to think fast. He performed a feint. This was a skill that he had perfected as a last resort action. While pretending to attack, he laid bare his chest for a split second knowing this would be taken advantage of by the opponent. Tobie's lack of experience led him straight into the trap. While Tobie leapt and aimed high at the chest, Master Wei stooped low and punched hard at Tobie's abdomen. Instinctively, Tobie sucked in his abdomen, and it became so soft that Master Wei felt as though he was hitting into a bale of cotton. His fist became embedded and he could not withdraw it. Without warning, Tobie shot out his abdomen and flung Master Wei to the ground.

Master Wei leapt up and grabbed a sword. He had felt it beneath him to use a sword, but Tobie left him no choice. He risked a great loss of face and now the sword was his only hope of salvaging his pride.

He planned to perform his famous sword sequence, the '*Qi Men Jian*'. Tobie used his index and middle finger to form a sword finger. He had read the '*Qi Men Jian*' manual and was able to anticipate Master Wei's movements. The *Qi* flowed to his fingers, diverting Master Wei's sword. Then he used his index finger to fire the One-Finger Zen. The *Qi* from his finger shot like an arrow from a bow.

Master Wei was stunned. The 'One-Finger Zen' was a fundamental kung fu of Shaolin but Master Wei had never seen such a powerful demonstration of it. What Master Wei did not know was that Tobie's 'One-Finger Zen' did not come from Shaolin but from the Duan family in Dali. Duan family's 'One-Finger Zen' was legend in the Brotherhood of River and Lake. Master Wei would not in his wildest dreams have connected the fat boy before him with the superior Duan family.

Soon Master Wei had finished the whole sword sequence, and he had no choice but to repeat the sequence. He seized an opportunity to thrust his sword at Tobie's throat, but the sword stopped dead an inch from its target. Tobie clipped the tip of the sword with his index and middle fingers, snapping it, then threw Master Wei to the floor. Quick as lightning, Tobie slammed his foot onto Master Wei's chest. 'Will you surrender, Master Wei?'

Master Wei would rather die than surrender to his pupil. But Master Wan marched over to them. 'Take your foot away. We surrender this match.'

Master Wei was a good coach. He was meticulous in his approach and took great pains to ensure that every movement was exact. He was incorrigibly stubborn when it came to correctness of form and as a result, he lacked flexibility and creativity. Tobie had demonstrated how within the general mode of form, one could move hands, legs and any parts of the body to meet the situation. Tobie had advanced to a higher level, so he had won the match.

The second match was between Bussie and Master Zheng. Master Zheng's Internal Kung Fu had already surpassed that of the present Abbot Xuan Kui, the result of the thousand-year ginseng soup. He knew Bussie had been born with super human strength, but he was confident of his own prowess.

Bussie was fearless. He fought without regard for human life including his own, single-minded in attack and never worrying about defence. He dared his opponent to attack, and his attacks in return were relentless and powerful. He used his own life as bait, prepared to die together with his enemy. Inevitably opponents were reduced to concentrating on their defence because they valued their lives more than Bussie valued his.

Bussie's size and strength was ideal for the Shaolin Lohan kung fu. This kung fu style was created by Bodhidharma and contained a series of 18 fighting poses known as the 'Eighteen Lohan Hands'. Bussie was looking forward to meeting his challenger.

'How quickly boys grow up!' Master Zheng muttered to himself. He had not seen Bussie for several months, and he seemed to have grown taller. At fourteen years old, Bussie was already as tall as Master Zheng, but broader. His muscles bulged from his arms like iron balls and his legs were thick as tree trunks.

Master Zheng was tall with a pear shape body, the upper part long and slender and from waist downwards, big and heavy. His arms were long and strong with nails like those of a monkey. His back was hard as tortoise shell and his waist trim and firm. Master

Zheng owed much of his body form to years of practising the White Crane kung fu. He had every reason to be proud because he was a master of this kung fu style, and there was no one in the Brotherhood to match him.

Master Zheng stood with his back slightly arched and his chest sunk inwards. When he looked at Bussie standing there like a fearless tiger cub, he felt a sense of unease.

Bussie began with the greeting pose, putting his hands together before his chest, fingers pointing upwards, and bowed low in deference to Master Zheng as the senior instructor.

Master Zheng adopted the fundamental pose, wrapping one hand over the fist of the other to protect his chest. He held his head upright, sank his shoulders, dropped his elbows and relaxed his hips. The external posture was relaxed but Master Zheng's mind was concentrating on the internal force in readiness to commence the attack.

With a sudden burst of speed, Bussie adopted the pose 'Lohan Emerges From Cave' and delivered a right punch below the right ribs of Master Zheng. So quick was his pace that it seemed his bowing in greeting and his punching out was simultaneous, throwing Master Zheng off guard. Master Zheng evaded the punch, stepping back with his right leg and defending by adopting 'White Crane Flies Into The Sky'. He stretched out and flapped his arms like the wings of a crane. When Bussie punched again, Master Shang evaded by moving to a long range position. The White Crane Kung fu was designed for short range combat. The kicking was kept low, aiming at the groin, the knee, the shin and below the waist, with the power generated and directed from the waist. To direct the power to strike in different directions, the waist and the entire body must be soft as a whip, the spine strong yet relaxed.

The tactic of the White Crane kung fu was to 'defend first and then attack'. A White Crane martial artist would stay to the side, patient and calm, waiting for an opportune moment when his body could shoot out like a whip to attack the opponent. Master Zheng waited for the right moment to move into short range to use his hands. He had refined and improvised the traditional

Shaolin White Crane kung fu, placing more emphasis on hand techniques. Several times he tried to use his 'Flapping and Quivering Hands', but every time he was forced back by Bussie. Bussie's punches followed one after another like waves of the sea. He attacked Master at the waist, in the chest and in the spine. Master Zheng was a bird caught in a thunderstorm.

A crane defends itself by swiping the enemy with the power of its wings, pecking with its beak and flapping its wings to stay high in the air. The punches from Bussie were so powerful and fast that Master Zheng was reduced to jumping up and flapping his arms. He was playing for time, hoping that the incessant punching would eventually wear Bussie down. He was wrong in his estimation of Bussie's strength. The attacks were relentless, leaving Master Zheng breathless. Soon they too had fought over 100 rounds.

Master Zheng grew impatient. He gave a ferocious yell. The sound used in the White Crane kung fu to help emit energy from the body and to raise the spirit of fighting was *Ha*, *Gen*, *He*, *Sha*, *Hei* and *Hu*. But his voice was drowned by Bussie who shouted out OM MA NI PAD ME HUM.

OM MA NI PAD ME HUM is the six-syllable Sanskrit mantra of the Buddha of Compassion, Guan Ying, originating from India. Its translated meaning is 'Hail to the Jewel of the Lotus'. When Bussie shouted the sacred words of the mantra, the internal force emitted was so powerful, it had a shattering effect on the eardrums of all those present in the hall. Everyone, including Master Zheng, had to muster his internal energy to combat the sound.

On the word 'HUM', Bussie hit Master Zheng in the chest and Master Zheng fell to the floor. Bussie placed one foot on Master Zheng's chest. He was about to increase the pressure of his foot, when he heard a whisper, 'I surrender!' Bussie removed his foot, and Master Zheng leapt from the floor. Adopting the pose 'White Crane Dips Beak in Stream', he moved his right leg forward and executed a left Phoenix-Eye Punch to strike at the energy point on Bussie's shoulder joint to immobilise his arm. This was followed quickly by a kick at the energy point 'Crouching Rabbit' to immobilise the leg.

White Crane martial artists often combine their kung fu with *Qin-Na,* a 'grabbing and controlling' technique which attacks energy points. Master Zheng, an adept in '*Qin-Na*', had immobilised Bussie by attacking his energy points. Bussie fell to the floor. Master Zheng put his foot on Bussie's chest. 'Do you surrender, Bussie?'

Bussie yelled, 'But you've already surrendered.'

Master Zheng turned to the audience. 'Did any one hear me say that I would surrender?'

True, no one had heard what Master Zheng had whispered to Bussie. However, everyone knew that there was an Internal Kung Fu skill with which spoken words could be passed to the ear of another without any one else being aware. The two abbots and Bussie's friends knew that Bussie would not lie. They believed that Master Zheng had used deception to win the match but there was nothing they could do about it. There is a saying 'All's fair in war, nothing is too deceitful'. They had to accept that Bussie had lost the match.

Master Zheng exerted more pressure with his foot. He asked again, 'Will you surrender?' Bussie refused. Master Zheng had cheated him. The old Abbot intervened. 'We surrender. You have won this match, Xuan Zheng.' Master Zheng released his foot and walked off, without displaying his usual triumphant smile.

The third match was between Flint and Master Wan. The fate of Shaolin rested on Flint. Master Wan looked at the young boy before him, a boy of only fifteen years old, and felt insulted. How could the old Abbot nominate a young boy to fight against one of the best martial artists in the Brotherhood of River and Lake? Master Wan had established his name before Flint was born. He had been a pupil of the legendary Wang Lang.

When Wang Lang was a lay disciple at Shaolin Monastery, he did not excel in kung fu because of his small physique. One evening he watched a fight between a cicada and a praying mantis. He saw how the cicada was caught by the long, powerful fore-legs of the praying mantis. He studied their fighting movements, and noticed how the insect was able to move its forelegs so quickly and so freely in attack and defence that it was able to defeat an enemy much bigger in size. This inspired him to create a new style of kung fu, the 'Praying Mantis' kung fu.

But Wang Lang knew there was still a weakness. The hand techniques did not coordinate well with the footwork. Then, walking through a forest, he saw monkeys jumping up and down from the trees. He noticed that the speed with which the monkeys moved was due to the free movement of their hind limbs. He was inspired to combine the movements of the monkey with those of the praying mantis. This adoption of the foreleg movements of the praying mantis and the hind limb steps of the monkey became a distinctive characteristic of the Northern Praying Mantis kung fu style. Later, Wang Lang made further improvement by selecting the best points of seventeen other kung fu styles and incorporated them into his Praying Mantis kung fu. He went on to develop several styles of the Praying Mantis kung fu. His first disciple practised the 'Seven-star Praying Mantis' and his third disciple practised the 'Flat Plate Praying Mantis'. Master Wan, being the second disciple, practised the 'Taiji Plum-Blossom Praying Mantis' style, suitable for both long range and short range combat. It combines the hard and soft style kung fu. When the fist hits out, it is 'soft as cotton', but the force emitted is 'hard as steel'. The application is flexible and the attack continuous. The movements can be 'quick as lightning, and still as Mount Tai Shan'.

Flint began with the Shaolin greeting pose. His right leg was placed slightly forward, and his left leg placed in front of the right leg to form a left False-Leg Stance[11]. He held his left palm and right fist in front of his chest, in the typical Shaolin greeting pose 'Dragon and Tiger Meet'.

Master Wan stood straight with his feet together, his shoulders dropped and loosened, fingers pointing downwards and palms facing the thighs. His head was straight and his eyes looked forward. This was his preparation pose before combat. He fixed Flint with a gimlet stare. He could not help being impressed by Flint's good looks and relaxed composure. Master Wan took no risks. His arms moved out, drawing an arc in the air. The

---

[11] The body weight leans on the back leg.

movement contained both open and hidden poses. He mustered all his internal force and struck out at Flint.

Flint stretched out both palms to take the blow. Master Wan's palm wriggled like a slippery fish through Flint's palms to strike at his chest. Flint was taken by surprise and his internal force automatically came to the fore to counter the attack. But before the two forces could meet, the force from Master Wan's palm disappeared. Flint was momentarily stunned and withdrew the *Qi* from his chest. Almost instantaneously, a powerful force rushed towards him aiming again at his chest. Flint's sixth sense helped him evade the punch. His animal instinct warned him of incoming danger and his body reacted, bending backwards and rolling like a ball out of hitting range.

The onlookers applauded. The movements of Master Wan's palm had been unpredictable, displaying no warning as to where he was going to strike. Master Wan had demonstrated the essence of the Praying Mantis kung fu where the *Qi* could 'expand like a bow and contract like a ball'. He could manipulate his internal force by emitting and withdrawing at will to confuse his opponent. When he had succeeded in diverting his opponent's internal force, he mustered all his internal energy to strike again at the same spot.

But Flint could bend and twist his body at any angle and in any direction. When Master Wan struck, Flint bent backwards, and borrowed the *Qi* emitted from Master Wan to roll away. As soon as he was out of striking range, he sprang up again. The act of borrowing internal force from an opponent was a skill from the 'Tendon Transformation' kung fu. It was similar in principle to the Taiji skill of 'using four ounces to defeat one thousand pounds'. Flint's lack of experience was compensated for by his intelligent application of the kung fu skills that he had learned.

Master Wan would not allow Flint breathing space. He closed in using the *Tagging, Clinging, Sticking and Leaning* techniques combined with quick footwork. The moment Flint was within striking distance, Master Wan unleashed the five chain-punches with his fist. The punches shot out like the 'Five Petals of the Plum-Blossom'. The force emitted from his palm was powerful and continuous. This was Taiji Internal Kung Fu incorporated into the Praying mantis kung fu.

Flint mustered all his internal energy and spread it round his body. When Master Wan's force reached Flint, it became submerged in Flint's stronger internal force, and disappeared like the river flowing into the sea. In theory, the 'Praying Mantis' is a comprehensive set of kung fu skills covering every point in attack and defence. But at the end of the day, speed and force are the deciding factors. Flint had stronger internal force and greater speed.

Master Wan immediately changed to a 'grabbing and controlling' technique by pressing Flint's 'Turtledove Tail' energy point located on the midline of the abdomen. Pressure on the vital point could cause the muscles around the lung to contract and seal the opponent's breath. The strike on Flint's energy point was accurate and the force was powerful, but it did not achieve the desired effect of knocking Flint off balance. Flint had already moved all his energy points, a skill which he had learnt from the three Shaolin elders. Instead of disabling his opponent, Master Wan felt his own arm gripped, and his shoulder became numb. Flint had struck Master Wan's energy point, the 'Front of the Shoulder' to disable his arm. He placed his palm on Master Wan's vital energy point, the 'Celestial Pillar', at the back of his neck, and asked, 'Will you surrender, Master Wan?'

Master Wan well knew that if Flint struck his 'Celestial Pillar' energy point, he would lose consciousness. He surrendered. He was well respected in the Brotherhood of River and Lake, and he accepted his defeat with grace. He had lost the battle, but the war was still to be won. Maybe he would be able to win Flint over to their side. Flint might be a good fighting opponent, but he had his weaknesses. An appeal to his feelings of loyalty to friends and country might be more successful than an outright challenge.

The result of the contest was as predicted by the old abbot. He had actually expected Tobie to lose and Bussie to win. Tobie had outperformed expectations, and he had failed to take into account Master Zheng's capacity for deception.

Just as the contest was over, Shaolin's three elders entered the courtyard. Master Zheng knew then that the game was up. While the contest had been waging in the courtyard outside the Abbot's Lodge, Master Wan's men and Shaolin monks had been fighting in the monastery grounds. Led by the three elders, the Shaolin monks brought down Master Wan's men and herded them into the courtyard behind the monastery. Master Wan found his followers tied together like a chain of crabs.

Master Zheng and Master Wei were immediately expelled from the monastery. There was only one remaining matter to be settled, that of the keys to the secret underground chamber where the 'Tendon Transformation' manual was kept. Master Zheng and Master Wei returned their keys to the Abbot.

Master Zheng offered to go with the Abbot and Master Fu to check that the secret manual was still safe inside the underground chamber. The floorboards in the Abbot's Study were removed. The Abbot, Master Fu and Master Zheng climbed down the stone steps and opened the door to the secret room. The manual was still there. They locked the door behind them and climbed back up the steps. The Abbot was the first one to exit, followed by Master Zheng and then Master Fu. But when Master Fu turned around to put back the floorboards, he felt a prick to his vital energy point at the back of the neck. He lost consciousness. When he came round, he saw it was the old Abbot Tong Ti who had released his energy point. The old Abbot explained that when the three men had not returned, he had come to look for them and found them lying unconscious on the floor. The underground chamber door was open, and the secret Shaolin manual 'Tendon Transformation' had been stolen.

A figure in black clothing ran from the Abbot's lodge, leapt over the walls of the monastery and raced uphill. He found a secluded spot, took out the manual of 'Tendon Transformation' and gleaned the pages. So many people had failed to get hold of this manual, but it had come to him effortlessly, all due to his clever daughter Minnie who had discovered the secret location of the manual. Ma QingLing could not suppress his pleasure.

Sometime after the contest, the old Abbot took Bussie to one side and asked him about the words he had chanted during his match against Master Zheng. Bussie had no idea what the words meant and said that Master Wei had once given him a Buddhist sutra to recite during meditation. The sutra was written in Chinese, and the words did not make any sense. When the old Abbot asked Bussie to show him the sutra, Bussie was embarrassed because he no longer had it. He had kept the sutra in his pocket because he found chanting the sutra helped him calm down. That night on the Five Breast Peak, when he and Tobie were being attacked, the sutra had been shredded by the powerful forces emitted from the palms of Master Wan, Master Zheng and Master Wei. The old Abbot thought it had probably been a sutra in the Sanskrit language. The chanting of sutras could have beneficial effects because of the rhythm of the intonation which could regulate the breathing and direct the *Qi* flow. The vibrations from the sounds, especially in Sanskrit, could help the *Qi* development. He encouraged Bussie to continue his daily recitation of the sutra.

The old Abbot also asked about Tobie's 'One Finger Zen' kung fu which he noticed was different from Shaolin's own. He realised then that Tobie must have learned it from a martial artist who was a descendant of the Duan family from Dali Kingdom.

XVIII

THE TARTAR CHAMPION

Oboi was in a foul mood. He had received two pieces of bad news. The Emperor had disappeared and the old eunuch Wang ChengEn had died. The Imperial Guard Songgotu, a close confidante of the Emperor, had not been seen for days. Reports had just come in of a sighting of Samara and the Princess on their way to Shaolin Monastery. Songgotu's men had also been seen in the vicinity of Shaolin.

Oboi summoned his two captains. The veins on his temples pulsed and his knuckles crackled as he clenched his fists. He looked as if he wanted to eat alive the two men kneeling before him.

'Damn, damn, damn,' he banged his fist on the rosewood side table. The table and the teacup on it shattered. The pieces were quickly taken away and another table put in its place with fresh tea.

'You blockheads, can't I trust you to do a simple job?'

He pointed to the captain on the right. 'You let the Third Prince slip through your fingers and dared report that there has been no sighting of him in Shaolin. The whole Brotherhood knew about the Triad Society's initiation ceremony at Five Breast Peak and the re-appearance of the two Ming Emperor swords. Yet you knew nothing. What on earth were you doing?'

He turned to the captain on the left. 'And you, you followed the Princess and Samara all the way to Five Terraces Mountain and didn't even notice that they had slipped away to Shaolin. You have made me look like an idiot.'

Oboi rose from his seat. At six foot five, he stood a giant of a man, a frightening figure. He was Manchu's Champion fighter and had been awarded the title '*Baturu*', Manchurian for 'Hero'.

153

Oboi walked towards the two captains. At each step, the floor cracked beneath his feet. The captains covered their heads with their hands and knocked their heads against the hard floor, begging for mercy. Oboe lifted them up and banged their heads together. The heads were crushed like two eggs and the men died instantly. He went back to his seat and ordered the bodies of the dead men to be removed.

He had found the memorial stating that the old eunuch had been ill with an infectious disease beneath his pile of papers. When he read it, he could not believe his eyes. It was dated nine days earlier, yet it had only just come to his attention. Then this morning he had received a further memorial informing him that the old eunuch had died. Again the memorial was dated three days earlier yet had only just reached him. He summoned the Prison guards and the Warden to be brought before him.

The twelve Prison guards and the Warden knelt before Oboi and kowtowed. Oboi's eyes blazed with anger. He asked the Prison Warden, 'Tell me exactly what happened in the prison, when and how the old eunuch died.'

'The old eunuch died of ... eh ... an infectious disease ... a few days ago.'

Oboi turned to his scribe, 'When was the prison report received?'

The scribe went forward and knelt. 'My Lord, the report was received three days ago.'

'Why was the report submitted to me only this morning?'

The scribe turned pale. 'My Lord has many more urgent matters to deal with.' Oboi smashed his tea cup to the ground.

'The first report that the old eunuch was ill with an infectious disease was dated nine days ago. Why was this report not submitted to me immediately?'

'The old eunuch was frequently ill,' the scribe squealed. 'He was getting old. The report was put along with less urgent ones so that My Lord could deal with it at a later and more convenient time.'

Oboi screamed, 'I have had enough of this.' He pointed to one of the prison guards. 'If you speak the truth, I will spare you with a less painful death. Tell me when and how the old eunuch died.'

The guard took his time. 'An intruder broke into the prison ten days ago. There were four of us on duty that night. But we were overpowered, our energy points were struck, and we lost consciousness. When we came round, we raised the alarm and chased after the intruder. We caught him, and he was seriously injured but he got away. We did not alert the Imperial Guards because we did not want anyone to know about the prison break-in. We searched for the intruder all over the Palace, but we could not find him.'

The Prison guard was so nervous he was gasping for breath. Oboi ordered another Prison guard to continue the story.

'When we returned to the prison, we found the old eunuch dead with a sword wound at the heart. Maybe it was a revenge killing and had something to do with the old eunuch's past. We knew that if news of the eunuch's death broke out, we would face punishment for failing in our duties. We covered up his death by saying that he was ill with an infectious disease. We waited a few days, had him cremated, and then reported his death. The scribe is a relative of our warden, and he agreed to put our report at the bottom of the pile of documents submitted to My Lord. Please have mercy.'

'You knaves, you almost had me fooled. Guards, take these prison guards outside for immediate execution by DECAPITATION.

He turned to the Prison Warden and the Scribe. 'Don't you expect such clemency. Guards, take these men out for immediate execution by QUARTERING.'

'Quartering' involved tearing the body into four pieces by tying the prisoner's limbs to four horses running in different directions. Sometimes five horses were used and the punishment was known as 'tearing apart by five horses'.

Oboi still could not understand how the Emperor could have left the Palace when he had his men reporting the Emperor's every movement. He ordered a review of all comings and goings of Palace Guards over the previous two weeks. An eagle-eyed officer spotted the name 'Speck', a Palace eunuch, leaving the Palace with a Guard on the night the old eunuch died. This was strange because the officer had met a young eunuch called Speck in the Palace's laundry only the day before. The officer summoned Speck and after questioning, the officer was satisfied that someone posing as Speck had left the Palace with a Guard. The name of the Guard was on palace record and he was summoned. The Guard confessed that he had been too drunk to report for duty that night. Someone must have stolen his identification tally. The officer duly reported to Oboi that two impostors had left the Palace on the same night the old eunuch died.

Oboi had almost forgotten about the eunuch's existence until the news of his death reached his ears. He decided to begin his investigation by finding out more about the old eunuch. All palace records about him were studied in detail. Old surviving eunuchs, retired officers, palace maids and palace guards were interviewed. By the end of the day, Oboi had received a comprehensive report.

The old eunuch's name was Wang ChengEn. He came from a poor family in Hebei. Driven by poverty, Wang was castrated at the age of ten and drafted into the Palace. By all accounts, his early career as a eunuch had been a successful one. He was the last Ming Emperor's closest confidante. His life had spanned the reign of four Ming Emperors and two Qing Emperors

As a young boy, eunuch Wang was intelligent. He was one of the select few to attend the palace school for the education of eunuchs during the Ming dynasty. As a learned eunuch, he was soon recruited to the Palace to serve under Emperor Wan Li's favourite concubine, the Honoured Consort Lady Zheng.

Emperor Wan Li was one of the worst emperors on the Ming throne. His only concern was to squeeze every ounce of silver from his subjects. During his reign, he accumulated so much money that it would have been more than enough to feed ten generations of his descendants. Emperor Wan Li's treasure became legend. Some thought that the hoard of money had been dissipated among soldiers and the hungry mob when the city of Luoyang was captured by the rebel chief Li ZiCheng. But others believed that Wan Li's treasure was still hidden somewhere in the country.

After the death of Emperor Wan Li, eunuch Wang was sent by his mistress to serve the new Emperor Tai Chang. Emperor Tai Chang died after only 30 days on the throne, so he returned to serve his old mistress Lady Zheng. Seven years later, Emperor Chong Zhen came to the throne. Eunuch Wang had been close to Chong Zhen even before he became Emperor, and he went on to become the Emperor's Chief Eunuch and his closest confidante. When Emperor Chong Zhen hanged himself on Coal Hill, eunuch Wang too tried to hang himself. But he was found in time and revived, and had since been held secretly in a prison in the Inner Court of the Forbidden City.

The old eunuch had no known enemies. His family had been wiped out during the Manchu invasion. His only relation was a nephew named Storm. The report contained an account of Storm, including his killing of a nephew of Wu SanGui. The Palace maid's involvement in Storm's reunion with his uncle was uncovered. Oboi was now sure that the intruder was the nephew Storm, and that he had sought sanctuary at Shaolin Monastery.

Oboi suspected that Storm had kidnapped the Emperor and taken him to Shaolin. The Grand Empress Dowager must have known about this or why else she had despatched Samara and the Princess there? The Emperor had been absent from the Palace for more than ten days without his knowledge. He thought he had the Emperor firmly under his thumb, but recent events had made him wonder.

Oboi thought the Grand Empress Dowager a 'sly old fox'. Soon after Regent Soni's death, the Grand Empress Dowager had manoeuvred to allow the young Emperor to rule in person. It was difficult for Oboi and the other two Regents not to agree when the Grand Empress Dowager had hinted that the Regents would be able to continue to rule for all practical purposes for a few more years. It was suggested that an auspicious day be chosen for the Emperor to begin his personal rule. The surviving regents had mistakenly believed such a date to be several years in the future, but the auspicious day chosen by the Minister of Rites turned out to be just four days after the Regents had agreed in principle to the Emperor's rule. So Kang Xi began his personal rule at the age of thirteen.

Oboi had laughed at the Grand Empress Dowager for her efforts to promote the Emperor. The Emperor was only a boy, and he remained on the throne only because he, Oboi, allowed it. He admitted that it was shrewd of the late Emperor Shun Zhi to appoint four Regents. Oboi was the most junior of the regents. Now two Regents had gone. Soni had died of illness and Oboi had engineered Suksaha's death. The remaining Regent Ebilun was a weak man and generally went along with his decisions.

Oboi was a warrior and had little respect for men of literature. He thought the Emperor spent far too much time reading Chinese Classics, and that he should behave more like a Manchu warrior, a *Baturu* like Oboi himself. The Manchus won their battles because they fought hard, not because they read well. He was contemptuous of the Emperor's pursuit of knowledge and dismissed the Emperor as a weakling raised by a doting grandmother. Yet recently Oboi had begun to doubt his own judgment. There had been promotions and several new faces in the Palace, arranged by the Emperor without consulting him. He had also noticed that some of his closest allies had been despatched by the Emperor on missions to places far from the Capital city. The Emperor was taking his personal rule seriously and had begun to interfere in the running of the country. Perhaps it was time to replace him with a younger, more compliant prince.

With the Emperor now in Shaolin, Oboi was presented with a golden opportunity. The more he thought about it, the more he felt he had to move fast. If his plan was successful, he could blame the murder of the Emperor on Shaolin Monastery and accuse the monastery of conspiring with the Triad Society in the movement to 'Overthrow the Qing and Restore the Ming'.

Oboi summoned the two Vice Commanders-in-Chief of the Bordered Yellow Banner. The Commander-in-Chief of the Bordered Yellow Banner was Oboi's younger brother, but he had been sent by the Emperor on a mission to Mongolia. Oboi would have to rely on the Vice Commanders.

The first Vice-Commander knelt before Oboi to receive his instructions. Oboi said, 'Go to Shaolin Monastery. Take with you fifty men adept in kung fu and bring back a man called Storm. I want him brought back alive. Go immediately on the fastest horses that you can find. Bring him to see me as soon as you return.'

The other Vice-Commander was to take banner troops and he too set off for Shaolin immediately. In view of the fact that Shaolin Monastery had 800 fighting monks, to play safe, Oboi ordered him mobilise three regiments, a total of 4500 men, to seal off the monastery and search for the Emperor.

Oboi then went to hold an audience with five other men. These five men were Oboi's secret weapon. They had been in his service for many years, but they never came to his residence and were not seen openly with him. No one except Oboi and his retainer knew of their existence.

The five men looked nothing but ordinary. One was a haberdasher selling the finest threads and needles in the Capital city. He owned a small, insignificant shop in a side street which was frequented by maids and ladies from the Capital's rich and noble households, including the Imperial Household. A second man was the innkeeper of an inn to the north of the Imperial Palace, and the third man was the innkeeper of an inn to the south. The two looked every bit like any innkeeper from an inn anywhere in the country. Their inns were in the seedy parts of the city, popular with guards, minions and coach drivers because of good food served at very reasonable prices. The innkeepers were kung fu brothers from the same school of martial arts. One was fat and short, the other tall and thin. The fourth man owned a small shop in the side street of a major shopping area, selling bowls, plates, spoons and cutlery. There was always a plate, or bowl or spoon in his shop to match a broken piece in a household, so his shop was frequented by housekeepers, maids and servants from the Capital's famous households. The last man was an itinerant hawker peddling deep fried smelly bean curd.

All were masters in martial arts. They had provided Oboi with valuable information over the years collected from the grapevine of maids, servants, guards and coach drivers. They had also eliminated many of Oboi's enemies. Oboi had spent money on keeping them. Now the time had come for them to make a final repayment for Oboi's generosity.

Oboi promised the men that this would be their last job, and irrespective of the result of their mission, they should come back for a final bonus before they retired. The men set off for Shaolin monastery immediately, as instructed.

After the meeting with the five assassins, Oboi went back to his residence. The report on the old eunuch Wang ChengEn was still lying on his desk. It was clear to Oboi that the interest shown in eunuch Wang by his captors was connected to the story of Emperor Wan Li's treasure. There were no surviving descendants of Wan Li's concubine, Lady Zheng. Her son, the Prince of Luoyang, had been killed by the rebel chief, Li ZiCheng. Her grandson, the Prince of Fu was beheaded when Nanjing fell to the Manchus.

Oboi believed that Wan Li's treasure remained hidden, and suspected that the old eunuch knew its location and had passed on the secret to his only surviving relative, his nephew Storm. Storm must be captured alive.

XIX

THE LAST MISSION

Kang Xi, still disguised as Speck, realised that the time had come for him to leave Shaolin Monastery. Oboi's men had been seen at the foot of Mount Song. He admired the two abbots, they were true men of religion, and he was happy that the monastery was in good hands. He was appreciative when the Abbot asked Flint, Bussie and Tobie to accompany him on his journey back to the Palace.

To the boys, Speck was a Palace eunuch, and they thought the Abbot was being overly cautious. Who would want to harm a Palace eunuch? Nevertheless they were excited about their trip as this was the first time they had been allowed to venture outside the precincts of the monastery. There is a saying, 'a new born calf is not afraid of a tiger'. They were young and full of confidence and nothing could daunt their spirits.

They were well armed for the voyage. The Abbot gave Bussie the best pair of twin axes in the monastery's possession. Flint had a fine sword, a birthday present from Storm, and Tobie a dagger, given to him by the Chef. The Chef told Tobie that the dagger had belonged to his father. He felt that Tobie was now old enough to know more about his parents.

The Chef and his younger sister had been brought up by their widowed mother in a village near Hangzhou. The Chef left home at a young age to learn kung fu. After his *Shifu* died, he had tried to save enough money to go home again, but it was difficult to find a job as the country was still in turmoil. It was early days of the Manchu Conquest, and there were uprisings and riots everywhere. He did not want to serve under the Manchus, but neither could he get along with the anti-Manchu factions. The Chef turned to thieving but was very much a loner. He became known in the Brotherhood and was nicknamed 'Shadowless Man'.

When he did manage to return home, he found his mother very ill. His younger sister was thirteen years old. His mother knew she was dying, and sent her daughter to work as a maid with a rich family in Hangzhou. The Chef was happy with the arrangement because his sister was with a good family well known for their kindness and generosity to employees.

Some years later, the Chef found himself ambushed by soldiers. His life was saved only when the old Abbot Tong Ti happened to pass by. He took the Chef to Shaolin Monastery. There the Chef determined to turn over a new leaf. After settling in at Shaolin Monastery, he wanted to visit his sister and tell her of his new job, but was surprised to find his sister at their family home, no longer working as a maid. She was heavily pregnant. The Chef demanded to know whether it was the old master or one of the young masters who had made her pregnant. But his sister insisted that her pregnancy had nothing to do with the family. The father of her child had promised to come back to marry her.

The Chef's sister had died giving birth to Tobie. She left behind two bequests for him, things that had been given to her by Tobie's father. One was a dagger with a gold sheath, the sharpest dagger the Chef had ever seen. It could cut through bricks and metal like cutting through bean curd. At the base of the blade was a gold band and the haft was decorated with rungs of gold wire. A large 'dove-blood-red' Burmese ruby was embedded in the pommel, and a tassel of white cord attached to the end of the handle. There were drawings of dragons, tigers and eagles on the sheath, and two loops which could attach the dagger to the girdle. Tobie's mother had also left behind a gold necklace from which hung a gold coin. The obverse of the coin was inscribed with the Chinese characters 'Long Life and Live a Hundred Years', and the reverse with the characters 'Shun Zhi 11th year February 8'. The Chef placed the necklace around Tobie's neck before Tobie set off on his journey. His sister had never told him the name of Tobie's father. The Chef hoped that if he was still alive, the dagger and the necklace might bring about a reunion between father and son.

The three boys went to the Abbot's Lodge to take leave of the two abbots. They found Speck, Samara, the Princess and Songgotu inside the Abbot's room. Speck was explaining, 'We did not come here to plunder. We want to become part of this great country. In addition to Manchus and Han Chinese, we have Mongols, Muslims, Tibetans, Jews and ethnic minorities, all of whom have lived here for hundreds or thousands of years. The land is big enough to accommodate all of us. We may be of different races but we are one nation.'

The old Abbot nodded. 'Do you think that people from different races can live together in peace?'

'Emperor Kang Xi believes in 'assimilation' and 'good government'. We try to involve as many Chinese as we can in our administration. The Grand Secretariat and the six ministries are staffed with equal numbers of senior Chinese and Manchu officials. The triennial examinations are based on the Ming curriculum with emphasis on Confucian Classics, yet many eminent and capable scholars shy away from the examinations.'

The Abbot listened attentively. 'Chinese society has been influenced by Confucian thinking for over two thousand years. The scholars may have taken a narrow interpretation of the moral virtue of 'loyalty', and to them, joining the Qing government might amount to betrayal of Ming memories.'

'This is a great pity. The Emperor is a great admirer of Chinese culture. He wants to promote Confucian thinking because he believes that Confucian values of loyalty and filial piety will bind officials to rulers and children to parents, and will lay the foundation for good government.'

Both the old Abbot and the present Abbot were men of wisdom. They were able to read a person's future from his physiognomy. In Kang Xi, they saw a man destined to be ruler. Kang Xi would enjoy a long life and would rule the country for a long time. They were satisfied that he was a wise, compassionate and magnanimous person and that he would make a good emperor. They also accepted that, as dictated by the law of 'Change' which governed the universe, the cycle of Ming Dynasty had come to an end and the cycle of Qing Dynasty had commenced. But they saw dark clouds gathering over Kang Xi's forehead, a sign of impending danger. This was why they had asked Flint, Bussie and Tobie to accompany Kang Xi on the road to protect him.

The group of travellers included Samara, the Princess and Songgotu, and they were joined by Toga who was also heading back to the Capital city. Samara dressed in man's clothing for convenience of travel.

Kang Xi wanted to say farewell to Storm before he left. The group headed towards Storm's hut in the vegetation plot behind the monastery. When they arrived, they found a scene of devastation, windows and doors blown open, the floor littered with broken furniture, and the walls splattered with blood. There was no sign of Storm. The fire in the stove was still burning. The kettle lay on the floor. Samara said quietly to Kang Xi, 'This has probably got something to do with Storm's visit to the Palace. When we get back, we must conduct an investigation. Time is running out. We really must make a move now.'

Reluctantly, Kang Xi and his party set forth on their journey. To avoid an encounter with Oboi's men, Kang Xi accepted the old Abbot's advice to take a short cut via the Chef's hut towards the Five Breast Peak. The scenery ahead of them was breathtaking, green hills, and tall, majestic trees. Kang Xi, Samara, the Princess, Songgotu and Toga rode ahead into the woods. Flint, Bussie and Tobie lingered, looking back in the hope of catching sight of Storm. Suddenly Flint shouted to the riders ahead, 'Stop, don't go any further.' He was too late. A large net fell down from the trees, trapping them, and quickly pulled back up into the branches.

As Flint, Bussie and Tobie rode forward to rescue their friends, five masked men jumped down from the trees. The five assassins sent by Oboi were surprised to find themselves facing three boys. This would be an easy task. They surmised that of the three, Bussie would be the strongest, and Tobie the weakest. Their strategy was to put forward their two best fighters, the innkeepers, to fight the second best opponent Flint, and their next best pair, the haberdasher and the crockery seller, to fight the weakest opponent Tobie. The hawker was thus left with Bussie. The haberdasher and the crockery seller were to finish Tobie off quickly and then join the hawker in the fight against Bussie.

Although the hawker was not their best fighter, it was he who was entrusted by Oboi to oversee the operation. He had started out as a hired assassin. Twenty years earlier he had severely injured a young child, and then killed the child's grandmother. The child was left brain-damaged. The hawker had been paid to kill the child by the concubine of a rich man, who wished to get rid of the son of the principal wife so that her own son could become heir. At first people blamed the killing on the Dark Way. Their spokesmen were forced to come out and condemn the atrocity. Men from the Dark Way were hardened criminals and convicts known for their callousness and brutality, yet even they abided by a basic code of decency and would not harm the old, the sick, young children and pregnant women. They swore to find the killer and bring him to justice. They nicknamed the killer 'The Hyena' to reflect their disgust. The hawker was a wanted man by the authorities, the Brotherhood and the Dark Way.

Tobie could not believe his luck. In just a matter of few hours, he would get to use his martial arts skills again. As he watched the two men circling him, he had not a clue how to fight them. To make matters worse, one was using a short weapon, a flute, and the other was a long weapon, an iron rod. The crockery seller performed a left to right sweeping block known as 'Beating a Snake Out of Bush' to force Tobie to retreat. Simultaneously the haberdasher shot to the back of Tobie, first to paralyse his legs and then to finish him off with a strike at the back of his neck.

The moment the rod was raised, Tobie anticipated the sweeping block, and from the corner of his eye, he saw the movement of the haberdasher. He leapt high up into the air using his *Qingong* step 'Arrow Shoots Into Sky', and instead of retreating, he moved forward. Before the rod had completed the arc from left to right, Tobie used his dagger to cut the rod through, reducing it to barely a foot long. Then he stepped back to a long range position. The two men were caught by surprise. They circled Tobie again, trying to pin him down. But Tobie was as slippery as a fish, deploying his elusive *Qingong* steps. One moment Tobie could be seen, the next, he disappeared, like a wisp of wind. The two assassins felt as though they were playing a game of hide-and-seek.

Meanwhile Flint was facing both the innkeepers. They were experts in *Baguazhang* or the 8-Trigram Palm. The *Baguazhang* is based on the *Yin-Yang* theories of the Doctrine of Change, the Five Elements and the Eight Trigrams. The kung fu skills emphasise the cyclical changes of motion, thus the movements are circular. The stepping techniques such as yielding, neutralizing, sticking, adhering and coiling are designed to coordinate with the circular movements. There are only eight basic movements but the movements are capable of unlimited variation. The *Baguazhang* was created by a Daoist and was practised by Daoist schools of martial arts. Over time, the *Baguazhang* was varied by different martial arts schools. Although the basic principles remain the same, the practising routines of each school were different. Attack and defence are equally important in *Baguazhang*. *Baguazhang* is externally soft and internally hard and is effective at all ranges: short, middle and long.

The two innkeepers were kung fu brothers and had practised the *Baguazhang* together for many years, developing their own unique routine. Their movements were light and swift, the palms followed one after another, direction constantly changing. They were two roving dragons, unpredictable and mighty. Indeed, this style of kung fu was also known as 'Roving Dragon *Baguazhang*'. Their routine of 64 palms consisted of eight palm movements each with eight variations. The 64 palms could be used by both the Left Hand and the Right Hand. An opponent would face 128 palm movements. While one was defending, the other would attack, and they switched roles continuously. They were nicknamed the 'Invincible Duo'.

They began to move in a circle. One would move from left to right and the other from right to left. Sometimes they would be back-to-back and move like a rolling ball. In a succession of palm movements, quick as lightning, the fat innkeeper completed a sequence of eight variations of 'Golden Pin Points to the Sky',

'Two Immortals Point the Way', 'Brush Against the Body and Turn Back', 'Green Dragon Turns Round', 'Phoenix Closes Its Wings', 'Immortal Twists His Waist', 'Phoenix Spreads Its Wings', and 'Tumble Backwards to Heaven's Gate'. While he attacked, the thin innkeeper defended.

Flint returned the eight strikes using identical poses. He was quicker than the innkeepers. His strikes were delivered later, but reached the opponent first. The fat innkeeper was quick with his palm movements, but Flint was even faster. Every time the fat innkeeper struck out, he was forced back because Flint's palm had already reached him. They could not understand how Flint could be using the same *Baguazhang* kung fu style.

Flint had earned this from Miao Shan *ShiTai*, successor to the Ice Maiden. The Ice Maiden was a Daoist who lived during the late Yuan period. She had learned kung fu from her father who specialised in *Baguazhang*. Her father had another pupil who was her *Shi-xiong*[12] and the two children grew up together. The Ice Maiden's beauty was widely known and young men from all over the country sought her hand in marriage, but she had eyes only for her *Shi-xiong*. Everyone expected them to marry. Then to everyone's surprise, her *Shi-xiong* married another.

Love turned to bitterness. The Ice-Maiden sought to kill the new wife. The couple ran from her but she stalked them. One day she tricked her *Shi-xiong* and he fell into her trap. She held a sword to his throat. 'Why have you not married me? Am I not beautiful or good enough for you?'

'You are the most beautiful and intelligent girl that I have ever met. You are extraordinary, and so superior in everything you do that I look up to you and I admire you greatly. But I cannot compete with you. My wife is nowhere near as perfect as you, but I am comfortable with her.'

How could her *Shi-xiong* reject her because she was too perfect? He was ready to die, but asked her to spare his wife because she was pregnant with their child. The Ice Maiden's heart was broken, and she dropped her sword and fled. Eligible young

---

12 Elder kung fu brother

167

men proposed marriage to her but she rejected them all, which was how she earned her nickname 'The Ice Maiden'. She became a recluse, living in a mountain cave. Meanwhile, her *Shi-xiong* and his wife became famous in the Brotherhood for their skills in practising *Baguazhang* as a pair, and they had never once been beaten. Since the Ice Maiden could not tear the couple apart, she decided that she would defeat them in kung fu so that she could tarnish their undeserved reputation in the Brotherhood.

It had in fact been the Ice Maiden and her *Shi-xiong* who had created the style of *Baguazhang* that could be practised by two people together to increase power and effectiveness. Eventually the Ice Maiden succeeded in finding a way to defeat the *Baguazhang* when it was executed by a pair. Practising *Baguazhang* as a pair had its strength, but it had weaknesses too. Whilst fighting together increased power, coordination needed to be perfect. They had to fight as two merged into one. Someone with greater speed could exploit any split second delay in coordination.

The fat innkeeper was down to the last two of the 64 palms. The force from his palms roared towards Flint like thunder. Flint summoned his *Qi* and deflected the force from the innkeeper to a nearby tree, which snapped into two.

The innkeepers were compelled to use their weapons. Each held a pair of 'Zi-Wu Mandarin Duck Axe'. 'Zi' which meant 'midnight, was 'Yin', and 'Wu', 'noon', was therefore 'Yang'. A 'Zi-Wu Mandarin Duck Axe' consists of two hooks shaped like deer antlers. The hooks are joined together with a gap in the middle. Four fingers can slip into the gap and grasp the hook from the inside, and the thumb can then grasp the hook from outside. Once the hooks are joined, they are inseparable like a pair of Mandarin ducks. The axe is capable of executing techniques such as hooking, sliding, seizing, cutting, drilling, chopping and mincing.

The innkeepers' axes spun. Flint took up his sword and waited for them to commence their attack.

Meanwhile, Bussie was fighting the hawker. Like a cunning fox, the hawker revealed neither his real kung fu nor his weapon.

He began with the Eagle Claw kung fu, which had become famous during the Song Dynasty when General Yue Fei used it to train his soldiers to fight the Jin invaders. General Yue Fei learned the kung fu from Shaolin Monastery and adapted it to include '108 Locking Hand Techniques'. Strong sharp claws coupled with smooth movements are powerful and effective for both long range and short range combat. The kung fu includes high kicks and sweeps. However its strength lies in grabbing, locking and striking vital energy points, all performed at very close range.

The hawker soon found that he could not get close to Bussie, whose only tactic was 'attack and die together with the enemy'. He valued his life and was not prepared to sacrifice it for Bussie's. He took out his weapon, a three-sectional staff, a weapon which could be used at both long and short-range. Different sections could be used at the same time to block, strike or stab, and the chains could entangle an opponent or his weapon. The hawker had excellent foot technique, and was capable of delivering swift, powerful high and low kicks from all angles. He would fool his opponents into focusing on his hands, while his feet would deliver the deadly kicks. He performed false poses with his hands to confuse Bussie while looking for an opportunity to move in to use his feet.

Bussie brought his pair of axes. He was irritated by the hawker's false moves, and he let out a yell. The *Qi* that was emitted was so powerful that the hawker almost lost grip of his staff. The hawker leapt to long range position. He extended his staff to its full length and made a sweeping movement towards Bussie, trying to entangle Bussie's legs in the chain. He whipped the staff until one of Bussie's axes was caught up in the chain, but before he knew what had happened, Bussie broke the chain with a powerful chop from his other axe. It was Bussie's speed and power which enabled him to keep ahead of the hawker's every move. Soon the hawker's three-sectional staff was reduced to one section.

The haberdasher was becoming frustrated with Tobie's elusive steps. Inside the hollow of his flute were hidden poisonous steel needles, and he released them. But Tobie had exceptionally sharp observation and fast footwork. The moment the needles were released, he moved behind the crockery seller. The crockery seller dropped down dead, and one needle pierced Tobie's arm. Another hit him on the shoulder, and his shoulder turned numb. The haberdasher did not waste a second. He delivered a downward looping strike with the end of the flute aiming at Tobie's head. But the flute stayed in the air, and a sword was plunged into the haberdasher's back, killing him instantly. A figure leapt forward and whisked Tobie away.

The rescuer's face was covered by a piece of cloth tied around his face. He carried Tobie up a tree, and used his internal force to press out the two needles. He put powder on the wounds and a tablet into Tobie's mouth. He told Tobie that he would recover shortly.

'Who are you?'

'You will know when the time is right.'

The man disappeared back into the woods.

The two innkeepers continued to circle around Flint, spinning and rotating their weapons. The thin innkeeper executed a series of fighting poses in quick succession. He brought together his two axes and faced his palms to his chest with the tips of the hooks pointing at each other. Without warning, Flint's sword was locked by the axes. The fat innkeeper moved behind Flint and flung both his 'Zi Wu' axes at Flint's back. The timing was perfect but Flint reacted fast. The moment his sword locked, his body shot up, his feet in the air, his head hanging downwards, and his hand still holding the sword. The axes missed Flint and hit the thin innkeeper in the chest. The thin innkeeper collapsed to the ground, releasing Flint's sword. Flint spun round in mid-air and aimed his sword at the fat innkeeper's throat.

The hawker was relying on his footwork. He sprang high and performed a succession of butterfly kicks. His chest close to the ground, and his back arched, the right leg kicked high and hard from behind, quickly followed by the left leg. Bussie rushed forward with his axes. The hawker realised that while his kick might injure Bussie, he would probably lose his leg in the process. He was forced to change course. He was finding it more and more difficult to fight Bussie. He was reduced to defensive moves and had received several axe cuts. From the corner of his eye he saw the bodies of the haberdasher, the crockery seller and the thin innkeeper. When he saw Flint's sword at the fat innkeeper's throat, he did not hesitate. He performed a feint, and threw a blade at the back of the fat innkeeper, killing him. He could not allow anyone to be captured and implicate Oboi in the plot. Then he disappeared into the woods.

The group continued their journey hoping to reach a government postal relay station in Zhengzhou before dark. Songgotu despatched four of his soldiers to escort the dead bodies of the four assassins to Beijing for investigation into their backgrounds.

XX

THE GREAT ESCAPE

Tobie's life had to now been simple and comfortable. Apart from good food, he made no demands. The Chef had regretted his neglect of his mother and sister while they were alive, and lavished all his love on Tobie. He made sure that he lacked for nothing. Tobie was a placid, happy and contented boy. Then he met the young eunuch, Huang Ding, and he had to learn to argue and fight his own corner. He did not realise that Huang Ding was the Princess in disguise, but he did feel a strange attraction to the young eunuch, and it confused him. He did not know how to deal with Huang Ding. Nobody had ever treated him like this before, and worst of all, there was no uncle here to protect him. Whenever Huang Ding lost a game or argument, he kicked out at Tobie or punched him. Tobie's elusive footwork saved him many times from unwarranted assault.

Samara and Huang Ding were responsible for the food on the journey. They took every precaution. They cooked all meals themselves and drank only water they had brought with them. They carried with them cooking utensils, bowls and plates, and chopsticks, to avoid being poisoned on the road.

When the group stopped for a rest, Tobie sat alone under a tree. He was in low spirits, upset by a rumbling stomach which reminded him that he had not eaten for hours. He dreamed of the smell of chicken roasting, and then realised it was not a dream. Someone really was cooking chicken nearby. He followed his nose and found Huang Ding taking two clay balls from a pit in the ground. He cracked open the clay and the fragrant smell of chicken broke through. This was 'Beggar's Chicken' invented by a beggar who had stolen a chicken but had no stove to cook it in. He had cleaned the chicken, covered it in mud, dug a hole in the ground and baked the chicken in the hole. The mud around the chicken hardened like a clay ball, and when the ball was cracked open, the feathers came off and the chicken was tender and delicious.

Everyone was drawn by the smell of chicken. Huang Ding tore two legs from a chicken and gave them to Kang Xi. She tore two legs from the other chicken and gave them to Tobie. 'Are we still friends?'

'Yes, as long as you don't try to hit me again.'

The others shared the remains.

After their meal, Kang Xi and his party rode ahead towards the government Postal Relay Station to change their horses and find some clean rooms for the night. Songgotu's men followed some distance behind. But when Kang Xi and his friends reached the postal station, no-one was there. Flint sensed that something was wrong. He called to the others to get out fast by the back door and through the courtyard. Behind the courtyard was a stable for the horses. The stable too was empty.

They heard the deafening clamour of clattering hooves. A barrage of incendiaries shot into the station building from front and back. Fire flared instantly, engulfing everything. Toga handed everyone a tablet to swallow, and then spread yellow powder all around the courtyard. They climbed up into the branches of a tall tree. The flames ignited the yellow powder, and the courtyard filled with smoke.

When the attackers poured into the courtyard, one by one they collapsed. The smoke from Toga's yellow powder was an effective opiate. When the last man fell, Kang Xi's party jumped down from the tree. Songgotu's men arrived, and they chained and manacled the highwaymen. When Songgotu pulled one of them over for questioning, he confessed he was leader of the group and that they took their orders from the Black Dragon Gang. Whenever the Gang Master gave an order, a messenger would come bearing a solid gold plate inscribed with a black dragon. The bearer of the gold plate would relate the Gang Master's orders. Those who refused to comply met with a cruel death, and so did their entire families. The Black Dragon Gang was the most feared gang in the

Brotherhood of River and Lake. Before he could say more, an arrow appeared from nowhere, piercing him in the throat and he fell down dead. Songgotu sent a team of men to escort the remaining highwaymen to the Capital for interrogation. Kang Xi and his party were now left with barely 30 soldiers to protect them.

After a night's rest at the Relay Station, they abandoned the government routes and headed for the hills. They travelled many miles, and when the day was at its warmest, stopped under trees to drink the water they carried with them.

An old man smoking a long pipe sat with an old woman in the shade near where they were resting. They were old, wrinkled and weathered. Beside the couple stood two large wooden barrels and a carrying pole. The woman scooped chilled green bean soup from a barrel into a bowl. The old man took the bowl from her and drank the soup. 'Da Lang's mother, when I first met you, I was such a poor young man. I had nothing, not even a cow to help me plough the fields. You were the daughter of the village teacher. I never dreamed that I would one day marry you. I am still a poor man. Do you regret marrying me?'

The old woman replied, 'When our Da Lang was born, you sold your flute to buy a chicken to make chicken soup for me. The flute was the only thing that your father had left you and yet you sold it for me. I became ill and you did not sleep for three days and three nights to look after me. I would have died if you had not given me the strength to recover. I am a lucky woman.'

The old man said, 'No, I am the one who is lucky. You have been an excellent wife, and what a wonderful cook you are.' The old woman smiled back at him like a young girl.

The mint flavour of the sweet bean soup hung in the air, and the travellers were desperate for a taste, especially Tobie who loved the lily-roots in green bean soup. They had listened to the conversation between the old man and his wife and were touched. Samara went over to them and asked to buy some soup. She tested the soup with her silver spoon and was satisfied that it was not poisonous. Toga took out his kit to test the soup, and he too was satisfied it contained no poison. As an extra precaution, Samara used her own bowls and ladle.

The group sat sipping hungrily from their bowls, but Flint felt uneasy. He looked around and saw Toga go behind the bushes to relieve himself. The old man filled his pipe and began to smoke. The smoke formed little circles in the air and drifted towards them.

On his way back from the bushes, Toga happened to look across at the old man. He saw that the man had only four fingers on each hand. Toga took out a dart and threw it at the old man, then dashed forward to disable him by striking at the vital energy point in his back. When he saw this, Flint jumped up and overpowered the old woman.

Toga knew all the users of poison in the Brotherhood, being an expert user himself. He had long heard of a man nicknamed 'The Scorpion Sting', whose skills with poison were legendary. Toga knew that the 'Scorpion Sting' had a special feature, he had only eight fingers, and realised that the poison was not in the green bean soup, but in the smoke from the pipe.

Toga demanded the antidote, but the old man refused. He forced a tablet down the old man's throat, and he immediately bent over in pain. Toga told him that he would not die, but that the pain would not go away until he handed over the antidote. The old woman broke down and took from her husband's clothes a phial fitted with a nozzle. She told Toga to spray once into the nostrils of those afflicted by the poison.

Toga tested the antidote. When everyone had recovered, he put another tablet into the mouth of the old man to relieve him of the pain.

Flint pricked the *Qi* storage cavities of the old man and his wife so that they could no longer exercise internal force. But when Songgotu started to question them, two blades flew from the bushes killing the old couple instantly. Reluctantly Songgotu had to dispatch two more of his men to escort the bodies of the 'Scorpion Sting' and his wife back to the Capital for further investigation.

Songgotu thought it too dangerous to continue by land, and suggested travelling by river. They were near Kaifeng which had waterways linking the city to other ports. They managed to acquire three boats. The first boat would carry Kang Xi and his companions while Songgotu's men would travel in two boats behind them.

They set off down the river, travelling for many miles without incident. But when Flint saw a fleet of boats behind them, he realised that they were to be attacked again. There was no way they could succeed against such a large fleet. Ahead of them was the thunderous roar of a waterfall. They headed for it at full speed, but the torrents of water bashed against the rocks, making it impossible for their boat to sail through.

Flint told those in the boat to hold on tight to each other. Then Flint, Bussie and Tobie jumped into the river. Bussie held the front of the boat in the air with his hands, Flint held the middle and Tobie the rear. The three of them faced the waterfall with the boat lifted high over their heads. They leapt up, using their internal force to push the boat into the air and over the waterfall. The boat flew over the rapids like a giant bird, landing safely on the other side.

Their relief was too short for celebration. Another fleet of vessels was heading towards them on this side of the rapids. The boat was surrounded. A vessel pulled beside them and a man jumped aboard and saluted respectfully. 'We are from the 36 Caves. We have come to escort you. Without our help, you will never reach Tianjin. All roads, rivers and ports leading to the Capital are heavily guarded by soldiers. We know how you can get to the Capital. Trust us and follow.'

The 36 Caves formed a subterranean network of caverns inside the mountains. Each Cave had its own leader, and the Caves formed a close alliance. They belonged to the Dark Way.

Songgotu asked, 'Who sent you here?'

'I cannot tell you. He is a benefactor to the 36 Caves. He has helped our brothers and we are in his debt. We will do whatever he asks to repay his kindness to us.'

They followed intricate subterranean passageways and narrow mountain tracks, deep winding valleys surrounded by high cliffs and steep rocks. Sometimes the scenery was exotic and breathtaking. Other times, the trek was rough and dangerous.

They were well looked after by their hosts. When they reached a cave, they were entertained by the chieftain, and given sumptuous meals. As usual, Samara and Toga would test the food for poison, but now they felt more relaxed. If these men had really wanted to kill them, they could have done so already.

When they reached Tianjin, they were handed over to other men from the 36 Caves. All roads to the Capital were by now heavily guarded by Oboi's men. Kang Xi asked the men to take them to the game reserves of Nan-Yuan outside the Capital, where he would meet up with his brother Fu Quan.

The Grand Empress Dowager had asked Imperial Prince Fu Quan to take a hunting party with him to the game reserves of Nan-Yuan and wait for the Emperor there. Nan-Yuan was a favourite hunting spot of the royals and Fu Quan's hunting party left the Capital without arousing suspicion from Oboi's men. At that time Oboi was not aware that the Emperor had left the Palace. The Grand Empress Dowager had once again out-manoeuvred Oboi.

When Fu Quan met up with Kang Xi, he disguised Kang Xi and his friends and took them back with the hunting party to the Imperial Palace. Flint, Bussie and Tobie were housed in the Wu-Ying Palace where they were disguised as eunuchs, because men were not allowed inside the Inner Court. Toga stayed at Songgotu's house. Kang Xi himself went back to his own palace, the Qian-Qing Palace. Samara and Huang Ding returned to the palace of the Grand Empress Dowager.

XXI

THE EMPEROR'S GAMBIT

As soon as Kang Xi reached the Palace, he went straight to see his grandmother, the Grand Empress Dowager.

Kang Xi had been concerned about Oboi for some time. Oboi was arrogant and domineering, and had not taken him seriously as Emperor. He reflected how Oboi made decisions without consulting him, moving personnel without his approval, blocking submissions from ministers, and forming a clique to promote his own interests. But what upset Kang Xi most had been the execution of Regent Suksaha.

Animosity between Oboi and Suksaha went back a long way. After the Manchu Conquest, each of the eight banners was granted land and settled in a territorial zone outside the Palace walls so that the Emperor and his family could be protected by their most loyal troops. The Chinese residents were forcibly relocated to the Outer City in the southern part of Beijing. The land belonging to each banner was encircled and referred to as 'circled land'. Rich farmlands from the Chinese were seized or swapped by bannermen. But Oboi also desired better land from other banners. He swapped inferior land from his Bordered Yellow banner for rich land belonging to Suksaha's Plain White banner. Suksaha objected to Oboi's bullying tactics, and they argued over 'circled land'.

Of the four regents, Soni was the most senior and the most trusted by Emperor Shun Zi and the Grand Empress Dowager. As the senior regent, Soni was responsible for drafting edicts and approving memorials submitted by ministers. Oboi dared not challenge Soni's authority. After Soni died, Suksaha, who ranked second in seniority, was expected to take over Soni's duties. Oboi could not allow this to happen and he looked for an opportunity to remove Suksaha.

The opportunity came six days after Kang Xi had begun his personal rule. Suksaha submitted a memorial for retirement on grounds of illness. In fact Suksaha was unhappy with the increasingly dictatorial ways of Oboi. He was supportive of Kang Xi's personal rule, and thought it time to submit his resignation as a regent. His intention was to set an example to the two remaining regents to give Kang Xi a free hand in the ruling of the country. Oboi accused Suksaha of acts of arrogance and disloyalty. He succeeded in gaining the support of the Council of Princes and High Officials in finding Suksaha guilty of 24 offences. The Council recommended that Suksaha and his eldest son be executed by the 'slow process of slicing', the cruellest death penalty. The 'slow process' is a lingering death in which flesh is cut from the prisoner until he bleeds to death.

The Council also recommended that Suksaha's six other sons, a grandson and two nephews be executed by decapitation, and that family members be taken into slavery. Seventeen Imperial Guards connected with Suksaha were to be demoted. Kang Xi was too young and powerless to disagree. He reluctantly approved the penalties, with the exception that Suksaha and his elder son's executions by 'slow process' be commuted to death by strangulation.

Oboi had won a victory and the young Emperor made to look a weakling. The execution of Suksaha had given Kang Xi his first lesson in the cruelty of politics and from that point he determined to seize back power from Oboi.

A battle ensued between Kang Xi and Oboi in the moving of personnel. Oboi put the Grand Secretary Bambursan in charge of the Veritable Records for Emperor Shun Zhi's reign, and named Marsai as the third co-president of the Board of Revenue. He imprisoned Adam Schall and his Christian astronomer colleagues on charges of incompetence and treason, and filled the Bureau of Astronomy with new appointees.

Kang-Xi responded to Oboi's moves by replacing Bambursan with the new Grand Secretary Duikana as chief editor of the Veritable Records. He ordered Ferdinand Verbiest, a Jesuit priest, to point out errors in the calendars submitted by Oboi's appointees. A commission set up to investigate the priest's claims was packed with Kang Xi's own men. Verbiest was then appointed assistant director of the Bureau of Astronomy. Kang Xi also fast-tracked the promotions of a number of young officials such as Songgotu, Mishan, Li Wei, and MingZhu, who were loyal to him.

The battle for power escalated. Just before Kang Xi left the Palace with Storm, he had sent several of Oboi's closest allies on missions away from the Capital city. Oboi's brother, Commander-in-Chief of Yellow Bordered Banner, Oboi's cousin, the Imperial Guard, and Oboi's brother in-law, the Vice-Minister of the Court of Colonial Affairs were sent on special missions to Mongolia. He had also sent Oboi's ally, the Minister of Works, to Fujian to patrol the coastal region.

The Grand Empress Dowager was always the first person Kang Xi turned to for advice. Kang Xi reported to his grandmother everything that had happened on the journey back from Shaolin Monastery. They decided that they had to act fast. They took out a map of the Capital City, and they studied it together.

The Capital city was made up of two smaller cities: the Inner City and the Outer City. Within the Inner City was the Imperial City, an irregular square in the centre. Within the Imperial City was the Forbidden City, another walled rectangle situated in the centre and slightly east. The Outer City had seven gates, the Inner City nine gates, and the Imperial City four gates.

The Forbidden City was divided into Outer Court and Inner Court. The Emperor and his family resided in the Inner Court.

Kang Xi reviewed the Imperial Guards in the Palace. The Imperial Guards Brigade was an elite force selected from members of the Upper Three Banners. The three banners were normally under the command of the emperor, but during Kang Xi's minority, they had come under the control of the four regents. After the death of Soni and Suksaha, the control of the Upper Three Banners had effectively fallen into the hands of Oboi.

Kang Xi realised he could not rely on the Imperial Guards. The Outer Court of the Palace would be guarded and controlled by Imperial Guards loyal to Oboi. The situation in the Inner

Court was better. Some of the Imperial Guards had been there since the reign of Shun Zhi, many others had been selected by either Kang Xi or the Grand Empress Dowager.

Kang Xi then reviewed the position of banner troops. The capital troops were divided into Inner Banners and Outer Banners, made up of bannermen drawn from all Eight Manchu Banners. The Inner Banners guarded the Forbidden City, while the Outer Banners remained in garrisons in and around Beijing, the Capital City. The Outer Banners were co-ordinated by a Commander-General chosen in annual rotation from among the Commanders-in-Chief of all the Banners. The Grand Empress Dowager had summoned the Commander-General during Kang Xi's absence. The Commander, an Imperial Prince, was her step-son. He swore his undying allegiance to the Emperor and would ready his troops and await instructions.

But Oboi's men already had control of the key roads and the seven gates of the Outer City. One man was very important at this crucial time, the Commander-in-Chief of the Nine Gates which led to the Inner City. This Commander-in-Chief was one of those in position since the reign of Shun Zhi. He was a quiet man, not associated with any Palace factions, nor involved in any scandal. He kept to himself while others around him were embroiled in palace intrigue.

After Kang Xi had begun his personal rule, Oboi had submitted a recommendation for the Commander-in-Chief of the Nine Gates to be promoted to the Ministry of War, his existing post to be taken over by a protégé of Oboi. Kang Xi had rejected his recommendation, saying that he had heard rumours that Oboi's officer was involved in corruption. After investigation, the officer was found guilty and executed.

A few months later, Oboi once again recommended the promotion of the Commander-in-Chief of the Nine Gates. The vacancy created was then to be taken up by Oboi's cousin, an Imperial Guard. Oboi was then surprised to hear that his cousin had been sent on a special mission to Mongolia, and the recommendation would only be considered after he had completed his mission and returned to the Capital.

As Kang Xi reviewed the strategic locations of key roads and gates, he remembered what his father had said to him before he died.

Emperor Shun Zhi's great love was the Imperial Honoured Consort Lady Dong. After her death, Shun Zhi lost all interest in life, and he died six months later, one month before his 23rd birthday. Manchu emperors married early. When Kang Xi was born, his father was only sixteen years old. Kang Xi himself married the grand-daughter of Soni at the age of eleven, and the girl was formally made Empress. The marriage was arranged by the Grand Empress Dowager for political reasons, firstly, to gain the undying loyalty of Soni, and secondly, to prepare Kang Xi to rule in person, which he could only do after marriage.

Shun Zhi was very ill when he appointed Kang Xi as his heir. He summoned his son to his sick bed. 'Son, you must try to be a better emperor than I. We Manchus must learn to co-exist with the Han Chinese if we want to remain in this vast country. You must learn the Chinese language and their culture. You must promote capable Chinese men to help you govern the country.

I do not have many days left. I was younger than you when I ascended the throne. I lived the years of my childhood under a powerful regent. I will appoint four regents so that after I die, power will not concentrate in the hands of just one. The four regents will come from senior officials so that they will be able to keep in check the ambitions of powerful Imperial Princes.

Son, you must remember that for your own safety in the Forbidden City, the most important person in times of trouble is the Commander-in-Chief of the Nine Gates. Whoever holds this post must be trusted. His official rank is not high but he holds a key position in the Capital by controlling the nine gates leading to the Inner City. The present Commander-In-Chief of the Nine Gates is a protégé of Soni and can be trusted. Do not remove him until you are secure in your throne as Emperor.'

Kang Xi summoned the Commander-in-Chief of the Nine Gates. 'How long have you been in post?'

'Twelve years, Your Majesty.'

'Lord Oboi recommended your promotion to the Ministry of War. I overruled his recommendation.'

'Yes, Your Majesty.'

'Were you disappointed?'

'No, Your Majesty. Your humble servant values his position as the Commander-in-Chief of the Nine Gates and would prefer to stay close to Your Majesty.'

'Your promotion is long overdue.'

'Your Majesty, your humble servant is content with his post. Your humble servant does not seek promotion.'

'The post of Commander-in-Chief of the Nine Gates is not high in the pecking order of the government hierarchy, but it is a very important position. The holder must be a very trusted person.'

'Your humble servant swears by oath his loyalty to Your Majesty. Your humble servant swears this upon his own life and the lives of all his family members.'

Satisfied with the loyalty of his Commander, Kang Xi gave his instructions. He then summoned Songgotu and two Imperial Guards.

After hearing Kang Xi's plans, the Imperial Guards took their leave. The Emperor asked Songgotu, 'Your men were escorting the bandits who ambushed us on our route back to the Capital. Have they yet arrived?'

'Sire, none have arrived.'

'What of the soldiers escorting the bodies of the four dead assassins. Have they arrived at the Capital?'

'No, Sire.'

'One of the five assassins escaped. Has he been found?'

'No, Sire.'

'What of the soldiers escorting the dead bodies of the 'Scorpion Sting' and his wife, have they arrived at the capital?'

'No, Sire.'

'And the soldiers in the two boats behind us? Have they arrived at the Capital?'

'No, Sire. They have not arrived.'

'So we have absolutely no evidence of Oboi's involvement in the plot to kill us.'

'That is correct, Sire. We have no evidence at all.'

Kang Xi summoned his wrestling team of young eunuchs and revealed to them his real identity. He took them into his confidence and explained that he wanted them to help him arrest Oboi. The young eunuchs had lived in the Palace long enough to know all that was going on between Oboi and the Emperor. They needed no further explanation, and swore their allegiance to the Emperor.

Huang Ding explained to Tobie, Bussie and Flint that the men who had tried to kill them on the journey from Shaolin had been sent by Oboi. They could not understand why Oboi would go to such lengths to kill a Palace eunuch. Samara explained that it was to do with Palace politics. The boys had grown up in the monastery and had no knowledge of the outside world so they took her word for it. Toga told them that Oboi was an evil man. It was Oboi who had instigated the literary inquisitions in which tens of thousands of innocent Chinese scholars and their families were imprisoned, executed or taken into slavery. Farmlands had been seized by Oboi for his own bannermen reducing the farmers and landowners to poverty.

So when Kang Xi, still posing as Speck, told the boys of the Emperor's intention to arrest Oboi and asked them to join the wrestling team, the three boys did not hesitate and gladly offered their assistance.

XXII

FINAL JUSTICE

Oboi rose early in the morning to review the situation. All key roads leading to the Capital were guarded by his men. Most of the Imperial Guards patrolling the Forbidden City took their orders from him. He had at least a dozen men keeping a close watch in the Inner Court, especially around the Qian-Qing Palace.

Oboi had also infiltrated the Grand Secretariat, the Six Boards and the military by placing his men in key positions. Among his closest allies were the Minister of War, the Minister of Civil Office, the Minister of Revenue, the Grand Secretary Bambursan, and at least two Imperial Princes.

He was confident of his political strength. He had been angered when the Emperor refused to allow him to reverse a decision which had been approved through proper court procedure. He suffered further humiliation when the Emperor openly rebuked him for not paying attention when memorials were read out in court. The young Emperor was getting out of control and must be removed. Oboi's plans were flawless 'as a seamless heavenly robe'. But there is a saying, 'Human Connivance cannot defeat the Will of Heaven'. It is all in one's destiny, whether to rule or be ruled.

When Oboi rose from his bed, he felt a twitch in his left eye. A superstitious man, he wondered if something unlucky was about to happen. The first bad news came when he received a report that the Emperor had left Shaolin Monastery, and his whereabouts was unknown. The Abbot acknowledged that a palace eunuch by the name of Speck had stayed for a short while, but he had already left when the soldiers arrived. A search of the monastery had produced no results and the Vice-Commander and his troops were now on their way back to Beijing.

Soon afterwards Oboi's retainer returned. He had been with the Regimental Commander in the inn at the foot of Mount Song. It was he who had killed Shaolin's traitor monk, pierced Master Wei's shoulder with a dart, and advised the Regimental Commander how to conduct the raid on Shaolin Monastery in the search for the Third Prince.

The retainer reported to Oboi that the five assassins had failed in their mission. Four assassins had been killed and only the hawker had escaped. The retainer had tracked down the hawker in the woods, and together they had found the soldiers who were transporting the bodies of the four assassins to Beijing. They had killed the soldiers and buried their bodies, along with the dead bodies of the assassins, deep in the forest.

When the ambush at the postal relay station was unsuccessful, the retainer and the hawker had followed the soldiers escorting the attackers of Kang Xi. When the soldiers and prisoners rested for the night in an abandoned house, the retainer blew opiate in through the windows to drug them. The retainer and the hawker killed the soldiers but released the prisoners. The retainer had produced a gold plate inscribed with a black dragon and claimed that he was a representative of the Black Dragon Gang. He asked the men to return to their hide-outs until they received further instructions. He then set fire to the house. He told the hawker to return directly to Beijing and wait for further orders.

The retainer had seen 'Scorpion Sting' and his wife under arrest and it was he who had thrown the blades that killed them both. He later killed the soldiers who were transporting their bodies, and again buried all of them deep in the forest.

He had caught up with Kang Xi and his retinue on the river trip. He had seen the boat of Kang Xi attacked, and watched it being lifted over the waterfall. When he reached the other side of the waterfall, he found the boat capsized and floating on the river. There were no signs of Kang Xi and his retinue. He killed the soldiers in the boats following Kang Xi and threw their bodies into the river.

The retainer reported cautiously, 'My Lord, your humble servant suspects that 'Mystic' has been drowned.' 'Mystic' was their codename for Kang Xi.

'Have you found his body?'

'No, My Lord. It was a huge waterfall. The body may take time to resurface.'

'Has the hawker returned to Beijing?'

'My Lord, he has returned to Beijing and I have asked him to come to see you. The man's weakness is his fondness for money. My Lord has promised him a bounty even if the mission failed. He will come to claim his bounty.'

Oboi was immersed in thought when his guard reported that a man waited outside. The hawker came to see Oboi with some trepidation. It was the first time he had set foot inside Oboi's mansion, and he was taken straight to the Study. He was dazzled by its grandeur and magnificence. A beautiful black tiger skin lay on the floor. The walls were hung with swords, bows and arrows, buffalo horns and elephant tusks, and the shelves stuffed with precious artefacts and antiques.

Oboi welcomed the hawker warmly. The hawker had not expected the smile, and felt a little better. He kowtowed to Oboi, and reported that he and the other four assassins had failed in their mission. But he had erased all traces of evidence.

Oboi asked the hawker to take a seat. 'It is true that you failed in your mission. But you did the right thing. You did not let the fat innkeeper fall into the hands of our enemy. I have good news for you. We have achieved what we set out to do.'

The hawker felt much relieved. 'Congratulations, my Master.'

'Would you like to claim your bounty and retire in comfort for the rest of your life?'

The hawker said gratefully, 'Oh, yes, my Master. Your slave is looking forward to his retirement, although he'll greatly miss the pleasure of serving under his Master.'

Oboi asked his Chief Steward to bring out a chest. Inside the chest were gold bars worth 15,000 taels of silver. The hawker had never seen so much money. He could not take his eyes from the chest and could hardly believe that the money was to be his.

The retainer came in with a tray, on which stood a jug of wine and three wine cups. He said to the hawker, 'We won't be seeing each other again. Let's drink to your good health and retirement.'

The retainer asked the hawker to pick up a cup. He and Oboi then took the remaining cups. To set the mind of the hawker at ease, he allowed him to pour the wine.

Oboi said, 'To your retirement!'

The hawker was not a man to be easily deceived. He waited for Oboi and the retainer to drink first before he touched his wine. He swirled the wine slowly in the cup and put it to his nose to smell the fragrance. This was Oboi's best wine. He saw Oboi and the retainer drink from their cups and he was satisfied. Nevertheless he was anxious to leave. He drank his wine quickly and put down the cup. Immediately he felt irritation all over his body, his face and his arms. He scratched until blood seeped from the broken skin. His hands turned purple and the blood that trickled out was black. He knew then that he had been poisoned, and that even if he had succeeded in his mission, he would not have been allowed to live. After his death, his entire family would be killed. The last words he heard were the retainer saying, 'You see, the poison was on the surface of the wine jug, not in the wine.'

A guard announced the arrival of an Imperial Guard with a summons from the Emperor. Oboi was taken aback. Had the Emperor managed to return to the Palace?

Oboi was not concerned about seeing the Emperor at Qian-Qing Palace because he knew that this palace was surrounded by his own men. When he arrived with his three bodyguards, he was met by Grand Empress Dowager's bodyguard who told Oboi that the Emperor was waiting for him at the Palace of the Grand Empress Dowager, the Ci- Ning Palace. This meant he would not be able to take his bodyguards with him. No one was allowed to enter the Palace of the Grand Empress Dowager without her permission. Still Oboi was not worried. Ci-Ning Palace had at any one time only four guards. Oboi, being the Champion of Manchu, had very little regard for the so-called kung fu masters in the Palace. He could handle four or five of them easily. His men were nearby, and at a command from him, they would come.

The Emperor was seated next to the Grand Empress Dowager. Everything looked normal, with the usual eunuchs and palace maids. There were no Imperial Guards.

Oboi kowtowed to the Emperor, 'May Your Majesty live ten thousand years!' He kowtowed to the Grand Empress Dowager. 'May the Grand Empress Dowager live a thousand years!' No one should live a longer life than the Emperor. If the Emperor were to live ten thousand years, the next in rank, the Queen, Prince or Princess, could live only one thousand years.

'Rise, Lord Oboi, and take a seat.' The Emperor behaved as if nothing had happened. He was so young and yet he was unfathomable. A slight unease came over Oboi. Was this the same young boy whom he had dismissed as a weakling?

Kang Xi said amiably, 'Lord Oboi, recently I have been getting bored with reading Chinese classics. I have been amusing myself with other things, such as wrestling.'

Oboi was pleased to hear that the Emperor was giving up his studies. 'Your Majesty has become wiser. We Manchus are warriors and not scholars. Reading books makes a person weak and he will lose the will and strength to fight.'

Kang Xi nodded. 'My young eunuchs have formed a wrestling team. I am very proud of them. There is no better person than you, Lord Oboi, to test their achievements in wrestling. You are our Champion fighter, our *Baturu*. The boys would be honoured if you could show them how to perfect their skills. There are 15 boys in the team between the ages of 14 and 15. Will you accept the challenge, Lord Oboi?'

Oboi bowed. 'The honour is mine, Your Majesty.'

The wrestling room was set up at the Wu-Ying Palace, to the south of Ci-Ning Palace. To avoid Oboi's guards, Songgotu took Oboi through the Ci-Ning Garden. Oboi changed from his court dress to wrestling clothes and Songgotu led him to the wrestling room.

The Emperor and his two Imperial Guards watched the wrestling from a window outside. Oboi was not at all worried about the presence of the Imperial Guards. Even if they fought together, they would not be his match.

The Emperor had not deceived him. The boys were all very young. Oboi's attention was immediately drawn to Bussie who stood head and shoulders above the others. 'How old are you?'

Bussie replied, 'Fourteen, My Lord.'

Oboi took a liking to the boy. He would be good material to be trained as a bodyguard.

While Oboi spoke with Bussie, twelve eunuchs grabbed him from behind. Some seized his arms, some his legs, some wrapped their arms around his waist, and some tried to grab him at the throat. Oboi flung the eunuchs from him and sent them crashing to the floor. He was about to hit out at the eunuchs when he noticed Songgotu standing in the corner smiling. He thought that perhaps this was a game, and he had better not use too much force and harm the Emperor's playmates.

The eunuchs got up from the floor and came forward again. This time they clung steadfastly to Oboi's legs and arms. While Oboi was entangled with the eunuchs, Songgotu rushed towards Oboi with his sword. Oboi ducked but his leg was pierced by the sword. This was not a game. The Emperor wanted to kill him.

Oboi sneered at the Emperor's plan to send a team of young and unskilled boys to kill him. He let out a cry of battle. He spun round and flung the eunuchs across the room with such strength that several of them died instantly. He punched out at Songgotu, who collapsed to the floor. When Oboi advanced towards Songgotu to finish him off, Flint, Bussie and Tobie surrounded him. Bussie hit out hard and fast. Oboi was caught unaware. He summoned up all his internal force and received the full blow on his chest, staggering back a few steps.

Oboi was shocked. He had very powerful internal strength and was adept in the Iron Shirt kung fu. His body was harder than bricks. He stood like an Iron Tower and no one before had ever forced him to budge.

Bussie quickly followed up his attack. Like Bussie's other opponents, Oboi would not choose to 'die together' with Bussie. He moved away defensively. Tobie leapt forward to strike at the energy point located at Oboi's shoulder, disabling his arm. Flint followed with two quick blows with his right and left fists, striking Oboi on the back. Oboi crashed to the floor. He heard the cracking sound of his ribs as they broke and he spat blood. Where had the Emperor found three such young fighters?

The kung fu practised by Oboi depended on internal force, which was wrapped around him like an Iron Shirt. However, it had its weakness. If the practitioner fought someone with greater internal force, the protective 'iron shirt' shield could be pierced, and he would then not be able to exert his own internal force to defend himself. Flint had stronger internal force than Oboi, something which Oboi had not seen before.

Oboi bellowed like a wounded animal. He struggled to get up from the floor, but Flint and Bussie jumped on his back, pinning him down. Tobie struck Oboi at the back of his neck at the vital energy point 'Celestial Pillar', causing him to lose consciousness.

The Imperial Guards came with ropes, tethers and chains and arrested Oboi under the orders of the Emperor. The Emperor returned to Qian-Qing Palace where the Commander-in-Chief of the Nine Gates, the Commander General of the Outer Banners, the Imperial Princes and the ministers were waiting for him.

The Commander-in-Chief of the Nine Gates had closed all nine gates leading to the Inner City. The Commander-General of the Outer Banners marched into the Outer City and arrested Oboi's men. He met up with the Commander-in-Chief of the Nine Gates and they went together into the Imperial City and then to the Forbidden City. The final victory came when Oboi's men who were guarding the Qian-Qing Palace and other Inner Court palaces were taken down.

All the ministers, military officers and Imperial princes inside Qian-Qing Palace knelt before Kang Xi and kowtowed. 'May Your Majesty live ten thousand years, ten thousand years, ten thousand of ten thousand years!' At the age of 15, Kang Xi was finally in control of his own government.

Oboi was charged with 30 offences, including holding the Emperor in contempt, manipulating official appointments, blocking ministers' memorials to the Emperor, and organising a clique to promote selfish interests. The fourteen members of Oboi's clique, all senior military and civil officials, were arrested together with Oboi's son. They would be tried by the Council of Princes chaired by the Imperial Prince Giyesu.

During the twelve days of Oboi's trial, Tobie, Flint and Bussie looked everywhere for Storm. They looked in Oboi's mansion which had been impounded by court order, with no success. They knew only that Storm had brought to Shaolin a Palace eunuch named Speck.

While the trial was on-going, the boys were given a guided tour of the Forbidden City by Songgotu. Kang Xi, still known to them as Speck, took time off to take them to the hunting grounds at Nan-Yuan for three days. There they spent the days hunting and shooting, and the spoils of the day became their food in the evening, roasted over an open fire.

The boys stayed on in Wu-Ying Palace. One day in the palace, Huang Ding was plaiting Tobie's hair. Huang Ding looked into the mirror and saw their reflections. He said softly, 'If I were a girl, would you marry me?'

Tobie teased, 'No, I wouldn't marry you. If you were a girl, you would look so plain that no man would want to marry you.'

Huang Ding slapped Tobie and ran from the room crying. Tobie was confounded by the outburst of tears. How could a boy be so vain? Perhaps because eunuchs were not real men, they behaved like women.

The boys' meals were prepared by imperial cooks, which by all standards were of high quality. But no one could match the cooking of Tobie's uncle except perhaps Huang Ding. Tobie begged Songgotu to ask the young eunuch to come to see him. He said he had something very important to say to him.

Huang Ding was still angry, and Tobie tried to placate him. 'Huang Ding, I was only joking. If you were a girl, you would be a very pretty girl. Men from all over the world would come and propose to you. They would queue all the way from the Palace Entrance Gate to the Great Wall and over the Great Wall until it ends at … er…'

'Stupid! The Great Wall is 4,000 miles long and runs from Shanhaiguan pass in the east to Jiayuguan pass in the west.'

They made up and became friends again.

On day twelve of Oboi's trial, the Council of Princes found Oboi guilty of all thirty offences. Ten of Oboi's men were also found guilty. The Council recommended that they be executed, in many cases together with their family members. The guilty men's property was to be confiscated and their women and children enslaved. Kang Xi had not requested such severe punishment. He ratified the death sentences of nine of the men, and sentenced the others to a hundred lashes. The death sentences of Oboi and his son were commuted to imprisonment, and Oboi's other family members released. The officials involved in Oboi's clique were pardoned provided that they repented for what they had done.

The boys wanted to find out from Oboi if he knew where Storm was. Toga found out where Oboi was being held and took them there, but when they arrived they found the prison doors open and guards lying on the floor, dead or seriously wounded. Two men, holding Storm by the arms, emerged from a cell. Oboi was with them.

This was a high security prison. Oboi had arrested Storm and hidden him in this prison, but he had never expected to be imprisoned there himself. One of the men holding Storm was a fake prisoner planted by Oboi to keep Storm under 24 hour surveillance. The other man holding Storm was Oboi's retainer who had broken into the prison to rescue his master.

Toga, Flint and Bussie rushed forward to the two men, killing one and wounding the other. The moment Oboi saw the boys, he thrust his sword through Storm's chest. 'I would rather have you dead than let the others have you.'

Tobie ran to help Storm. He could not let Oboi withdraw his sword, or Storm would die. The sight of Oboi was frightening. He was a different person from the man in the wrestling room. Then Oboi had been arrogant, dressed in the finest livery, projecting an image of elegance and power. The Oboi before Tobie now was a wild animal, dirty, sweaty and smelly. Bristles protruded wildly from his chin, and blood-shot eyes bulged from his eye sockets. He was raging like a mad man. Oboi's large hands grabbed at Tobie's neck until he could not breathe. It was probably his fat neck that saved him. Tobie pulled out his dagger and thrust it into Oboi's heart. Oboi staggered back. He looked at the dagger embedded in his chest. Pointing a finger at Tobie, he laughed hysterically, 'This is my judgment, my just dessert.' Tobie pulled out his dagger. Blood gushed from Oboi's wound and he dropped dead to the floor.

Bussie carried Storm in his arms. Toga advised the boys to go back to Shaolin monastery immediately. Tobie had killed Oboi in self-defence, but there was no knowing how the Emperor would react to the death. In any case, Storm needed urgent medical treatment. There was no time to say good bye to Speck. The horses were ready outside. Flint sat Storm in front of him on the horse, and hastened towards Shaolin monastery.

Men from Heaven and Earth Society also found the prison where Oboi was being held. When they made their way into the prison, Oboi was already dead and the prison in chaos. The Triad members slipped away disappointed. They had lost the honour of killing Oboi and the chance to show their leadership of the anti-manchu movement.

XXIII

THROUGH THE WOODEN MEN LANE

The Emperor was woken in the middle of the night and told about the death of Oboi. He guessed that the short fat intruder who killed Oboi must have been Tobie. Tobie had killed out of self-defence and he would not take any action against him. The prison break-in was inexcusable, but it had been the boys who had helped him to arrest Oboi, and they had stopped Oboi escaping from the prison. Their merits more than compensated for their offences. He decided not to further the investigation into Oboi's death. He was fond of the boys and would miss their company. After the death of Oboi, Kang Xi released Oboi's son from prison.

The boys made their way towards Shaolin Monastery, with Storm slipping in and out of consciousness. The first night of the journey, he woke and called for Flint. He whispered something in Flint's ear. He waited until Flint gave his promise, then he closed his eyes and died. The boys were distraught. Storm had been a father figure to them. His farmhouse had been their home. When they had problems, it was Storm that they went to. They carried Storm's body back to Shaolin Monastery and buried him near his farm house.

The boys had broken a rule of Shaolin monastery by leaving the monastery before their graduation. Although they had left at the Abbot's request, they still had to bear the consequences. They were punished with six months' confinement in a secluded place.

The Abbot said to them, 'You should look at the six-month confinement not as a punishment, but as a blessing. Use this period to hone your skills and reflect upon your fighting tactics, and be ready for your graduation test. The most important test in the graduation will be the Wooden Men Lane. Try to visualise all possible forms of attack from the wooden men and think about your strategy. At the end of the six-month confinement, I will call for you and explain the tests we have set for you.'

None of the boys had ever seen the wooden men, but they had heard stories about them. The 'Wooden Men Lane' had long been used as a final test for pupils who wished to graduate and leave the monastery. The wooden men were known for their size, the toughness of the wood and the clever mechanical devices attached to them. Those who wished to graduate had to fight their way through the 'Wooden Men Lane'. Indeed, the expression 'Through the Wooden Men Lane' had come to mean graduation from Shaolin kung fu.

Songgotu was sent by Emperor Kang Xi to Shaolin Monastery to look for Storm and the boys. He learned that Storm had died and that the boys were confined for breaking the rules of the monastery. The Emperor did not wish to exert pressure on them to disclose Storm's secret. He knew that the secret must have to do with Emperor Wan Li's treasure. He valued his friendship with them and hoped one day that they would give him their loyalty and respect. The boys had been brought up in the martial arts world, a world in which honour and loyalty were placed above everything else, including one's own life. As far as the Emperor was concerned, the case of Emperor Wan Li's treasure was closed.

The boys worked hard during their six month confinement, meditating and practising kung fu. This period proved most difficult for Tobie. He found the food unpalatable. He refused to eat for the first day, then his stomach got the better of him. Soon he forgot about food as Flint pressed him on with exercises. Tobie joined in reluctantly. His old problem of 'mental blocks' came back. He could not summon up his internal force. On the one hand, Tobie was anxious to pass the Shaolin test. On the other, he was stubborn in his refusal to practise kung fu. The *Qi* flow was directed by a person's will. As a result of Tobie's aversion to kung fu, he had mentally blocked his *Qi* flow. No matter how hard Flint and Bussie tried to persuade Tobie, it just did not work.

One morning before dawn, Flint and Bussie dragged Tobie out of bed. They had prepared some wooden blocks shaped like the arms of the wooden men and began to hit out at Tobie. 'What do you think you are doing?' Tobie yelled.

Flint and Bussie said nothing and continued the attack. They were merciless. 'Stop, stop, why are you doing this to me?' Flint and Bussie ignored him and went on hitting him.

Tobie tried to run away with his superb *Qingong* steps, but Flint caught up with him. When the pain became too much, he began to defend himself. The pain dissolved his mental block. He spread the *Qi* around his body and began to strike back, kicking out with force and strength. They fought until Tobie was flat out, collapsed on the ground.

They took him back to the hut. He was badly bruised. Flint applied wound powder, and he and Bussie transferred their own internal energies to him. Flint told him that he was only suffering from external injuries and he would soon recover. Tobie was angry. He refused to speak to his friends and he refused to eat. But by night time he was hungry. He slipped out of bed, helped himself to three bowls of rice, and finished the food left out for him on the table.

The next day, Flint and Bussie let Tobie rest for the morning. In the afternoon, they dragged him out again. The whole process was repeated with Tobie again ending up badly bruised. This went on for days. He started to coordinate his movements with Flint and Bussie. He knew his friends were trying to help him pass the test so that he could leave the monastery together with them. He also discovered that he could summon up his *Qi* at will.

At the end of the six months, the boys were released from their confinement and told to ready themselves for their graduation test. They were taken to the top of a high cliff overlooking a deep ravine. A rope was tied from the top of the cliff to the other side. The Abbot said, 'Walk across the tightrope. When you reach the other side, you will head north. There will be further challenges on the way. Each time you overcome a challenge, head north again until you find Wooden Men Lane. We have made the wooden-men test exceptionally difficult for you.

Normally we design only 18 wooden men, but for the three of you, we have designed 108. However, instead of going in one by one as is normally the case, we will allow the three of you go into the Lane together. You have learned all of the 108 movements of the wooden men, but the combination of their movements will be very different from what you have been practising. You will need to apply your skills intelligently, and to think fast on your feet.

'Pass through Wooden Men Lane, and you will enter a court yard. There you will face your final challenge. You must complete all your tasks within two hours. At the end of two hours, the Tower Bell will chime and the gate at the courtyard will open for one minute only. If you fail to go through the gate within the time, the gate will close. This will mean that you have failed your test and you will have to return to the monastery to retake your test in another six months.'

Walking across a tightrope posed no problem for the boys. They had practised this skill soon after they had learned to walk. Nevertheless, the sheer height of the cliffs was daunting. When they had walked halfway across, they heard a loud rolling sound behind them, and looked back to see a team of wooden men on wheels locked on to the rope, sliding towards them at speed.

Flinted shouted, 'Jump down and grip the rope with your hands. Tobie, use your dagger and cut the rope.'

They clung on and Tobie cut the rope in the nick of time. The wooden men fell down into the ravine. The rope swung towards the cliff on the opposite side and the boys gripped on to the rocky surface with their feet. They scaled the mountain using the rope, until they reached the top of the cliff. Tobie looked down at the ravine. 'Wow! Our *Shifus* are cruel. What if we had fallen?'

Flint laughed. 'Don't be silly. Our *Shifus* would surely have found a way to save us. They wouldn't let us die.'

They headed north as instructed by the Abbot, and came upon a stretch of swamp land. They threw a twig into the swamp. The twig was swallowed. Flint lopped down a tree with the side of his palm. The tree was chopped into rectangular wooden blocks by the boys, using the force of their palms. The plan was to use the *Qingong* step 'Dragonfly Skims the Water Surface'. A dragonfly lightly touches the water surface and propels itself up again into the air. One boy would throw a wooden block high into the air so that the next boy could land lightly on the block with his foot. He would then muster all his internal force and propel himself into the air before the block sank into the swamp, and another block would already have been thrown by the time he touched down. Flint reckoned it would take three wooden blocks to reach the other side.

Flint was the one who threw the blocks. Bussie and Tobie successfully jumped across the swamp to the other side. Flint threw more wooden blocks across the swamp to the grassland on the opposite side. Tobie then threw the blocks back across the swamp and Flint too crossed successfully. It was an act of perfect timing combining pace, agility, internal force and accuracy.

They were now at the Wooden Men Lane. During their six months in confinement, the boys had spent long hours discussing the tactics they would use. They decided that Bussie's tactic of 'dying together with the enemy' would be useless against the wooden men. Even if the wooden men broke an arm or leg, they could carry on attacking with that broken limb. As the wooden men had no energy points, Tobie's skill in striking the energy points to disable an opponent would also prove useless.

One good thing about the wooden men was their lack of internal force. Their strength depended solely on the hardness of the wood. They could not project over a distance. Their power to injure was limited to actual contact. The wooden men could not think. They were machines and their movements were pre-set according to a fixed pattern.

The boys had learned all the 108 Wooden Men movements. The routine contained 108 fighting poses. Some of the poses would not work against the wooden men. Poses which aimed at jabbing eyes, striking the temple, slapping the ear, locking the throat, pulling the hair, pressing the hands, or attacking the face, chest and jaws, would be ineffectual. Even if their heads, chests, or faces were broken, the wooden men could continue to attack. A number of poses attacked the genitals. These too would be ineffectual against the wooden men. Furthermore, the Shaolin masters discouraged the use of such fighting poses, as attacking a man's genitals might affect his virility, and a man's inability to procreate was a shame and a curse upon the family. Shaolin disciples were banned from using such fighting poses except as a last resort. The boys were confident the wooden men would not be designed to use such poses on them.

They expected that the wooden men would use more attacking poses and not be too bothered with defending. There were 108 men and most of them could be sacrificed. After all, these were only machines.

The three boys' internal force was stronger than that of the wooden men. Their force could break through brick walls. It was the large number of wooden men that was the problem.

The Wooden Men Lane ran through a cave. The boys peered inside. There stood the wooden men lined six in a row, a total of 18 rows. They were bigger than the boys had imagined, over seven-foot tall and broad. They filled the cave with barely any space between them. The ceiling of the cave was low with less than a foot over the head of the men. The low ceiling was designed to discourage the deployment of high leaps and *Qingong*. The whole purpose of the wooden men test was to test the pupils' fundamental kung fu skills in kicks and punches.

The boys knew that once they crossed the threshold, they would trigger the wooden men to action. They had worked out a strategy. Before they stepped in, they put forward their left legs to adopt the fighting pose 'Twin Dragons Rise from Sea', thrusting their palms towards the wooden men. The force from their palms was so powerful that immediately several of the wooden men were sent crashing to the ground. They advanced into the cave using the same pose, grounding more wooden men.

Once in the cave, they formed a circle and moved round to defend each other and to attack the wooden men at the same time. They changed to the fighting pose 'A Hundred Birds Return to Their Nests', a sweeping movement, where the right and left arm move in continuous semi-circles to hit as many wooden men as possible.

The wooden men marched towards them. Some were punching out continuously alternating between a left and right punch. Some moved sideways, hitting out with their fists. Some kicked out continuously, alternating between the right and left leg. If an opponent tried to move to avoid the punches, he would be met by wooden men on left and right. If the opponent tried to step back, a wooden man would kick from behind.

The first wooden man came towards them with straight left and right punches. Bussie moved in quickly and crouched down to grab hold of both of its legs. Flint and Tobie each grabbed hold of one of the arms and the three of them flung the wooden man towards those men lined up in the back rows. The wooden men were unable to distinguish who was their real opponent and they began to fight amongst themselves.

Flint and Tobie quickly turned to tackle the wooden men moving sideways with fists. Bussie used his fists to break the knee joints of the wooden man kicking from behind. The wooden man fell to the ground and the three of them again threw him towards those wooden men in the back rows.

The success of the boys' tactic depended a lot on their pace. The throwing of wooden men, then turning round and attacking the wooden men at the side and back, was done in a flash. No matter how skilful the mechanic was with his design, the wooden men he created were unable to move or turn faster than the boys.

The most difficult to tackle were the wooden men fitted with continuous windmill palms. The normal defence was to make continuous kicks at the genitals, but wooden men were immune to such kicks. The boys had to kick instead at the knee joints to bring the wooden men down.

They kept together and moved in circles. They aimed only at breaking shoulder joints, knee joints and hips. Eventually they brought down all the wooden men, and left them lying, detached from their limbs.

They reached the end of the Wooden Men Lane. Their exit was blocked by a huge burning cauldron. Tobie peered beyond into the courtyard to find out what lay ahead for them. He was surprised to find that for their final test they were to fight the 18 Lohans.

The 18 Lohans were 18 Shaolin senior monks. People had heard of Shaolin's 18 Lohans but very few had seen them. They lived in seclusion and spent their days meditating and practising kung fu. The 18 Lohans were Shaolin's most lethal striking force, called to action only if Shaolin Monastery needed to defend itself from serious attack. Even when Shaolin was under siege by the Heaven and Earth Triad Society, the 18 Lohans had not been summoned. So the Lohans were surprised when they were called upon to assess pupils' abilities in the graduation test.

They had no knowledge of Flint and Bussie, but they knew Tobie from when he was a small child. They remembered that the fat little boy always had a sweetmeat in his hand, perched on his uncle's shoulder, watching them practise their Lohan Kung Fu. The monks were fond of the child and had not objected to his presence. Tobie had always looked younger than his age. It was only when he had reached seven years that the monks forbade Tobie to visit them anymore. The Lohans would have been shocked if they knew that Tobie had learned their practising routines, their formation line, their ways of grouping and regrouping, and their attacking and defending tactics. What Tobie had seen when he was a child had been stored in his head.

Tobie told the others what he knew about the 18 Lohans. They quickly devised a strategy. But they had to pass the cauldron first. The boys grasped the burning cauldron with their hands, turned it round, and squeezed past one by one. The one who exited would continue to turn the cauldron. It was like walking through a revolving door.

Inside the courtyard, the Lohans lined up opposite the boys. They were a formidable sight, all of them Bussie's size. They looked like the 18 statues of Lohans flanking the Trinity Buddha in the *Daoxiongbaodin*, the Grand Hall of the Shaolin Monastery.

The Lohans had varied their 18 Lohan Hands and created new sequences. The sequences were linked but forever changing, making it difficult for the opponent to anticipate their movements. When the eighteen of them fought together, the force they generated was tremendous. Their open palms followed one after another, like the tidal waves of the roaring Yellow River, ferocious and unstoppable. Their movements were so well co-ordinated that even if their formation was broken, each one knew exactly where the others were and they could regroup immediately. This was the result of many years of practising together.

If it was a fight of one against one, none of the Lohans could have matched the boys in power or pace. But the boys were greatly outnumbered. They saluted the Lohans with the Shaolin greeting pose. Keeping their hands together with finger tips pointing upwards, they bowed low, a courtesy shown by junior disciples in deference to their seniors. The boys had summoned up their internal force and spread it around their bodies to protect themselves. Almost as soon as the greeting was over, the boys thrust both their palms and struck at the Lohans. This was the same fighting pose 'Twin Dragons Rise from Sea' which they had used as their opening strikes against the wooden men. Flint then leapt in mid-air, and kicked out successively with his right and left leg, while Bussie defended Flint by making wide sweeping movements with his arms, punching out in all directions. Tobie followed swiftly, striking at the vital energy points of the Lohans. Before the Lohans knew what was happening, six Lohans had been disabled and brought to the ground.

The boys did not waste a second. While the Lohans were dazed, and before they were able to regroup, the boys used the same technique again, with Flint kicking out in mid-air, Bussie defending and Tobie immobilizing the Lohans. Another six Lohans were felled. The remaining six Lohans realised that they had greatly underestimated the boys. They had started out half heartedly, planning to form two circles round the boys, but they took their time in summoning their internal force. They were greatly taken aback by the first strike which saw six of them fall. They had never faced the need for such a fast regrouping. After another six fell, the remaining Lohans turned serious. They summoned up their internal energy and circled round the boys.

The boys also formed a circle. The Lohans lashed out their palms, this time without reservation. The moment their arms were raised, the boys anticipated their movements, and leapt high up and out of the Lohan circle. Flint and Bussie kicked from behind and Tobie quickly struck their energy points. Another three Lohans fell to the ground.

Bussie and Tobie brought down two more Lohans. It was now only Flint against the best of the Lohan fighters. The monk struck out hard at Flint, but the internal force rebounded and hit him in the chest. Flint was using a technique he had learnt from the 'Tendon Transformation' kung fu, by which he borrowed the internal force from the monk and diverted the force back to him.

The monk looked to be seriously injured. His face turned blue and he gasped for air. Flint sat the monk down. He sat behind him, legs crossed as in meditation, and put his palms behind the monk's back to transfer his energy to him. Bussie and Tobie sat behind Flint. Bussie put his palms behind Flint and Tobie put his palms behind Bussie. In this way, the internal force from Tobie, Bussie and Flint passed to the monk.

The tower bell chimed. The monk opened his eyes. 'Go, the door will close'. But Flint would not leave him. The three boys were of one heart, they could not ignore a dying man. The other monks cried out for Bussie and Tobie to go, and to leave Flint to look after the monk. How little the Lohans knew them. The boys were as close as brothers. They ignored the pleadings of the monks.

The door at the end of the courtyard remained open for one minute and then slowly closed. The monk's colour returned, and he thanked them. 'I'm sorry that I have delayed your departure.'

The door opened again, and in walked the three Elders, the old Abbot and the present Abbot. The boys kowtowed. They apologised for failing their graduation test.

The yellow-faced elder Qing Wang said, 'If you had exited when the door opened, you could have left Shaolin monastery.' He paused, and his voice cracked. 'But you would have had to leave behind all the kung fu skills you have learned from us.'

Seeing the bewilderment on the boys' faces, the elder explained. 'We would have had to take away all your kung fu skills by breaking your tendons. A person who puts his self interest before compassion walks in the path of darkness. He will be blinded by greed and desire until he brings his own destruction.

'You have reached such a high level of kung fu that few people in this world could hope to subdue you. For this reason, we designed the toughest graduation test for you. We can not create a monster and let it loose to harm mankind.'

Elder Qing Wang smiled. 'The final test was a test of your character. You are good boys, you are brave and intelligent and most importantly, you have compassion in your hearts. We are proud of you. I now announce that you have successfully graduated and are free to leave the monastery. Remember always that you are disciples of Shaolin. Once you are a disciple, you remain a disciple to the end of your life. You must abide by the rules of the monastery and the teachings of Buddha. If you ever do a bad deed or break the rules of Shaolin, our disciples will go after you no matter where you are, to bring you back to Shaolin monastery to face your punishment.'

The boys knocked their heads repeatedly on the ground, vowing that they would never break a rule of Shaolin, nor do any deed that would bring shame to the monastery.

'When you leave this monastery, you will carry with you the spirit of a true martial artist,' said Elder Qing Wang. 'You will oppose the wicked, you will seek out the weak and relieve the oppressed, and you will uphold justice at all times. You will be Heroes of Shaolin.'

The Abbot had thought the boys would be unable to defeat the Lohans. He had therefore asked the Lohans to feign defeat. In the end the boys performed much better than expected. The injured monk was not nearly as badly hurt as he made out to be. If Tobie had not known about the Lohan's practising routine and their strategies, and if the Lohan had prepared their combat seriously, the three boys would not have been able to defeat the 18 Lohans fighting together.

When the boys returned to the monastery, they learned that Leo had passed his graduation test and had already left the monastery. The boys were keen to follow Leo and to venture into the world of 'River and Lake' now that they had graduated in

Shaolin kung fu. The Chef urged them to stay on for a while. The New Year was round the corner, the weather was cold and unpleasant for travel, and it would be better for them to set out in spring.

The boys went to stay with the Chef in his hut. They had graduated and could no longer use the pupils' dormitories. Snow began to melt, the weather turned warmer, and finally spring arrived. The boys were preparing for their journey when Toga called on the monastery. He was looking for Haidi. Haidi had left home without Sir Qin's knowledge and had gone missing. The boys were anxious to help.

And so the next morning the friends, no longer boys but recognised masters of Shaolin kung fu, set off together to join in the search for Haidi. The Chef prepared them dried food and provisions to take with them on their journey. He walked with them until they reached the border of Henan Province. Then after embracing Tobie, he turned sorrowfully back to Shaolin.

The friends barely looked back, so keen were they to experience the adventures of the world. The search for Haidi, who had become their friend while he was at Shaolin, would be their first opportunity to show their skills and courage to those beyond the monastery. With their packs on their back and their weapons at their waist, they marched forward with excitement.

Flint's two sparrowhawks flew behind, following them as they embarked on their journey.

AUTHOR'S NOTES

(All weights and measures, units, time and dates are converted to English standards. The actual age of the characters is used instead of the Chinese age. Chinese age could be one or two years older than this age.)

PROLOGUE

1. *Han Chinese.* Han Chinese people are Ethnic Chinese. They are supposedly descendants of the Yellow Emperor who reigned from 2696 to 2589 BC.

I
THE BROTHERHOOD

2. *The City of Kaifeng.* Qin Guan, a poet of the Song Dynasty (960AD to 1279AD), described Kaifeng as 'surrounded by level land in all directions, with a convergence of roads which connect it with the Chu river to the south, the Han river to the west, the Zhao river to the north, and the Qi river to the east ... These waterways teem with boats, the bow of one touching the stern of another, while men, carts and animals jam the roads in an endless flow from every corner of the country.' (Xu Xin: The Jews of Kaifeng, China.)

3. *Beijing.* When Ming dynasty was first established in 1368, the capital was moved from Dadu (meaning 'The Big Capital) to Nanjing. The name 'Dadu' was then changed to 'Beiping' by the founding emperor of Ming. In 1406 when Emperor Yong Le ascended the Ming throne, he changed the name 'Beiping' to 'Beijing'. In 1421 he moved the capital from Nanjing to Beijing. Nanjing means 'The Southern Capital' and Beijing means 'The Northern Capital' During the Ming and Qing dynasties, Beijing

was also known as 'Jingshi' meaning 'The Capital'. For convenience, the capital is referred to here as 'Beijing'.

In 1927 Beijing was renamed 'Beiping' when the Nationalist Party established the capital in Nanjing. On 1st October 1949, the Communist Party was formally established. The capital moved back to Beiping and the name changed back to 'Beijing'.

4. *Tartar Barbarians*. Manchus were called 'Da-Zi' by Han Chinese, meaning 'barbarians from the Tartar race'.

5. *Li ZiCheng*. He came from a poor rural family in Shaaxi, and later became leader of an insurrectionary peasant army. His rebel army grew in size and seized Beijing on 25th April 1644. The Ming Emperor Chong Zhen committed suicide. Li had established his kingdom in Xian a few months earlier, and called it 'Da Shun'.

Li ZiCheng, Wu SanGui & Chen YuanYuan. Li captured the Ming general Wu SanGui's father to force Wu to surrender but Wu was undecided. At the time Wu had the important job of guarding the north-east to hold off the invading Manchus. According to popular tales, it was only when Li claimed Wu's favourite concubine Chen YuanYuan for himself that Wu joined forces with the Manchus and defeated Li at Shanhaiguan. Li retreated to Beijing and retaliated by beheading Wu's father.

Death of Li ZiCheng. On 3rd June 1644, Li proclaimed himself 'Emperor' under the reign title 'Yong Chang'. The next day, on the 4th June, he fled Beijing. Li first fled southwest to Xian, then to Wuchang, and finally a year later, in the summer of 1645, he was surrounded by pursuing Manchus in the mountains of Jiangxi Province, known as the Nine Palaces Mountain, where he died. He was said either to have committed suicide or to have been beaten to death by villagers by mistake when he was trying to steal some food.

6. *Chen YuanYuan*. She was popularly known as the woman who brought down the Ming Dynasty. Originally a singsong girl from Jiangnan, she was first procured for Emperor Chong Zhen when

his favourite concubine died, but the offer was declined. She was then presented to Wu SanGui who fell for her at first sight and made a payment of one thousand taels of silver as his betrothal gift to the bride. Wu then rushed back to the northern front on orders of Emperor Chong Zhen to defend Ningyuan and Shanhaiguan pass against the Manchu troops. Before Wu and Chen YuanYuan could meet again, Beijing fell to the rebels. Chen YuanYuan caught the eye of the rebel chief Li ZiCheng who took her and claimed her for himself. The popular tale went on to say that when Wu heard this, he was so furious that he defected to the Manchus to get his lady back, and so caused the downfall of the Ming Dynasty.

7. *Hooked Spear*. This hooked spear was a weapon invented by the Song General Yue Fei to chop off the legs of the enemy's chained horses, and it had enabled him to defeat the invading 'Jins'.

8. *'Jins' and 'Manchus'*. The 'Jins' were ancestors of the Manchus. They originally came from the Jurchen tribes which settled in the vast territorial region of Manchuria in north-east Asia. At the time, Manchuria bordered Russia in the north, Mongolia in the west, China in the south and south-west, Korea in the south-east and was separated from Japan in the east by the Sea of Japan. It was traditionally the homeland of the Qidans, Jurchens, Tungus and Eastern Turks. After the Manchu Conquest, Manchuria became part of China. Now, the region previously known as Manchuria is divided between China and Russia, the Russian half known as 'Outer Manchuria' and the Chinese half as 'Inner Manchuria'. The Chinese half comprises the provinces of Jilin, Heilongjiang and Liaoning.

Nurhaci united the Jurchen tribes and created the 'Later Jin Dynasty' in 1616. Abahai who succeeded him was aware of the Chinese hatred of the 'Jins' who invaded China in the twelfth century and occupied northern China for over one hundred years. When he became emperor in 1636, he changed the name of the Dynasty to 'Great Qing' and banned the use of 'Jins' in favour of 'Manchus'.

In 1643 Abahai died without setting foot in the Forbidden City. The Manchu Conquest was led by his younger brother Dorgon eight months later. The Manchu troops entered the Forbidden City on 6 June 1644. Abahai's ninth son, Emperor Shun Zhi, became the first Qing Emperor to rule in China. At the time, Shun Zhi was six years old and his uncle Dorgon became the Regent.

After the Manchus entered Beijing, the Ming Princes continued to fight in the south. It was only in 1662 when the last Ming Pretender, the Prince of Gui, was executed that the Ming Empire came to an end, and China was unified once again by the Manchus.

9. *Haohan*. Literal meaning of *Haohan* is 'good fella'. *Haohans* are brave men who put their honour and loyalty before their lives.

10. *Taiwan and Koxinga*. Marshall Zheng ChengGong's hometown was in Fujian Province, but he was born in Japan. His father Zheng ZhiLong was originally a maritime merchant and a pirate, and was eventually offered amnesty by the Ming court and rose to the rank of Regional Commander. The Manchus seized Beijing in 1644, but the Ming princes were fighting back in the south-eastern coastal areas. The father Zheng ZhiLong arranged for his son Zheng ChengGong to serve the Ming Pretender, Prince of Tang. However, the father was also an opportunist who defected to the Manchus in 1646 and opened the way for the capture and execution of Prince of Tang. The son Koxinga greatly disapproved of his father's doings. They went their separate ways.

Zheng ChengGong was popularly known as Koxinga, a Dutch romanization of the Chinese title '*Gao Xing Ye*' meaning 'The Lord with the Imperial Surname'. He was given the honour to use the Imperial surname 'Zhu' by the Prince of Tang because of his loyalty to Ming. The Prince further bestowed upon him the title 'Field Marshall of the Punitive Expedition'. After the death of Prince of Tang, Koxinga supported another Ming Pretender, the Prince of Gui, who awarded him the title 'Prince of Yanping'.

Koxinga continued to wage war against the Qing armies and raided the coastal regions of Fujian, Zhejiang, Guangdong and Jiangsu. He had his operational bases in Xiamen and Jinmen. In 1959 he made the fatal decision of attacking Nanjing and suffered a huge defeat. He gave up Xiamen and Jinmen and turned his attention to Taiwan. At the time Taiwan was occupied by the Dutch.

In 1661, Koxinga's father and brother were killed by the Manchus when Koxinga refused to surrender. His Japanese mother was raped by Manchu soldiers while on her way to join Koxinga in Taiwan and she committed suicide. To rub salt into the wound, the Manchus desecrated Koxinga's family ancestral graves. All this greatly angered Koxinga. He determined to fight the Manchus to the end.

In April 1661, Koxinga and his army landed in Taiwan. After nine months of intense fighting, in February 1662, the Dutch surrendered and left the island, ending 38 years of Dutch rule in Taiwan. The Dutch left Koxinga 'trade goods and cash estimated to be worth 1 million ounces of silver.' (Jonathan Spence: The Search for Modern China)

Koxinga died four months later in June 1662 at the age of 38. There were differing opinions regarding his sudden death. Just before his death, he had learned that his eldest son, Zheng Jing, was having an affair with his younger brother's wet nurse and the relationship had produced a child. Koxinga ordered the child to be killed but the order was not carried out. Koxinga died shortly afterwards. Some said that he killed himself. Some said that he died in a fit of madness after he learned of his son's affair. But the most likely cause of his death was probably the malaria which was prevalent in Taiwan at the time.

The former name of Taiwan was Formosa. The Portuguese were the first westerners to arrive in the island at the beginning of the 16th century. They were impressed by the beauty of the island and named it 'Ilha Formosa' meaning 'beautiful island'. However the Portuguese withdrew from the island and chose instead to keep Macao, a tiny piece of land at the tip of the peninsula 70 km south-west of Hong Kong and 145 km from Guangzhou, as their main operational base in south-east Asia.

After the Portuguese, the Dutch came to Taiwan along with the Spaniards. The Dutch drove out the Spaniards and occupied the Island for 38 years before they too were driven out by Koxinga.

In ancient Chinese documents, Taiwan was referred to by various names including 'Peng Lai', or 'Liu Chiu'. The name 'Taiwan' was termed near the end of the Ming Dynasty.

II
YIN AND YANG

11. *Acupuncture and Chinese Medicine*. Acupuncture is based on the theories of *Yin* and *Yang* (literary meaning of *Yin* is shade and *Yang* is light), the *Qi* channels and their interconnection with the internal organs Five Viscera and Six bowels (The five viscera are the heart, spleen, lungs, liver, and kidneys. The six bowels are the stomach, bladder, gall bladder, large intestines, small intestines, and the Triple Burners '*SanJiao*'). There are numerous energy points on the external pathway of the *Qi* channels. Originally only 365 such points were identified, but the number identified has now increased to about 2,000. (Stephen Barrett, M.D.: Acupuncture, Qigong and 'Chinese Medicine')

The treatise on *Yin* and *Yang* is expounded in an early medical book known as 'The Yellow Emperor's Classic of Internal Medicine'. This is the earliest and the most important book on Chinese medicine. It develops the theory that a man's health and illness are related to the balance or imbalance of the *Yin* and *Yang* in his body. It inspires the use of moxibustion and acupuncture to cure illnesses. Although the book is attributed to the Yellow Emperor who reigned from 2696 to 2589 BC, many scholars believe the book was written at a much later date, around the 5th century BC.

12. *Daoism*. Daoism is China's ethnic religion with its own cosmology and a pantheon of deities. Its exact date or place of birth is not clear. The Daoists believe the religion started in China some 4700 years ago when revelations of the *Dao* or the Way were first made to the Yellow Emperor by Guang ChengZi, an incarnate of Laozi.

214

The Daoist Bible, the *Daodejing* or The Way and Its Power, is attributed to the work of Laozi, an archivist during the late Zhou Dynasty (1046BC to 221BC) around the 6th or 5th century BC. Laozi is generally accepted as the Father of Daoism. According to Daoist myths, the universe began with the *Dao* and Laozi is the incarnation of the *Dao* or the Way itself.

Through the ages, the Daoist religion evolved, constantly changing, adapting and reinventing itself. The Daoist religion itself is not a unified religion and consists of a combination of teachings. There is much borrowing from Buddhism and Confucianism. By the time of the Qing Dynasty, the Daoist fusion of Buddhism and Confucianism was so thorough that its pantheon of deities had included the Daoist Immortals, Buddhist bodhisattvas and Confucian sages. (Isabelle Robinet: Taoism; L.Kohn: Taoist Mystical Philosophy: The Scripture of Western Ascension; Eva Wong: The Shambhala Guide to Taoism)

Daoist Philosophy. Daoism is basically concerned with good health, longevity and immortality. These aims can be achieved by following Daoist ideology and practices.

The fundamental philosophical concept is '*wuwei*' or 'non-intervention'. It advocates a state of harmony between human, heaven and earth by letting nature take its own course without human intervention. It rejects established values as being too artificial and favours '*ziran*', which means natural or spontaneous. The ideals of a Daoist sage are therefore total serenity and tranquillity of the mind bereft of emotions and passions, withdrawal from the affairs of the world and following the course of nature without intervention. Daoist sages are often hermits living in seclusion in mountain caves.

Daoist Practices. Daoist practices can be roughly divided into External Alchemy and Internal Alchemy. Most Daoists practise both Internal Alchemy and External Alchemy. External Alchemy involves the use of furnaces and cauldrons with which the ingredients, mainly minerals and herbs, are compounded into a pill or elixir which is believed to bring immortality. In Daoist Internal Alchemy, it is believed that all essential ingredients are found inside the human body which can be refined and which can achieve the same effect of longevity without the external use of elixir. The Daoist Internal Alchemy is therefore concerned with the cultivation of *Qi* and *Qi* flow.

Qi, Yin and Yang. The universe, according to Daoists, develops from a single component, the Primordial Breath (*Yuan-Qi*). The creation began when the Primordial Breath was split into *Yang* and *Yin*. 'The *Yang* was a pure, light breath which moved upward and created Heaven. The *Yin* was an opaque, heavy breath which moved downward and formed the Earth' (Isabelle Robinet: Taoism). The make up of the human being is parallel to the universe. Each human being is a small universe and is therefore made up of *Yin* and *Yang*. The theories of *Qi* based on the pattern of *Yin* and *Yang* give rise to the development of the style of kung fu known as Internal Kung Fu as opposed to External Kung Fu.

13. *Qi and Qi Flow. Qi* is the vital and intrinsic energy in a person's body. Like blood which flows in blood vessels, *Qi* flows in *Qi* channels. There are twelve primary *Qi* channels, eight extraordinary *Qi* vessels, and twelve divergent channels. There are also numerous smaller energy pathways branching from the energy channels. The twelve *Qi* channels are connected internally to the organs and externally to the limbs. The *Qi* channels are divided into six *Yin* channels and six *Yang* channels. The six *Yin* channels are connected to the six *Yin* organs and the six Yang channels are connected to the six *Yang* organs. Each *Yang* channel of the hand is paired with a *Yin* channel of the hand, and each *Yang* channel of the leg is paired with a *Yin* channel of the leg.

Energy Points. All the energy points lie on the external pathway of the channels. Of the eight extraordinary vessels, only the Conception Vessel and Governing Vessel have energy points of their own.

Extraordinary vessels. The eight extraordinary vessels have no direct connection with the internal organs. They link the twelve *Qi* channels and supplement the function of circulating *Qi* throughout the body. They also act as reservoirs as they absorb excess *Qi* from the primary channels and return it when *Qi* becomes deficient.

Of all the *Qi* channels in the body, the most important are the Conception Vessel and the Governing Vessel. While the other channels are compared to streams and lakes, these two vessels are like seas. The Conception Vessel is the 'sea of *Yin* energy' to where all *Yin* channels flow. The Governing channel is the 'sea of *Yang* energy' to where all the *Yang* channels flow.

Energy Fields. The vital energy, *Qi,* is accumulated and stored in energy fields, the most important being the *Dantian* located two inches below the naval. The two other energy fields on the Conception Vessel are the *Tanzhong* located above the heart and the *Huiying* located just before the anus. There are also two important energy fields along the Governing Vessel, the *Mingmen* located at the centre of the back waist and *Baihui* located at the crown of the head.

14. *Fighting Pose.* Each kung fu style has a practice routine which is made up of a series of fighting poses. The number of fighting poses varies with each style of kung fu. There is no minimum or maximum number of fighting poses. Fighting poses can be joined together in sequences and the sequences can be varied. Each pose is given a descriptive phrase. For example, the 'Dragon And Tiger Meet', 'Dragon Rises From Sea' or 'Roving Dragon Plays In Water' are some of the basic fighting poses in the Shaolin kung fu style 'The Five Animals Set'.

III
ALL ROADS LEAD TO SHAOLIN

15. *Foot binding in China.* Foot binding began in China in the tenth century, sometime between the end of the Tang Dynasty and the beginning of Song. The feet were usually bound to a length of 3 Chinese inches when the girl reached the age between three and five. Chinese men became obsessed with small feet and nurtured an erotic desire for the 'three-inch golden lotus'. After the Manchu Conquest, foot binding was banned but many Han Chinese families still upheld the tradition, and attempts to enforce the ban were unsuccessful during the

Manchu rule. It was only in the first half of the 20th century that footbinding was finally eliminated in China. (Chinese describe small feet as 'three-inch golden lotus'. 'Three-Inch' here is the Chinese inch, and 3.4 Chinese inches equals 5 English inches.)

IV

NUMBER ONE MONASTERY UNDER HEAVEN

16. *The Story of Buddha.* Buddha Sakyamuni was born in 563 BC in the kingdom of Kapilavastu at the foot of the Himalayan mountains, in what is now part of Nepal. Sakyamuni was born a prince and the sole heir to the kingdom. His early life was one of luxury and comfort. At the age of sixteen, he married and his wife bore him a son. However the mysteries of old age, sickness, and death troubled him and he resolved to find the Truth and put an end to human suffering. At the age of twenty-nine, he secretly left his home to start his search for Truth by adopting the life of a wandering mendicant. He studied under two yoga masters who failed to give him an answer. He left them and spent another six years as an ascetic. Five mendicants came and joined him. The prolonged fasting weakened his body and put his life in danger. Yet his efforts were in vain, he finally gave up asceticism, and his five companions abandoned him. He was all alone, when one evening, under a fig tree (called a 'bodhi' tree after his Enlightenment) he reached 'Enlightenment' which led to 'Buddhahood'. He acquired three insights. In the first, he saw each of his previous existences. In the second, he surveyed the deaths and rebirths of all living beings. In the third, he identified the Four Noble Truths and the Eightfold Path. He then understood the cycle of birth and death, the chain of cause and effect, and the steps to 'Enlightenment' and finally 'Nirvana'. After 'Enlightenment', Sakyamuni realised that all sentient beings in this universal life have the potential to become Buddhas. There were two alternative paths; he could enter 'Nirvana', which is final cessation and an end to all suffering, or he could stay on earth to spread 'enlightenment'. He chose to stay and spread his teachings. He died in 483BC at the age of 80. He finally passed

into Nirvana, breaking out from the cycle that can cause rebirth in this or any other world.

The Buddhist religion does not regard Sakyamuni as a creator of the universe or as a founder of the religion. Rather, Sakyamuni is revered as the Supreme Teacher, an example to all human beings of how to attain 'Buddhahood'.

V
CLOSE ENCOUNTER

17. *Vermillion Finches*. Rose finches are called 'Vermillion finches (*Zhuque*) in Chinese.

VI
MASTER WEI'S GROOVE

18. *Shaolin 'Fighting Monks'*. Shaolin monks are sometimes known as 'fighting monks'. It is a tradition of Shaolin Monastery to train 'fighting monks.' The tradition originated from an edict issued by the Emperor of the Tang Dynasty. In 621AD, when the Emperor was still the Prince of Qin, thirteen Shaolin monks saved his life from a rebel leader. The Shaolin monks rejected the Emperor's gifts, and would accept only a grant of 300 hectares of land, one water-powered grain roller and purple cassocks for the monks. The Emperor was shrewd enough to realise that the Shaolin monks could form a powerful reserve force in times of need. He allowed the monastery to train 500 'fighting monks' to assist in the defence of the country. According to popular tales, the Tang Emperor further exempted the Shaolin monks from adherence to a strict vegetarian diet as he considered that meat was essential to strength. Hence Shaolin monks could drink wine and eat meat. But by Qing Dynasty, Shaolin like other Buddhist institutions had resumed their vegetarian diet, and meat and wine were prohibited. (The story of 13 Shaolin monks rescuing the future Tang Emperor is depicted on a mural in Shaolin Monastery's White Clothes Hall. The White Clothes Hall was built in the Qing Dynasty, but after the reign of Kang Xi.)

19. *Lohan.* The Sanskrit name for Lohan is 'Arhat'. In the Buddhist religion, there are three types of spiritually perfected beings, the Buddhas, the Bodhisattvas and the Arhats. Bodhisattvas are 'future Buddhas' who have attained 'enlightenment' but who choose to stay in this mundane world to help all sentient beings to attain 'enlightenment'. All other Buddhist saints and 'enlightened beings' are commonly known as 'Arhats'.

20. *Qing Hair Style.* The Qing hair style of shaving the forehead and wearing the hair in a plait at the back was resented by the Chinese men and led to uprisings even when the cities had formally surrendered.

Shaving off one's hair was in conflict with the doctrine of 'filial piety' observed by the Chinese Confucian Society. 'Human hair and body are bestowed by one's parents; no damage should be caused to them. This is the first step towards filial piety' (Classic of Filial Piety, Chapter 1).

Chinese men would rather lose their head than their hair. In the 'Three Slaughters of Jiading' nearly 100,000 men were slaughtered, and in the '81 days of Jiangyang', except for 53 survivors, the whole population of 97,000 was killed.

VII
HUNT FOR THE THIRD PRINCE

21. *Manchu Banner System.* In 1601, Nurhachi, founder of the Manchu state, organized his warriors into banners of different colours. The smallest unit was a *niru* or a company with 300 men. The next was *jalan* or regiment consisting of five companies. Five regiments made up a *gusa* or banner, a total of 7,500 men. Nurhachi had started with four banners of yellow, red, white and blue. In 1615 four more banners were added. These became the bordered yellow, bordered red, bordered white and bordered blue. All Manchu men were required to enrol with one of the banners along with their families. Each banner was headed by a Commander-in-Chief and assisted by two Vice-Commanders.

Ideally each banner should consist of 7,500 men but the actual numbers in a *niru* varied and the colour of the banner was also subject to change by the khan. For instance, in 1626 when Abahai succeeded Nurhachi as khan of Later Jin Dynasty, he swapped the white colour of the two banners under his control for the yellow colour, the colour normally reserved for the ruler. This was a simple process of just changing the colour of the banner and the clothes of the soldiers.

In 1634, Abahai added eight Mongol banners, and in 1642, he added another eight Chinese banners.

During the reign of Shun Zhi, the Manchu banners were reorganized. The two yellow banners and the Plain White banner were assigned to the Imperial Household and were known as the 'Upper Three Banners'. The other five banners were known as the 'Lower Five Banners'.

IX
A TEST OF STRENGTH

22. *Taijiquan.* '*Taiji*' is also translated as '*Tai Chi*'. '*Quan*' means 'fist'. Thus *Taijiquan* means *Taiji* Fist or *Tai Chi* Fist.

23. *Wudang Style of Kung Fu.* The Wudang style derived its name from Wudang Mountain in Hubei Province. Just as Shaolin is an important centre for the study of Zen Buddhism, Wudang is important for the study of Daoism. Wudang kung fu is influenced by Daoism and Daoist *Qi* practices.

24. *The Doctrine of Change (Yi-Jing).* Yin and Yang are opposite states but their interaction sets in motion the cycle of 'change' in all things. The notion of 'change' depicted in the ancient Chinese book '*Yi-Jing*' or 'the Doctrine of Change' emphasises that 'change' is the only immutable law of the universe. When things reach a peak, they begin to descend, and when things reach the bottom, they ascend. It is this continuous cyclical change which underlies all things in the universe.

25. *Five Elements.* Yin and Yang are opposite states but they are also

complementary. This gives rise to the theory of Five Elements, wood, fire, earth, metal and water. The Five Elements exist in a cycle of creation and a cycle of destruction. In the cycle of creation, wood creates fire, fire creates earth, earth creates metal, metal creates water, and water creates wood. In the cycle of destruction, water destroys fire, fire destroys metal, metal destroys wood, wood destroys earth, and earth destroys water.

All things in the universe are governed by the law of creation and destruction. Thus fire creates earth but is destroyed by water. The largest animal, the elephant, is feared by all other animals, but is afraid of a small animal, the rat.

26. *Eight Trigrams (Bagua).* The cyclical pattern of change is reflected in the Chart of '*Bagua*' or the Eight Trigrams which can be further developed into a 'Cyclical Chart of 64 Hexagrams'. The Eight Trigrams contain the eight directions, the four seasons and the five elements. The theories of *Yin-Yang*, Eight Trigrams, and Five Elements inspire many styles of kung fu, the most famous of which are Taijiquan, Baguazhang or Eight Trigrams Palm, and Xingyiquan.

27. *Zhang SanFeng, founder of Taijiquan.* The founder of Taijiquan was a Daoist, Zhang SanFeng, who lived during the Late Yuan and early Ming period. He spent his early years learning kung fu at Shaolin Monastery. He was familiar with all of the three most important schools of thought at the time, Daoism, Buddhism and Confucianism, but he chose to follow Daoism. He was intrigued by the mysteries of Daoism and its secrets of immortality. One day he saw a snake and a crane fighting and was inspired by the *Yin* and *Yang* qualities of their attack and evasion. This led Zhang to create a new style of pugilism which emphasised the use of *Qi*. The new style of kung fu created by Zhang SanFeng became known as 'Taijiquan', based on the *Qi* theories of *Yin* and *Yang*, the Eight Trigrams and Five Elements.

As Zhang SanFeng was a resident of Wudang Mountain, his Taijiquan Kung Fu became known as the Wudang style. Wudang style is an Internal Kung Fu and sometimes referred to as the 'soft style' in contrast to Shaolin style which is External and called the 'hard style'. Wudang is famous for its Internal Kung Fu just as Shaolin Monastery is famous for it External Kung Fu.

28. *External and Internal Kung Fu.* Nevertheless it is misleading to classify schools of martial arts as strictly Internal or External. All martial arts schools provide training in both External and Internal Kung Fu. The schools recognise that 'External' without 'Internal' lacks force and power, and such kung fu is derided as 'Flowery Fists and Embroidered Legs'. On the other hand, 'Internal' without 'External' lacks skills and techniques. Traditionally, therefore, Shaolin training has moved from External to Internal, while Wudang training has progressed from Internal to External. To become a master in martial arts, one needs to be skilled in both External and Internal Kung Fu.

X
A STRANGER COMES BEARING GIFTS

29. *'Thousand Year Ginseng' Folklore.* 'There is a Buddhist monk who mistreats his young pupil. Every time the monk goes out, a child with a red cummerbund comes to play with the pupil. When the monk learns about this, he tells his pupil to fasten a thread to the clothing of his visitor. This is done, and later the monk finds the thread on a ginseng plant. So he digs up the root and boils it. While the root is boiling, the monk has to go out for a moment; the pupil lifts the lid of the pot and eats the contents. He gives the soup to his dog. When the monk comes back, the dog eats him up.' (Wolfram Eberhard: Dictionary of Chinese Symbols)

XI
THE SECRET UNDERGROUND CHAMBER

30. *Imperial Surname 'Aixin Gioro'.* 'Aixin' means 'Jin' or 'gold', 'Gioro' means 'surname'.

31. *Qing Emperors' Consorts.* The hierarchy of Qing Emperors' consorts was composed of 8 ranks, headed by the Empress, followed by the Imperial Honoured Consort, Honoured

Consort, Consort, Concubine, Honourable Woman, Palace Woman of the 7th rank and Palace Woman of the 8th rank. Qing law forbids inter-marriage between the Manchus and the Han Chinese. The young girls must come from families of bannermen who belong to one of the three banner systems, namely the 8 Manchu banners, the 8 Mongol banners or the 8 Chinese banners. Every three years, all young girls between the ages of 11-16 from the three banner systems underwent a selection process for presentation to the Emperor before they were allowed to marry freely. Those not selected would be released. Those selected if not chosen for the Emperor would be allocated to other Imperial Princes or become Palace maids.

Once chosen for the Emperor, the girls can move up the ladder and become an 'Honourable Woman' if she is chosen to share the Emperor's bed. If she produces a child, she will be promoted to the position of 'Consort', and if the child is a boy, she will become an 'Honoured Consort'. If the boy is appointed the heir apparent, she will become an 'Imperial Honoured Consort'. When the heir apparent becomes Emperor, she gains the title 'Empress', the highest status of a woman in the land. There are many who never catch the attention of the Emperor and spend their lives in loneliness at the bottom of the ladder as a 'Palace Woman' of the 7th or 8th rank.

XII
THE HEAVEN AND EARTH TRIAD SOCIETY

32. *The Heaven and Earth Triad Society*. Chinese triad societies are said to have originated from the Heaven and Earth Society founded during the Qing Dynasty. The Society started as a movement to 'Overthrow the Qing and Restore the Ming' and over the passage of time gave birth to numerous triad societies, especially in Hong Kong and Taiwan, whose activities are now mainly criminal and a threat to society. For convenience of the readers, the Lodge Masters are referred to by their professions. Most triad accounts contain the five Front Lodges and five Rear Lodges, and the names of the Lodge Masters and the areas under

their control are given as:

Cai DeZhong, Master of the Green Lotus Lodge, in charge of Fujian

Fang DaHong, Master of the Hong Compliance Lodge, in charge of Guangdong and Guangxi

Ma ChaoXing, Master of the Family Posterity Lodge, in charge of Yunnan and Xichuan

Hu DeChang, Master of the Great Reach Lodge, in charge of Hunan and Hubei

Li SeKai, Master in charge of the Grand Sublimity Lodge, in charge of Zhejiang

Little else has been written about the Society, the Lodge Masters or the members. Even if written materials existed, they would be unable to be verified as historical fact. The personalities of the founder, the Lodge Masters and members of the Heaven and Earth Society in the novel are fictional.

Extensive research into Chinese triad societies has been carried out by a Dutch scholar, Barend J. Ter Haar in his book 'Ritual & Mythology of the Chinese Triads' published by Koninklijke Brill NV, Leiden, The Netherlands

The article on 'The Triad Society, or Heaven and Earth Association' by William Stanton published in the China Review Vol.XX1, No.4, p220 is also recommended.

33. *Literary Inquisition – the case of Zhuang YanLong*

The case of Zhuang YanLong took place in 1663. The investigation was one of the most extensive ever carried out and many people, whether directly or indirectly involved, were executed.

The crime of the Zhuang family was to publish a book on Ming history which was originally written by a Ming Grand Chancellor. The Ming history book fell into the hands of Zhuang YanLong, son of a wealthy family from the Huzhou Prefecture. He organised well-known scholars to edit the book and then he published it. The book instantly won acclaim among the literati of the day. Unfortunately, the book contained criticisms of the Manchu invasion, as well as careless mistakes whereby Ming reign years were used instead of Qing reign years. Even after the

Manchu Conquest, the book continued to use the reign years of 'Long Wu' and 'Yong Li' which were the reign titles of Prince of Fu and Prince of Gui. The book caused fury in the Qing court and was interpreted as an act of sedition. The publisher Zuang YanLong by this time was already dead, but his coffin was broken up and his corpse mutilated. Led by the Regent Oboi, Zuang's brother and those scholars who had contributed to the editing, commentaries, or who had written a foreword, were executed and their family members taken into slavery. The net widened to engravers of the wood prints, the printers and book-binders, the sellers and purchasers of the books, and even to next door neighbours who had known about the book but had not reported it to the authorities.(Bo Yang: History of the Chinese People)

XIV
THE SECRET MANUAL OF 'TENDON TRANSFORMATION'

34. *Shen or Mind and Spirit.* The emulation of Buddha's compassion to neutralise the lethal effects of kung fu is also explained by Louis Cha in his novel '*Tian Long Ba Bu*' p.181 5–182.

XV
MUTINY AT SHAOLIN

35. *Kingdom of Dali.* The Kingdom of Dali was established in 937AD and located in what is now Western Yunnan Province. The founder, Duan SiPing, came from an aristocratic family of the 'Bai' ethnic minority race. The 'Bai' and the 'Yi' minorities had settled in the region over 4000 years before. The Dali Kingdom lasted 317 years and was a tributary of China during the Song Dynasty. In 1253, the Kingdom was destroyed by Mongol armies under the command of Kublai Khan. Despite the might of the Mongolian force, it took a traitor to lead the enemies through a secret pathway across the Cangshan Mountains into the Erhai Valley and finally break through the defence of the Bai warriors. In 1274 the Province of Yunnan was

created, and the region was incorporated into China.

36. *Four Books and Five Classics*. Candidates for examinations held in Imperial China were expected to be tested on their knowledge of the Four Books and Five Classics. The Four Books are: The Great Learning, The Doctrine of the Mean, The Analects of Confucius, and The Works of Mencius. The five Classics are: The Book of Poetry, The Book of Historical Documents, The Book of the Doctrine of Change, The Book of Rites and The Spring and Autumn Annals.

XVI
HIDDEN DRAGON

37. *Number of eunuchs and palace maids*. During the Ming Dynasty, the number of eunuchs and palace maids reached 100,000 and 9000 respectively. The number was greatly reduced in the Qing Dynasty. According to records, in 1690 during the reign of Kang Xi, the number of eunuchs was 500 and palace maids 134 not including the palace maids in Ci-Ning Palace. (Bo Yang: History of the Chinese People)

XVIII
THE TARTAR CHAMPION

38. *Death Penalty: The Slow Process*. This was the cruellest penalty in Imperial China. It was a lingering death as small bits of flesh were cut from the prisoner until he bled to death. This penalty is also called 'Death by a Thousand Cuts' although the actual number of cuts could amount to over 3300.

XX
THE GREAT ESCAPE

39. *Imperial Prince Fu Quan*. Imperial Prince Fu Quan was the second son of the late Emperor Shun Zhi, and Kang Xi was the third son. He and Kang Xi had the same father but different mothers. He was only 8 months older than Kang Xi. Before Emperor Shun Zhi died,

he had to choose between his two eldest surviving sons, Fu Quan and Kang Xi, to succeed him on the throne. Shun Zhi eventually accepted the recommendation of the Grand Empress Dowager and of the Jesuit Priest Adam Schall, and appointed Kang Xi as the Heir Apparent. The recommendation was based on the fact that Kang Xi had survived an attack of small pox whereas Fu Quan had not yet had small pox. Small pox had a high mortality rate. Fu Quan's chances of surviving a small pox epidemic were unknown making him unsuitable to be Heir to the throne. However Prince Fu Quan was a mild and modest man, and he bore no grudge against Kang Xi. He showed Kang Xi the greatest respect and remained loyal to him to the end of his life. (Zhen Yang: Kang Xi's Family)

XXI
THE EMPEROR'S GAMBIT

40. *'Circled Land'*. When Manchus moved their capital to Beijing, they needed land for their bannermen. It was Regent Dorgon who issued the order for 'circled land'. Manchu bannermen were allowed to ride their horses round and encircled the pieces of land they wished to own. The original order was to 'circle' only wastelands, and lands abandoned by landlords or owned by former Ming officials. Very soon, the practice of 'circled land' went out of control and spread to the whole country. Rich fertile lands were seized from Chinese farmers leaving them with no means of livelihood. This caused great grievance to the Han Chinese and led to uprisings and riots.

Soon after the arrest of Oboi, Emperor Kang Xi abolished the practice of 'circled land'.

41. *Upper Three Banners*. The Upper Three Banners consisted of the Plain Yellow, Bordered Yellow and Plain White Banners. Kang Xi as Emperor belonged to the Plain Yellow Banner. Soni also belonged to the Plain Yellow Banner, Oboi and Ebilun belonged to the Bordered Yellow, and Suksaha belonged to the Plain White.

42. *Emperor Shun Zhi's death*. Shun Zhi's death at the young age of 22 gave rise to many tales. Some believe that he abdicated the

throne after the death of his favourite consort Lady Dong, and became a monk at a Buddhist monastery at the Five Terraces Mountain. However, the generally accepted version is that he died of small pox.

43. *Regent Dorgon.* He was the fourteenth son of Nurhaci. He missed at least two chances of ascending the throne of the Manchu Empire. Some historians believe that Nurhaci had intended Dorgon to succeed him, but when he died, Dorgon was only 14 years old, and his eighth son Abahai was 34. With the support of Nurhaci's second son, Abahai was elected the khan of the Later Jin Dynasty.

When Abahai died in 1643, there was power struggle between Dorgon and Abahai's eldest son. Dorgon was more powerful at the time, but he did not wish the bloodshed which would weaken the Manchu army because his ambition was to conquer China. So he and Abahai's eldest son settled on a compromise candidate, the ninth son of Abahai, who was to become Emperor Shun Zhi. Dorgon became the Regent during Shun Zhi's minority.

Dorgon had only one daughter from his ten wives and concubines. He later adopted the fifth son of his younger brother to be brought up as his own son.

Grand Empress Dowager and Regent Dorgan. It was Dorgon who led Manchus troops to China. He was the most powerful man after the Conquest, effectively ruling the country, but he had never claimed the throne for himself. Some historians believe that after the death of his elder brother Abahai, he married Abahai's widow, the Grand Empress Dowager. Marrying a deceased brother's widow was Manchu custom. But their wedding remained one of the mysteries of Qing history. The Grand Empress Dowager gained the title 'Empress' when her son Shun Zhi became emperor, and came to be known as 'Empress Xiao Zhuang Wen' after her death.

Regent Dorgon and Emperor Shun Zhi. Shun Zhi never got along with Dorgon and resented his dictatorial manner. Dorgon became very ill after falling from a horse during a hunting accident, and died aged 38. Shun Zhi was then 12 years old and assumed full power as Emperor. Dorgon was charged with treason two months after his death. Under orders from Shun Zhi, Dorgon's grave was destroyed, his corpse whipped, the head severed and the torso exposed to public. His title was forfeited and his property confiscated. His supporters were executed, exiled or removed from their posts. 128 years later, in 1778, under the reign of Emperor Qian Long, the great grand-son of Shun Zhi, Dorgon was cleared of the charge against him. His grave was rebuilt, his title and property restored. His fifth generation grandson inherited his title and became one of the eight Iron Hat Imperial Princes. (Wang Si Zhi: The Historical Characters of the Qing Dynasty)

XXIII
THROUGH THE WOODEN MEN LANE

43. *Wooden-Men Lane.* According to popular tales, Shaolin pupils had to go through the Wooden-Men Lane test before they could graduate and leave the monastery. Stories of the test differed. Some describe the Wooden-Men Lane as a maze with deadly traps. Some describe the wooden men as armed with deadly weapons. The Wooden-Men Lane and its wooden men in the novel are fictional.

MING EMPERORS AND MING PRETENDERS

MING EMPERORS (1573-1644)

1. *Emperor Wan Li (1573-1620)*. Emperor Wan Li was a drug addict, an alcoholic, a money grabber and a cold-blooded killer. According to records from 1592, Wan Li had by that time already whipped to death one thousand palace maids, eunuchs and officers of his court. He killed at least one person a week, but some escaped death by offering large sums of money to the emperor, who would then spare their lives. (Bo Yang: history of the Chinese People)

For a stretch of over 20 years, Emperor Wan Li held no audience with his ministers. He did not emerge until one day when an intruder wielding a wooden baton was captured in the part of the Palace where the heir was staying. At the time, everyone thought that the intruder was an assassin hired by the Honoured Consort Lady Zheng, who had hoped to replace the heir by her own son, the Prince of Luoyang. The Emperor only showed his face because he did not want to involve his favourite concubine in this unpleasant incident. The matter was allowed to rest when he exacted a promise from Lady Zheng that she would make no further attempt to replace the heir.

After that incident, Wan Li did not show his face again until the day of his death five years later. During the last thirty years of his reign, no one governed the country. The administration and important decisions were often left to eunuchs who were not competent to rule, and not surprisingly, made a mess of it. Of the six ministries of the Central government, five had no one in charge of ministry affairs. Half of the government officers had left their posts. Prisoners languished in their cells as there were no judges to try their cases. When the families of the prisoners knelt before the Palace Gate, Emperor Wan Li remained unmoved. When the Manchus invaded Liaodong and captured several cities, all the ministers too knelt before the Palace Gate and begged the Emperor to issue military aid and food to the soldiers, who were dying of hunger and cold in the north. Again the Emperor ignored their pleading.

Nor did Emperor Wan Li reply to memorials submitted by his ministers. When the Senior Grand Secretary submitted his memorial for resignation, which he did 120 times, the Emperor still did not reply. The Senior Grand Secretary eventually just left his post. (Ray Huang: The Cambridge History of China Vol 7, The Ming Dynasty Part 1)

Yet there was one matter which Emperor Wan Li would always deal with promptly, and that was the matter of tax. There were many exorbitant taxes on the people, including salt tax and mineral tax. The tax collection process was corrupt and extortionate. Where money was concerned, Emperor Wan Li made sure that he squeezed every ounce of silver from his subjects. During his reign, he accumulated so much money that it would be more than enough to feed ten generations of his descendants. It later transpired that Emperor Wan Li was trying to amass as much money as possible for his son with Lady Zheng, the Prince of Luoyang.

When the city Luoyang was captured by the rebel chief Li ZiCheng, Li ZiCheng had the Prince of Luoyang chopped into mincemeat and fed to the dogs. Many believe that the hoard of money had been dissipated among soldiers and the hungry mob when the city of Luoyang fell. (Bo Yang: History of Chinese People)

2. *Emperor Tai Chang (30 days in 1620).* Emperor Wan Li was succeeded by his eldest son, the Heir Apparent, who became Emperor Tai Chang. He had been a promising emperor, but he fell into the trap laid by Wan Li's widow, Lady Zheng. She presented him with a gift of eight beautiful women. He began to

indulge in orgiastic sex, his health deteriorated and he fell ill. The medicine provided by a eunuch associated with Lady Zheng caused the Emperor frequent bouts of diarrhoea which further aggravated his illness. In desperation, the Emperor took some red pills claimed to be a miracle drug offered by a minor official. He died soon afterwards at the young age of 34, after only 30 days on the throne. Whether the medicine and the red pills had something to do with Lady Zheng remained a mystery of the Ming history. (William Atwell: The Cambridge History of China Vol 7, The Ming Dynasty Part I)

3. *Emperor Tian Qi (1620-1627)*. Emperor Tai Chang was succeeded by his 16 year old son who became Emperor Tian Qi.

Lady Ke and Eunuch Wei. Emperor Tian Qi was deeply attached to his wet nurse who was 18 years his senior. She received an honorific title and became known as Lady Ke. By then, her husband had already died.

Lady Ke had several lovers. One of them was Eunuch Wei who was to become a very powerful person during the reign of Tian Qi. Eunuch Wei was castrated at the age of 21. He had been married and had a daughter before castration. According to records, his castration was complete, but that did not prevent him from having an intimate relationship with Lady Ke which enabled them to forge a close bond in the struggle for power.

Tian Qi, the carpenter. The new Emperor Tian Qi's pastime was carpentry. He spent endless time building furniture and other wooden articles. His handiwork surpassed that of many of the finest carpenters in the country. Had he not been born in the Imperial household, he could in all likelihood have become an outstanding carpenter. Eunuch Wei and Lady Ke were only too pleased to encourage the Emperor to devote his time to carpentry, and leave the running of the country to them.

With Lady Ke exerting her influence on the Emperor, Eunuch Wei began purging ministers who stood in his way. The two of them held the country and even the life of the Emperor in their hands.

Emperor Tian Qi was physically weak and mentally deficient, and died after seven years on the throne. He left behind no heir. His three sons had all died during infancy. Furthermore, Lady Ke ensured that the Emperor would remain childless by mixing abortion drugs into the food of his Empress and his concubines as soon as they became pregnant. The throne thus passed to the nineteen years old younger brother who became Emperor Chong Zhen. After the death of Emperor Tian Qi, Eunuch Wei was persecuted and he committed suicide. Lady Ke was beaten to death. (William Atwell: The Cambridge history of China vol 7, The Ming Dynasty Part 1)

4. *Emperor Chong Zhen (1627-1644)*. Emperor Chong Zhen was hard working but he lacked the ability to rule. He had frequent outbursts of irrational temper and he killed recklessly. He executed the generals and officials whenever a city or prefecture fell to his enemies. He moaned his bad luck for not having good people under him, yet he failed to make use of good ministers and generals when he had them. He executed the national hero, General Yuan ChongHuan who had been fighting the Manchus with great success. Chong Zhen was the sixteenth and the last of the Ming Emperors on the throne in the Forbidden City before the Manchu Conquest.

In April 1644, the rebel leader Li ZiCheng seized Beijing. Emperor Chong Zhen committed suicide. He hanged himself from a tree, and let his hair fall over his face as a sign of his shame at losing the empire. He left a valediction, blaming himself for his own lack of virtue, as well as blaming his ministers for failing him. It was typical of Emperor Chong Zhen to blame others for his mistakes.

After Chong Zhen had hanged himself at Coal Hill, his eunuch Wang Cheng-En followed his master and he also hanged himself. (Johnathan D Spence: Emperor of China)

MING PRETENDERS (1644-1662)

After the Manchu Conquest, there were several Ming pretenders to the throne. Four of the princes were enthroned by their supporters as 'Emperor' with a 'reign title'; the Prince of Fu, the two Princes of Tang and the Prince of Gui. There was also the Prince of Lu who was named as Regent by his supporters.

5. *Prince of Fu.* The Prince of Fu, a grandson of Emperor Wan Li, was son of Prince of Luoyang who was killed when the City of Luoyang fell to the rebels.

After the death of Emperor Chong Zhen, a group of senior Ming officials named Prince of Fu as successor. He was enthroned as Emperor Hong Guang in Nanjing. The new Emperor's first orders were the requisition of beautiful women and aphrodisiac drugs. Over the next few months, his court was torn by the same internal struggles for power and the inefficiencies that had brought down the Ming Empire. The kingdom lasted only 13 months. The city of Nanjing fell to the Manchus and Prince of Fu was captured. He was sent back to Beijing and beheaded the following year.

6. *Prince of Tang (Elder Brother).* With the death of Prince of Fu, two brothers who were descendants of the founding Ming Emperor, and both known as Prince of Tang, were successively enthroned as Emperor in the eastern coastal regions. The elder brother was enthroned in Fuzhou but was captured by the Manchus and executed in 1646.

7. *Prince of Lu.* In 1645, in the same month, August, of 1645 when the elder Prince of Tang had established his court, another group

named his nephew, Prince of Lu, as Regent in Zhejiang. But Prince of Tang and Prince of Lu did not get on and their supporters were constantly fighting and disputing over the issue of succession. Lu commanded the smallest territories and armed forces. In early 1652, after defeats from the Qing armies, he went to Xiamen and was received by Koxinga. In 1653, he renounced the title of regent and settled in Jinmen Island. He died of asthma on 23 December 1662.

8. *Prince of Tang (Younger Brother)*. The younger brother of Prince of Tang was enthroned in Guangzhou in December 1646. When it was heard that Prince of Gui had set up his own court in Zhaoqing in the same month, battles broke out between the supporters of the two groups in early January 1647. The forces of Prince of Gui were almost completely wiped out. Yet for the new Prince of Tang, there was little time for rejoicing, for soon afterwards Guangzhou was seized by Qing armies. He was captured and later executed. His regime lasted only 40 days.

9. *Prince of Gui*. The last hopeful claimant to the throne was Prince of Gui. He was a cousin of Prince of Fu. His ancestral estate was in Hunan. After war broke out, he fled southwest to Zhaoqing, west of Guangzhou, and there he was enthroned with the reign name Emperor Yong Li by a group of fugitive officials. His court, like the others, was torn by factional strife. His regime was characterized by the constant moving of its base from the south to the west and then back to the south again. In early 1650, the Qing forces attacked his southern base. Prince of Gui was forced to flee again, westward to Guangxi, then into Guizhou province, from Guizhou to Yunnan and finally across the Chinese border into Burma. The Ming General Wu SanGui who had defected to the Manchus attacked Burma and compelled the Burmese King to hand over Prince of Gui. In 1662 Prince of Gui and his only son were executed by strangulation in Yunnan Province. The regime of Prince of Gui had survived for 15 years mainly due to his successful evasion of his pursuers. With the death of Prince of Gui, the Ming Empire came to an end.